I0586512

DEATH IN THE VALLEY

BAER CHARLTON

Copyright ©2017 by Baer Charlton
Death in the Valley
By Baer Charlton

ISBN-13: 978-0-9971795-3-8 [Paperback]

All rights reserved.

No part of this publication may be reproduced or transmitted in any form or by
any means, electronic or mechanical, including photocopy, recording, or any
information storage and retrieval system without the prior written consent of
the author, except in the instance of quotes for reviews. No part of this book
may be scanned, uploaded, or distributed via the internet without the
permission of the author and is a violation of the International Copyright law,
which subjects the violator to severe fines and imprisonment.

Rogena Mitchell-Jones, Editor
www.rogenamitchell.com
Cover Creative Art by Nina Golemi
Cover Design by Baer Charlton

Published by Mordant Media, Portland, Oregon

MORDANT MEDIA ™©®
A Division of Charlton Productions

10 9 8 7 6 5 4 3 2 1

CONTENTS

01 Learning Early   1
02 Hung Judge   3
03 Homecoming   6
04 Silver Canyon   13
05 Message from Beyond   17
06 Old Wounds New Cuts   24
07 Puzzles   32
08 Burn In the Night   40
09 Stick a Pin In It   50
10 Morning Light   61
11 Single File   69
12 New Whore in Town   78
13 How Dare You   85
14 Who is Who   89
15 Your Uncle   99
16 Records Aren't Always Reports   107
17 Old Paper   118
18 Not What It Appears   126
19 Hornet's Nest   135
20 Read Carefully   145
21 Side of the Road   154
22 Water and War   168
23 War for Water   172
24 The Hills are Alive   185
25 Nevada   193
26 Hot Water   201
27 Pipe Dream or Down the Tubes   205
28 Old Fight Same War   211
29 Heather   221
30 Deep Mine   233
31 Come Back   244

32 Heading South   252
33 Brief   258
34 Alliances   270
35 Crickets Are Loud   280
36 Old Paper   287
37 The Pass   296
38 Hammer   303
39 What Now   314
40 Harold   318

Acknowledgments   323
Baer Charlton   328
About the Author   329

ALSO BY BAER CHARLTON

NOVELS

The Very Littlest Dragon: NEW 2019 Editions

(Newly edited editions available: an all-new full-color ebook, a paperback with coloring pages, and a full-color Collector's Edition hardback)

Stoneheart
(Pulitzer Nominee 2015)

Angel Flights
What About Marsha?
Pirate's Patch
Dry Bridge of Vengeance

—

SOUTHSIDE HOOKER SERIES

Death on a Dime – Book One
Night Vision – Book Two
Unbidden Garden – Book Three
Boomtown – Book Four
One Day Under the Grass – Book Five

Southside Hooker Series: Books 1–5 Box Set
(Collector's Edition hardback & ebook available)

—

THORNY WALLACE SERIES

Death in the Valley – Book One
Light to Light – Book Two

01 LEARNING EARLY

She watched her grandfather as he bent over to work on the tractor. She was sure they were the same age. She knew the dent on the cowling was somehow connected to the large scar separating his hair along the one side of his head.

He reached into his back pocket. Without looking, his fingers selected one of the half-dozen wrenches. The spider-web of cracks on his hands were stained permanently black from the farm. Thorny had wondered as a small girl if her claw of a hand would become a marked but usable hand like his. His head never moved as the hand swapped one wrench for a larger. The pocket on the faded bib overalls had been patched many times.

Her gaze slid to the other back pocket. Low on the large patch of a pocket was a small square, glazed black as the cracks of his hands, and framed by the whitish fray of wear. From experience, Thorny knew the small wallet contained only a few items. Money was only an occasional carriage. The two photos were of him with four other men in a place called Cuba, and Thorny's mother holding her one-month-old daughter. The two photos and a business card of the man from the farm bureau were all he carried about his life. His times during the war, any suggestion of his right to drive or to vote or about who he was were of no consequence to his person. Everyone in town knew him, which was enough.

His mustard-gas destroyed throat croaked. "We'll be needing them eggs afore lunchtime," he reminded her of her chores.

She grumbled lightly—hoping the stub of his mangled ear wouldn't hear her complain. "Ester, Ruth, and Sarah peck at me. It hurts."

He rolled around to sit on the small front tire. The patch of burned off flesh created pink on the tanned face. "Use your other hand. They will think they have pecked at you enough and leave you be."

Thorny sighed and stood. Her head and shoulders hung. The man watched the tiny feet leave footprints in the gray silt dust of summer. They matched the footprints in his heart.

02 HUNG JUDGE

The two small feet swung just short of the floor. The summer heat had begun to cook the small house. The cooler air from the crawl space, leaking up through the cracks between the floorboards, felt good on Thorny's feet. Since the fire when she was just a baby, she couldn't feel pain, but she could still feel the heat from the day and the cool through the cracks in the floor. Most times, the cracks were her salvation when she had to sweep the kitchen. The separation between the boards was large enough to sweep down the crumbs and dirt.

The five pale freckles wrinkled on her nose. "What does obs... obstin... ately mean?"

The old man stood barefoot, looking out the back screen door. He sipped on his warm coffee. His wet eyes looked along where the clothesline ran. His mind ran along the line to a time when Vida hung fresh wash there. The Owens Valley sun made the sheets smell like the best flowers he had ever smelled. He had smelled roses and honeysuckle, but they didn't smell as nice as when his aunt Vida made the bed fresh on Saturday nights.

He turned. "You know where the book is."

Thorny bit her tongue. She wanted to lash out. Saying he probably didn't know what it meant. She hated looking up words. She wanted to just know them and what they meant.

Her bib overalls shushed as she slid off the chair. Her bare feet were silent as she crossed into the sitting room and the squat bookshelf.

The man sipped and then looked at the article the girl had been reading. The judge had been found hanging in his own closet. He had been the only voice in the valley speaking out against the big city grabbing up all the drought-baked land—along with the water rights. Eustis rubbed his finger behind the stub of his ear. He had liked the judge. They had met when he ran off to go ride with Teddy Roosevelt down in Cuba.

Thorny lugged the large dictionary back to the table. Laying it down open to the right section, she started piecing the word together in the book.

Eustis listened to her wet licked lips spell out the word as he watched out across the alfalfa. The breeze was a day away from making the tops sway. For now, he would rest in the cool of the house until he needed to go change the traps on the irrigation ditch.

He looked at the last sip in the bottom of the battered enameled mug. He thought about his oldest friend. He mussed as he squinted out the back door again. "What does the second definition say for obstinate?" He had heard her sounding out of the word as it changed to reading.

"There is only one definition." Her finger moved. "But the second word—which is similar, says unyielding." She looked up as he turned.

His eyes were closed as he thought. She never could figure out if he also slept in those few stolen moments. His head nodded softly as his lower lip slid forward. "That would be Harold. When he knew something was right—he was unyielding."

"But he hung himself."

"What does the article say?"

"They found him in his bedroom closet—"

He softly cut her off. "But does it say he took his own life?"

She pointed at the newspaper. "It says…" She knew the next argument by heart.

"Only facts count. Everything else is just a story."

She slumped back into the chair. Her good hand wrapped around her claw. "Yes, sir."

He set the mug in the sink. As he walked behind her, he paused and held his hands on her forehead, hugging her head to his belly. He sighed softly. "You knew that. I didn't need to lecture you on it. I'm just sorely hurting. Harold was one of my few friends. I've lost my Vida, your mama, and now my friend. I'm just old and hurting, and I took it out on you. I'm sorry, Thorny."

She knew he was hurting. Remembrance Day was coming, and it was also the holiday he lost his aunt, Vida. She nudged her head gently.

He fluffed his hands at her hair. "After school, why don't you stop by the niggra and get him to cut your hair up for the summer. It's going to be a scorcher this summer. Tell him I'll pay up my bill at the end of May when I come in for my shave."

She closed her eyes. Her voice was little more than a whisper. "Mr. Geronimo isn't a darky."

The man turned with a deep sigh. "Run along before you're late for the bus and have to walk to school."

03 HOMECOMING

T he silver sides of the bus were a dull, dusty gray from the long day driving up from Los Angeles. The desert grime hung glued in a thin coating. The soft yellow blinker repeated its heartbeat each second as the forty-passenger Bluebird crept around the right turn. Four passengers lazed dopey in their seats from the heat.

The bus passed the string of mules standing under the long canopy. Twenty beasts, two abreast, could fit under the long tent affair at a single time. The father and son moved like agile squirrels among the patient pack team. Every inch of leather, every stitch, every buckle, would undergo the critical eyes of Victor and his son Vic. They knew the brutal loads depended on their skill and knowledge of the leather rigs. The summers spent trudging up the long trails of the Sierra Nevada Mountains took their toll on leather and beast equally. The beasts would survive, but it was up to the two men so the mule train wouldn't have to return to town before the next early spring.

The bus turned left, lumbering down the block separating the commercial block from the small homes. The driver kept the bus in slow gear. The dust could be thick on Back Street. The second house on the right was the widow Helms. The driver knew she purposely sat on her front porch at this time of day just to torment him. If the dust rose, the chief of police would receive a letter by the next day's post.

Taking the last left, the bus came to rest. Its nose parked twenty-three feet from the corner of Willow and North Main Street. The bus's front bumper was aligned with the small sign with a dog on it—one small car-length from the fire hydrant.

The driver reached over and took his bus driver's hat from the hook on the small wall behind his seat. Standing, he opened the door. He reached down with his left hand and took up the one-step stool. Carrying the battered wooden stool, he stepped down to the sidewalk. Turning, he placed the stool the prescribed three inches away from the last step in the bus. His eyes took in the polished brown riding boots with the army twill slacks stuffed inside. He hadn't heard the young woman step down the two steps, but she waited there nonetheless.

Each step was slow and pensive. The driver looked up the long legs covered in the pleated wool kakis. The starched white blouse did nothing to hide the slender body.

She turned and watched him through the green glass of her sunglasses. Her mouth slowly pulled back on the right side. "I guess I should say it's good to be back."

The driver stood erect and smiled as warm as the day. "It's been a longtime, Thorny. When you got on in North Holly-wood, I almost didn't recognize you."

She drew her left hand out of her pants pocket. She looked at her claw of a hand. It had never changed. "Hard to mistake me for Katherine Hepburn, eh, Phil?"

He blushed.

She ignored his discomfiture. She had stopped caring about what other people thought was polite or not. "My bags. Would it be okay to leave them here until I figure out how to get them out to the house?"

Phil glanced through the window of the office. "Mike lives out near the ranch. He could drop them off when he goes home at six."

She thought as she looked through the window at the man behind the counter. She wasn't sure who he was, but if he knew where the ranch was… "Thank you. I'd appreciate it. The Fergusons are in the house, but if he can just place them on the front porch, they'll be fine." She pulled a slim man's wallet from her hip pocket. "I can help with his petrol…"

Phil put his hand out. "He's with the Civil Air Patrol, so he's off ration. It's on his way."

She hesitated and then glancing once more, she put her wallet away. "Thanks, Phil."

The man slumped his hip to one side as he relaxed. His voice was almost a sigh. "Welcome home, Thorny." His face jittered. "I mean, you are here to stay this time, aren't you?"

"We'll see, Phil. I'll need to find a job. The ranch can't support much more than the Fergusons."

"Well, I for one would like to see you stay this time."

She studied his face. "I thought you were married."

His blush came with a smile and a soft shake of his head. "Debbie and I are about to celebrate our tenth anniversary. The girls are seven and nine. But I think Debbie would like to have you around too. In fact, we'd like to have you over on Sunday for dinner. I'm off, and I know the girls would find you refreshing as well."

The tip of Thorny's tongue snuck out along her lips. "I'll be sure to stop by and get your invite confirmed by Debbie. But Sunday dinner sounds nice. We have more than a few years to catch up on."

"I'll make sure Mike knows where to take your bags."

Thorny pulled at her hair curling around her collar. "Thanks... now I think I need a haircut. I hope Monte is still working."

"The niggra? Sure. He'll be there until six or so."

She smiled at the old mispronunciation of the Spanish word for black or dark: Negros. Some things are reassuring in their not changing.

THE MAN with gray at his temples and more salt than pepper in his curls looked up. The woman stood quietly in the door. Her hands were in her pockets, but the stance was a familiar defiant show of bravado.

"*¿Estamos en guerra?*" Are we at war?

Thorny leaned her head over and smiled softly. "Only if I don't get a hug." She stepped into the barbershop as the man rose. As she neared, she could see his eyes begin to tear.

"Oh, mi pequeño... I have missed you."

She hugged him. "I've missed you too, Monte." She pushed him back, removed her glasses and studied his face. "Tell me everything." She pulled at her hair. "And I need a haircut."

"Still want a tomboy cut?"

"Do you think you can cut it like Amelia Earhart?"

He pulled at her large lazy curls. "I can make you her twin. Do you have an airplane too?"

"I've been in one—twice. I also met Amelia my freshman year at UCLA."

"Then I will trade you a haircut for the stories of meeting the goddess of the wings."

Main Street torpidly drifted by in the afternoon sun. The few pedestrians hugged the shadier sidewalk and the occasional awning. At four-thousand-feet elevation, the summer sun can blister paint and skin alike. During the record heat of summer, some notable would have their picture taken with an egg frying on a sidewalk. Dogs were smarter and stuck to the cooler grass and shade of a large elm or cottonwood.

"Have you seen Flapjack and Sandbag, recently?" Thorny tried to sound casual in her inquiry.

Monte combed and snipped near her ear. "Ulysses, but Sandbag passed away years ago. He has a new burro..." He paused. "Hmm, I can't think of it now. It's some kind of flower. Not one we have here, though. I think it's from a poem or something. You know how Ulysses is with books and all."

"When was he in last?"

Monte fluffed at her curls. "He always comes in just before Thanksgiving. I spruce him up, and he goes to eat at the Copper Kettle." His hand stopped at her hair. The walnut of his fingers raking through the loose curling, contrasted in the sun-washed blonde. His face darkened in the mirror as he thought.

Thorny weighed the look. "He wasn't in for Easter—was he."

"No." His eyes slid shut as his body slumped. His hands rested heavy on her shoulders. "He didn't come down for graduation either. We've always sat along the low wall on the west side of the front lawn of the high school, to listen to the kid's speeches. I missed it. Ulysses never showed, and I missed it."

Thorny reached her right hand up to cover his hand on her

left shoulder. "I'll go look for him tomorrow. I haven't received a letter from him since before Christmas. I've been worried, but then he goes back up in the canyons and time for him... just seems to stop."

"If you need the T, you know where it is. I'm sure the key has rusted its way into the lock."

"That would save me some time. Would you mind if I use it for a few days until I get my feet under me?"

The dark man snorted softly and stepped over to one of the small drawers. "You're going to need some of these ration cards." He drew out a small stack of booklets and placed them on the narrow counter. Taking in the woman's one raised eyebrow, he pushed out his lower lip. "Where am I going to drive to? I walk the five blocks to home. The Copper Kettle is four blocks down Main, May's Bib is three blocks away, and I might have to clean the pigeon poop off the window so I can see the other three cars with gasoline."

"Are those ration stamp books good anymore?"

He lowered his head and looked through his eyebrows. "If not, then take them up to Bertha. I'm sure she can get you what you need."

Thorny's cheek pulled with conspiratorial mirth. "That isn't all I need from her."

His eyes grew wide as his face came up in possible revelation about Thorny and the town prostitute. His mouth formed the beginning of a small *o*.

Thorny growled. "Oh, stop it. I don't walk down that side of the street, and you know it. But, like you, she knows more about what goes on in this valley than probably the police downstairs." It never escaped anyone's attention that the town whorehouse was on the second floor, over the police station.

Monte leaned back against the high counter as his body started to jiggle. Soon, both were softly chuckling at Thorny being teased. The two shared a bond they had known since she was a young girl. Neither felt the emotions other people seemed to be fraught with. Monte's caring emotionally about other people ended as a young boy in the service to the cavalry as he watched his ancestors, both Apache and Mexican, as they were slaughtered. Thorny never knew if she was capable of feeling emotion, or if it was wiped away by the same fire that took her mother and part of her left hand. What they both shared was caring about others. Strong caring. Beyond was something estranged and left for others. Much like romantic or sexual relationships.

Thorny stood in the doorway sorting through the fist-full of ration books. The backlight of the day behind her reminded Monte of the last photo taken of Amelia Earhart climbing into the door of her airplane before she left to circle the globe. There were no other photos taken. She never reached the land of the kangaroo.

"There are probably several fill-ups left in these." She held up some books in her right hand. "The rest I'll take over to Bertha." She slid the good rations in her right pant pocket. Her claw was left clamping the others.

Monte smiled softly at the now tall, slender woman in the door. He nodded and commented softly. "You look just like her." He knew how much Thorny admired the pilot for her following her heart, but he also remembered Thorny's mother. The two could be twins.

04 SILVER CANYON

Thorny removed her shoes. She drove the battered old Model T as far up the canyon as she knew she dared. The small flat allowed her to turn the car around and point it back down the canyon. She looked out across the wide valley toward the still snowcapped Sierra Nevada Mountains. The one cone of a mountain standing out front of the range was Mt. Tom. The late snowpack reached almost a third of the way down its sides. She knew from experience the last white would be gone with the end of June. Only the winter of 1917 had left snow until the Fourth of July.

Pulling the dark green glasses from her face, she cleaned the lenses on her shirt. Her thumb and finger moved the cloth unhurriedly. The valley seemed like another lifetime ago, and yet, as the heat wavered the valley floor, it was the seven years away which seemed like someone else's life. Every turn of the river below, every steeple of the town, and even the heat—hanging in the air—wore like a favorite shirt.

Her left foot reached out and sunk into the light gray-tan dust. The warmth squished up through her toes like an old friend. She reached behind the seat and pulled out the small rucksack with the four patches. The two of them had been up this road many times before. She hefted the weight of the two canteens and a double lunch over her left shoulder and fed her right arm into the other strap. Shrugging the straps into place, she pushed the creaking door closed.

Right hand shielding her eyes, she looked up the canyon. The small cluster of weathered buildings was another mile or so. She wasn't sure what she would find, but she had her suspicions. The canyon had changed her life before. She was ready for it to do so again.

The man known as Flapjack, with his wild white hair and a shaggy beard, were an occasional but accepted sight in Bishop. His hands were empty as he walked along Main Street. The mule followed with its lead draped over its neck. They were more partners than man and beast. Having no experience, teaching her fear, a four-year-old Thorny had walked over to the mule standing next to the sidewalk, and started petting the long nose.

When she turned to tell her grandfather how bristly the hair was, the old miner was standing next to her pop. The two men were smiling at Thorny making friends with Max, the mule. A few years later, and the old mule was gone, but the friendship with a free spirit named Ulysses Grant, but called Flapjack, was solidified.

Thorny paused at what Ulysses had always referred to as The Stone. In a mountain range of crumbling granite, the short stump of basalt stood out as nothing more than a seat to catch one's breath. She drew out a canteen and sipped on the still cool water. The galvanized metal taste bit at the back of her teeth. She took another sip and lazily screwed the cap back on.

Slipping the cool metal container into the rucksack, she thought about the next stop. The bench was outside the first building. The back of the building had disappeared in a fire. The remaining three walls created a wind shadow for whichever mule was Ulysses's current companion. Thorny had never thought about it, but the floor had always been covered with hay.

The bench was where Thorny and Ulysses had their important talks. The day she wanted to know why he lived alone, explaining the differences of boys and girls, the time she had asked if he had known her mother—all the important talks had been between her and him. Pop, her grandfather, had been too close for many of the questions about life. For the woman questions, she had gone to her friend, Bertha. She had learned early on there were knowledgeable people, and then there were experts.

The last serious talk on the bench was shortly before she graduated from high school. It was Easter, and Flapjack ran into her at Monte's. He took her aside and asked if she could meet him on the bench the following Saturday. He said he had some things to explain to her.

She had never seen him wear, to her knowledge, a new shirt or pants. She knew Victor and his son Vic looked after Flapjack's boots as well as the tack for the large mule pack. She never saw him spend money, nor even talk about money.

He talked about the silver, tin, mercury, and cinnabar in the White Mountains, and the gold in the Sierra's, but he never spoke of any running through his hands. At some level, she understood he needed money to pay for food... but any worldly possessions beyond his boots, he never seemed to need.

On the bench, she learned she was going to college. She had

only thought about college, but with the depression, Pop's farming was little more than field to table with little left to sell.

Ulysses had written to a friend. Those connections garnered a seat at the new college in Los Angeles. Upholding her grades and what she did with herself was up to her. Ulysses got her in with enough money to provide for a room at a nearby boardinghouse for young women. With her working small jobs on the UCLA campus and a scholarship here and there, it had been enough to see her through even a degree in law.

When she tried to explain it all to Pop, he had gently patted her hand with the bankbook in it and told her she had paid her way through her friendship. It was the closest she had ever heard him explain the human heart and relationships.

The grayed wood mass held the morning's heat. The thick lumber making up the bench was probably cut from ends of posts holding up the mine shaft. Thorny looked down the canyon before she sat, the makeshift envelope clutched in her left claw.

Her right hand washed at her face as she thought about the mummified body lying in the cabin Ulysses had always used. The damage to the hip and leg were obvious, even without a medical degree or removing any clothes. Any other insult to her old friend was long ago removed by the bone-dry air of the winter. A slightly damper spring left nothing to rot or putrefy. The desert air never rots, but only dries until the skin makes a tight bag around the brittle bones of a carcass. The old desert rat demonstrated this truth to Thorny many times on the small dry bags which formerly were rabbits or coyotes. A swift kick from a boot turned the contents to powered shards.

She looked at the delicate printing on the wrapping. She could imagine how hard it was to write while he was in so much pain—and on slippery oilcloth paper, no less. The handwriting was definitely the handwriting of the man on the bed. The precise form of the letters spoke of his years of study to be an engineer. The closest he had come to building anything was his making of Thorny's chance to get an education, but his degree in where water was had facilitated his livelihood and financed her degree in law.

She smiled as she turned the packet over to undo the folds making the large envelope. He knew she would come up here looking for him. The cover said merely her first name—Elizabeth. The old enameled coffeepot, sitting on half of the packet, was probably originally full of water. There were no mice at the mining camp, and lizards and horny toads wouldn't have held any interest in the oilcloth.

She opened the package and withdrew the sheets of paper. The writing was spare and concise. He had torn maps in sixths and written on the backs.

My Dearest Elizabeth,

I don't know when you will find this, but I am certain I will be gone.

I made a damn fool's error in judgment and reached out too far. If you go down to the third level, on the right branch, you will find my mark. Beyond, the same count as your address walking is what I was reaching for. Don't fall. You will probably need the services of an accountant just like Pop did the year you were born.

Eli at the bank is holding an envelope for you, along with some other stuff. I would have given it to you earlier, but after your grandfather passed on, I didn't have the heart. He was my best friend and saved my life down in Cuba when we four young fools rode with Teddy. No matter what you hear or learn about the four of us, we tried to be the best men we knew how. Show Monte this letter if he is still alive. He can tell you everything you want to know, or he wants to tell you.

If you are here, I would like to believe you have come home. Hopefully, it is for good. This valley has needed good people as long as I can remember. An honest lawyer would also be a blessing this town has prayed on for years.

This war has taken too many of the young men. Even the new tungsten mine behind Mt. Tom has a problem finding good men. This one is going to be as bad as The Great War, so I guess I could be grateful for not having to watch the best we raise be hewed down like so much alfalfa.

Elizabeth, I know lawyers aren't detectives, but you have a sharp mind. I would like to ask you to do something for us three. When we came back from Cuba, we brought a young lawyer with us. He became our fourth. Most Wednesday night's, he probably came out ahead by at least two bits or four. His saving grace was we played gin at his house and drank his whiskey. You probably wouldn't remember him, but he became the judge in town. When you were just about bellybutton high, he was found hanging in his closet. The police and newspaper said it was a suicide. None of us three ever thought he had a reason to do such a thing, but we never found proof to convince us of any foul play. But still, as I lie here facing my own end, it nags at me.

The new girl, Bertha, who is running the brothel over the police station, might know where Ethel is now. Back in those days, she went by the name of her favorite flower—Violet. If you can find her, she might have some insight into his state of mind. They were friends, and he used to visit her regularly and share tea while they talked about the new philosophy of the time—existentialism. Other than her and Monte, I don't know where to point you.

If you need a good mule, my newest love is named Heather. When I knew I couldn't take care of her, and my leg started turning black, I turned her loose and headed her down the canyon. She knows her name and will come if you call her. Look where the grass is lush down in the river bottom. She likes carrots and apples. I never loaded her heavier than two hundred on a side, but I also never rode any of my mules. So, I know she could carry you, but I don't know if she is ridable.

You will need to have my death corroborated by the coroner or the sheriff, so don't just burn the cabin down right away. Monte or Bertha can help you find the right person to come up here and verify things, and then you can burn the cabin down.

I spruced up the second cabin, next up from the bench you liked so much. The pump in the kitchen works, and the well is still sweet. This mine claim I registered a few years ago in yours and my name. You will need to file these other claim assessments down Independence way. Some are just land, but they carry full mineral rights. Water is considered one of them minerals. These are important and are likely to stir up a piece of trouble, but I know they will be good in your hands. So, now, I guess it's all yours. You won't want to live here, but when you need peace and quiet, you have a place to go.

If you need a good soak, you will need to cross the valley and go up to the pond in upper Buttermilk. I couldn't stand the mud anymore, so I dug it out and added a bunch of sand over the years. With the new depth and the sand, it makes a grand place to stay for a week. I think the minerals are good for the bones and the mind.

I don't know what else to tell you. My water is turned black, so I know I better think of anything else soon.

Your friend and uncle,

Ulysses

Oct 8, 1941

She closed her eyes and weighed her right hand on the

paper. She pictured his face from a time she liked to remember him by. The tears would never come. She wasn't capable of emotion, the same as her inability to feel pain.

She thought about the massive pain he must have been in when he wrote the letter. The first few paragraphs made little or no sense as she reread them for the third time.

She had buried her grandfather during her junior year at UCLA. He had been her only family. Her mother burned to death in the fire, even as she pushed her baby to safety. The fire had marked Thorny, but she only saw it as a reminder of her mother's dying love.

The Fergusons, who now lived in the farmhouse, Pop hired to come live with him, look after him, and sharecrop the farm. She had seen no reason to change the living arrangement, except they now paid her a small share of the harvest. The old tack room and groom's quarters in the large rarely used barn had long suited her solitary nature.

A small bird called from somewhere, and she opened her eyes. The afternoon shade was now burned away by the low setting sun across the valley. Her toes clawed loosely at the powdery dust. Folding the papers up, she noticed the pale writing on the edges of what she had thought were blank pages. The notations made no sense. She turned the page over to the map. There was still no rhyme or reason to the broken sentences and partial clauses. She folded it all back into the original oilcloth paper and shoved it all in the back of her pants. Standing, she fluffed out the back of her shirt over the packet. Looking down the canyon, she sighed deeply. Resolved, she started walking.

The mouth of the canyon broke from the shoulders of the mountains at the peak of the alluvial fan. The view was only four or five hundred feet above the Owens Valley floor, but it left an unobstructed view across to the Sierra Nevada range. The two parallel mountain ranges rose to matching altitudes of just over fifteen thousand five hundred feet. With the valley floor sitting way below at only four thousand, the eleven-thousand-foot difference made the Owens Valley the deepest valley in the world.

Thorny stopped and sat on the stump of basalt. The view of the valley was something she never tired of.

To the south, she could see well past what were apple orchards—now dried snags or stumps. The needed water was now kept back from anything growing in the valley. The precious liquid flowed down the Owens River until it funneled into a large wooden pipe emptying only in Los Angeles. Even the farms in the San Fernando Valley were restricted from growing useful food unless they paid Mr. Mulholland and his gang of thieves. The water stolen from the farmers, ranchers, and people of the valleys was used to make the lawns of mansions green. A few million people drank the water, bathed in the water, and flushed their toilets. What could have grown them and many others food was flushed out to sea. There were a few who had wells deep enough to withstand the brutal years of drought. Pops had been one of the few.

In the last light of the afternoon, she could pick out the two large orchards spreading across the low hills above the west side the valley. Further south were the two large family ranches. The green acreages were distinctive in what they raised. The cousins shared the alfalfa and wheat. When the water was low, they consolidated. They sold down the cattle herd, and only the sellable wheat was raised beyond the sustaining alfalfa for the smaller herd. They had also pooled their sources and paid a higher price for land and water rights from owners up the small canyon feeding a creek from an artesian well. Agents of Mulholland tried to burn them out for getting in the way of them stealing land at pennies on the acre.

Thorny turned her head north. Only because she knew where to look, she could see a tiny speck of reflected light. She knew it was the large nickeled headlight from a Pierce Arrow. The light hung over the barn door of her ranch. She rose and headed down the last few turns to the car.

The sun had long dipped behind Mt. Tom as she turned onto Highway 6. It would be dark when she pulled into the barnyard. The Fergusons would have long turned off the radio and gone to bed. The morning for them would start before Chester the rooster even thought about crowing.

06 OLD WOUNDS NEW CUTS

The thin stiletto slid carefully down the throat. Any good surgeon would have been proud of the edge of the blade. The work was almost silent. Clean. Deadly.

The man held the blade under the drizzle of steaming water. The soap foam slid off the steel, taking the stubble with it.

The stump of a finger pushed the battered nose up. The blade gently slid down the upper lip in concise short strokes. The scars on the man's face hadn't come from him mishandling the blade. The finger pushed at the tip of the nose as he glided the deadly blade to the other half of his lip. The wide scar running from his chin to his left eye had finally flattened, and he didn't nick the skin anymore.

The movement at the door caught his eye. His body screamed to move, but his brain paced the work at hand. The face was only almost familiar. The hair he knew he should place. The rest of the woman standing in the door to his bedroom was new.

Moving the blade up, he turned his head. The sideburn was square at the dead center of his ear. She crossed her arms and leaned quietly against the doorway. His eyes didn't have to focus. He would know her left hand from three blocks away.

"It's been a longtime, Thorny... or do you go by Elizabeth now?"

"Hello, Danny. Thorny is fine." She waved her hand back toward the rest of the house. "The door was open..."

He rinsed off the blade as he looked at the shave. "I guess I'll have to fire the maid."

"Is that what you thugs call it these days—fire? I thought you guys liked to rub people out or fit them for a set of concrete shoes, or maybe your style was of taking them for a drive in the desert."

His one eyebrow raised as he looked at her in the mirror. He slowly wiped his face with the damp towel and turned off the water. He paused and thought as he watched her. She didn't move.

"You know I never did that stuff." He turned and leaned against the vanity. "You watched too much Eddie Robinson and the Cagney fella."

He reached out and took a white shirt from a hook. He removed the hanger and placed it back on the single stub of a deer antler set into the knotty pine paneling. Holding Thorny's eyes, the slight man pulled on the shirt and buttoned it down. Fluffing the front, he reached for his pants and opened the fly. She didn't flinch or turn her eyes. He tucked the shirttails, closed the opening, and cinched his belt.

"Still the same Thorny." He stepped to a chair near the military-made bed. Sitting, he pulled on his black socks and shoes. "What brings you out to the dude ranch? I know you don't drink. It's too late for breakfast and early for lunch. The only thing else we have to offer is horses to ride... unless your tastes have turned to the other residents that we have here to ride." He placed both feet on the floor and leaned back in the chair.

Thorny's thin mouth pulled on the right side. The high school rumors of her playing for the other team. "Still fishing, Danny?"

He shrugged his face, shoulders, and hands. "Goes with the job."

She bounced her shoulder away from the doorway frame. Her hands slid down, and her thumbs hung in her front pockets. The man smiled. She was lost without the high pockets on her bib overalls or the lack of pockets. He remembered how she hung her hands in the tops of her bibs—the same as her grandfather had.

He reached up and curled the button-down collar where others would have a tie. "I don't think this is a social visit for old times' sake. What do you want, Thorny?"

"You."

He snorted softly as he stood. "You could have had me our junior year. Why now?"

"Not what I meant, Danny. I need your help—as the only honest criminal I know."

"Down in the big city, they would call using that insulting word slander."

"I just came from the big city, and I didn't use the term criminal in a slanderous way."

He smiled. "I meant the word honest. It carries an overshadow of someone who is a do-gooder."

"So now you're going to deny beating up Tommy Keselowski in the fourth grade because he tripped me and then tried to kiss me?" She noted the slight blush. "I need an honest cop. I need one I can trust to keep his mouth shut, do a legal job, but not say anything."

"But it's legal?" His eyes closed into a judging squint.

"Completely. I just need there to be complete discretion."

"Are you ever going to tell me what it is you need done?"

"No, because you are going to help and be the expert witness."

"Expert in what way?"

"How they were murdered."

His eyes opened. She had his attention. "Who was murdered?"

She smiled. "They weren't, but you will be the person to verify."

"Who's the stiff?"

"Stiff? Hmm... yes, very." Her face wavered. "Flapjack."

"Ulysses? The old miner? What happened?"

"He fell down a mine shaft last fall. Do you have an honest cop to corroborate the death?"

"Cop or sheriff?"

"It's up one of the canyons—"

"Sheriff. Yeah, I play bridge with him every Tuesday. He won't even lie about the trump—even if it would win the rubber and game. His name is Pete Pitchess."

They walked out onto the driveway. A white Cord sat alone on the pea-gravel. Danny looked around. "Where's your car?"

"I don't have one."

"How did you get here."

Thorny pulled out the pair of green, dark glasses. "I walked."

He swung around with a frown. "It's four miles from town..."

27

Thorny bumped her lower lip out. "It's almost eight from my farm to town. Are we going to go talk to this deputy?"

The Cord was smooth. Thorny ran her hand along the leather seat where Danny couldn't see. It felt cool and smooth on her hand.

"Why didn't you go out with me back then?"

"When?"

"High school."

"I didn't go out with anyone."

He glanced over at her profile. "Was it because it was me or because I was a guy?"

Thorny moved her weight into the back of the seat. Her sigh was soft. "I didn't date anyone. It had nothing to do with male or female. It wasn't about you or your father's business. I don't date."

"Then how will you ever...?"

She gently shook her head. "Find a husband to look after me, take care of me, provide for me?"

His lower lip drew in as he nodded.

"Yeah...kind of ..."

She turned slightly toward him. She leaned over and reached out before he could turn his head. The longer nail on what now would work as her index finger dented the skin over his carotid artery. He felt the pressure on his neck.

"Like you, I carry a small knife. A few more pounds of thrust, and it will sever your carotid artery. You'll probably bleed out before you can stop. My guess is you will be dead in less time than it will take me to get out and drag you from the car and into the weeds. I don't need a man to do it, either. I don't need a husband to point out to the nice Sheriff Peter how you made advances unbecoming a gentleman, and I simply defended myself."

Thorny could tell his eyes were ping-ponging from the road to her. His artery was pulsing under her finger.

"Wh… when did you start carrying a knife?"

She pulled her hand away and looked at the nail on her claw. "I don't. I just forgot to trim my nails this week."

He swallowed. "Point taken."

THE THREE STOOD LOOKING at the desiccated cadaver. Thorny didn't mention the letter.

The deputy turned his head to his bridge partner. Thorny liked him from their first meeting. The man was quiet in a shy way, but not because he was shy, but he was watching and listening. The entire walk up the canyon, he never asked more than a couple of questions—none were about why they were here.

"Verdict?"

Danny shrugged. He pointed at the protruding bump in the faded tan overalls. "If the shattered hip and leg didn't kill him, the dry would have. I don't have to remove his clothes to tell you he wasn't murdered." He looked at Thorny and back at the deputy. "And doing a nose dive down a mine shaft… just sounds like an ugly way to commit suicide."

The uniform swelled with a deep breath. "I concur." He looked past his friend at Thorny. "Well, counselor, what do you need from here?"

"Just the death certificate. I'll take it down to Independence and file it with a few other papers."

The man drew a white handkerchief from his back pocket and wiped his brow. He looked at the fragile baked remains. "What about—?"

She had been waiting for the question and cut him off. "I'll cremate him in place. This building was his home. The memories should go with him. It's what he would have wanted. I'll come back and do it at night, so then nobody sees the smoke."

Danny looked at his wristwatch. "Well, it looks like we can just make lunch at the Copper Kettle. Can I buy you two lunch?"

They stepped back out into the heat. The three looked around the old mine camp with its handful of broken-down shacks.

The deputy frowned. "What did they mine here?"

"They built the mine for silver, but mostly, they pulled cinnabar and mercury out of here. Silver was almost as elusive as gold. By the nineties, the price of mercury coming out of Arizona and Colorado turned this and other mines into just holes in the ground."

"So, Flapjack wasn't mining the claim?"

"Maybe more as a hobby than trying to make a living. He probably got more from panning for gold up Bishop Creek."

"There's gold up Bishop Creek?"

Thorny shook her head as she thumbed her hand back at the shacks. "Probably just enough to pay the rent here. There are four cans of red beans in the cupboard, and if the sack of flour weighs more than five pounds..."

She turned and stared down the broken road. "I don't know about you, but I hear the Kettle has some juicy steaks."

As they walked, Thorny could tell the gears were working in the deputy's head. He wasn't looking around but watching the road. Between rocks the size of heads and shoulders, there were trenches where the occasional wash had slashed the road. He knew no car was coming up this pass.

Thorny felt the question form. She had waited all her life as people thought about how to offer help to the girl with the mangled hand. Few had ever seen the rest of the scars.

"I have access to a jeep... if you need any help."

She lowered her head and snuck a glance at her oldest friend from the first grade. He never blinked. He knew better.

"I appreciate the offer, but I have a mule. She can haul anything I'll need."

Danny guffawed. "You've been in town only three days, and you already own a mule?" He started to laugh before she backhanded his shoulder. He sidestepped to be out of range for the next swing. His hand massaged the first hit. "What? You don't have a car, you walk eight miles into town, and then four more out to get me... but you have a mule?"

Thorny's look was a visual growl. Her voice was even lower and more threatening. "She's not a riding mule."

He continued to rub his shoulder. "I want to see this mule."

"Not unless you get down off your high horse."

The deputy smirked. "Check and mate."

Thorny gave him a smile, and they finished walking down the canyon in silence.

Thorny eyed the large rocks and wondered how much work it would take to make the road passable for a jeep or a Model A.

07 PUZZLES

Monte shuffled through the papers. Occasionally, he turned one over and looked at the map piece. He came back to the original start of the letter. The map side looked like it might be a part of the southwest section of Upper Buttermilk Canyon. The wide alluvial flow was familiar, but a small notation in pencil confirmed the location. The tiny graphite dot was captioned *warm spring*.

He remembered the small artesian well they had found. The three young bucks, fresh back from the war in Cuba, had built a small dam. The result was a three-foot-deep soaking pond with warm water year-round. And then, the century turned into the new one. Eustis found himself with a daughter to raise. Monte went down to the city to train as a barber, and Ulysses followed his heart and soul.

The barber leaned back in his own chair. His eyes closed. He wasn't thinking—he just let the sauce of old friends wash through his being.

The one and a half hands slid down on his shoulders and crossed over his chest. Her head rested alongside his. "You're the last of them. Ulysses said you have all the answers, but it's all up to you. I won't push. You can share, but I only want to listen if *you* want to tell me."

"We were just young kids. War wasn't the same. We didn't know what the Civil War was like. It was just something we read in schoolbooks. So, when the Governor of New York, Teddy Roosevelt, sent out this call, we came running from all over. Ulysses grew up at the Cerro Gordo ferry head across the lake from Olancha. His father was the boiler man on the Mollie Stevens. She was one of the ferries running the ore cars across Lake Owens. By 1880, the little ferry got hauled out, and they put the big engine in the larger ferry. During the fit out, a fire started on the main deck. Before the fitters in the boiler room could get out, the ship was ablaze and burned to the waterline."

Monte looked back to see if Thorny knew any of this. She shook her head.

"Well, the company looked after their own, and they paid the widow five hundred in company gold and enrolled the boy in the Bishop Academy."

Thorny's head raised. "Where the high school is now." He raised his right index finger and nodded.

"We met during his second term. My father landed a job as the powder monkey at the new tungsten mine above Round Valley. Uli's mother was a seamstress down in Independence, and so we were in the dormitory together. Because we weren't paying students, we were what they called charity. I think today, they would call us something else. We thought we were special because they put us up on the top floor. When the winter turned bitter cold is when we found out the heat never got up to the top. We explored and found the steam tunnels running the length of the building. We set up camp. I think that's when Uli found out he liked mines and caves. I found out I hated them, but Uli was there and made it all right."

He held the map up. "There were some nice times growing up, but we never knew how bad it all was until the three of us got back from Cuba in ninety-nine. It was still chilly in the valley, but your grandpa could see the beauty we saw. He decided to stay. We hiked up to the upper Buttermilk to just camp and do a little hunting. We knew the deer would still be down low for a few more weeks. When we found the warm springs, we decided to stay for a while."

A tiny dot of light caught Thorny's eye. She reached out for the paper. Holding it to the window, she saw a pinhole in the middle of the graphite dot marking the spring. She turned the paper over. The pinhole was in the middle of a letter.

"What do ya see?" Monte held his finger up to bend down the paper.

"There is a tiny pinhole in the map."

"Maybe it's where he tacked it to the wall?"

She held up one of the other maps. There was a hole. She confirmed there was a hole in every paper. The holes didn't seem to coincide with any marked landmarks. Some of the papers had no writing on their backs while others had writing but nowhere near the pinhole.

The pinholes randomly wandered around the territory of the papers. The punctures were in unique locations whether she looked at the map side or the plain side with the writings. Most of the writing was a simple random line of words. Something was wrong.

Thorny stepped over to the low wall running the length of the barbershop. On Saturday, the wall would be lined with young boys reading the magazines Monte left there. The well-thumbed magazines ranged from Boys' Life to the old standby National Geographic. Monte upheld subscriptions for both, but never put out any of the more graphic issues which might contain pictures a mother would find objectionable. Thorny smiled at the issues of the new magazine she had found while she was at UCLA. When she could get her hands on a few issues, she would take them over to the Greyhound station and send them north to Monte. Life magazine became a big hit and was now also reporting on the war with images from the bombings in London to the devastation in France.

She moved the magazines to one side on the seat-deep low wall. The afternoon sun was just starting to heat the concrete as it peeked below the wide awning. In the summer, the awning and the ceiling fans struggled to make the heat bearable in the shop. The entire western facing wall was windows.

Spreading out the papers, map side down, she arranged and rearranged them. Suddenly, she could hear Ulysses's voice. He had been reading a poem to her. The poem was written by a friend he made when they were in Cuba. The young Robert Service was there as a reporter for Hearst Publishing.

She carefully restacked the papers. The top fraction of an inch of each paper was exposed with a line of the poem. Holding the papers together, she stood, turned around, and sat.

She was sure the stack of map parts was not in order, but the poem beginning was. Something was still wrong, but she started to read aloud.

> *"There's a race of men that don't fit in,*
> *They range the field, and they rove the flood,*
> *And they climb the mountain's crest.*
> *Theirs is the curse of the gypsy blood,*

And they don't know how to rest.
And each forgets, as he strips and runs
With a brilliant, fitful pace,
Till he stands one day, with a hope that's dead,
In the glare of the truth at last.
Life's been a jolly good joke on him,
And now is the time to laugh.
Ha, ha! He is one of the Legion Lost.
He was never meant to win.
He's a rolling stone, and it's bred in the bone.
He's a man who won't fit in."

She lowered the stack of paper and looked at Monte. The man was pensively fingering his pursed lips. His head began to sway as his eyes closed. Finally, he stood and walked to a small cupboard located over the drawer he used for his cash. He removed a small key from his wallet and fitted it into a hole concealing a lock. The door swung open exposing a small library.

His finger swept until he found the slim book. There was no marking on the soft brown leather cover. Even from the window, Thorny could tell the book wasn't a commercial publication. This small edition would contain hand-pulled printing and hand sewn binding. There were a couple of such books out at the farm. She just hadn't taken the time to look at her grandfather's small collection. She now wondered if there was a matching twin or even a triplet resting on the farm and possibly the mine.

Monte sat as he read to himself. He harrumphed and looked up. "He picked and chose, but it's not the whole poem."

"Why would he..."

Monte's eyes rolled to the door as his tongue wet his lips. "He was saying good-bye."

Thorny frowned as she looked at the papers and the fifteen lines of the poem. "But why not just say good-bye? I mean other than he said as much in the letter on the other papers, which are..." she lifted the other two pages, "written a little wonky."

The man took a deep sigh as he gripped his face and ran his fingers and thumb down to his jaw. His hand floated to his lap as he looked to Thorny. "He was saying good-bye to his last friend. He was saying good-bye to me."

Thorny gently bit the inside of her cheek. She wanted the full answer, and she knew she was only getting the appetizer. Her gaze wandered over the face of the man she had known since her first haircut, one of the three people who never questioned her not having any interest in dating or going to a dance or any of the other parts of growing up. The three men never questioned her wearing pants instead of dresses. When she was sent home from school for not wearing a dress, her grandfather finished his farm chores, fed Thorny, and then rode into town.

He showed up at the principal's home. The man was just finishing his dinner and invited Eustis in. The man's wife came to the front room to offer their guest some coffee. Instead, Eustis asked her if she had a favorite dress and would she please fetch it. The woman thought it was strange, but Eustis just asked please again.

When she brought it to him, he held it out to the principal and told him to put it on. The man refused, saying it was preposterous. Eustis handed it back to the wife, telling her to make the man put it on. She only stood there gasping for breath like a fish out of water. The man growled about the visit getting out of hand, and it was time for Eustis to leave.

Eustis gently grabbed the man by his shirtfront and long tie. He stepped in until they were inches apart. Eustis looked down on the man from almost six inches above.

"So you refuse to wear her dress?"

"I most certainly will not. It is wrong to even think of such a thing."

Eustis let the man go. "Good. Remember this the next time you think about telling my granddaughter she has to do the same."

Thorny's slacks, bib overalls, and even dungarees were never a topic of conversation again. At the time, she chalked it up to the rural farming and kids getting to school after their farm or ranch chores. But looking back, it was more about a conviction held by a grandfather who believed in her right to dress and be the way she felt right.

Thorny looked at the sheaf of papers in her claw. She thought about the pinhole and wondered if they lined up as the poem now suggested. "I need a pin or needle."

He pointed at a drawer. "I keep needles and thread for the occasional button."

She pulled the drawer. There were a dozen spools of colored thread and a packet of needles. She pulled out a long but thin needle.

Carefully, she began to thread each paper onto the needle. The pinhole slightly changed the exposures, but the poem was kept intact. Confirmation the poem was correct and complete, even with Monte's verification of pieces missing.

Thorny thought about the other two pages only containing parts of the letter. She fed them onto the needle. They were fully covered by the others. They had needle holes but added nothing to the clues or good-bye poetry.

She withdrew the needle and placed it back in the packet. Closing the drawer, she turned and leaned against the cabinet —thinking.

Monte watched her. He had watched the same face and stance as she grew up. Even as a small girl, she never thought of what he would call frivolous girlie things. Monte never knew her to have, much less ask for, a doll. When she was six, she asked for a hoe her size for her birthday. Monte had taken the metal to the blacksmith to grind it down in size while Eustis carved down the length of the handle. That summer, the vegetable garden produced a bumper crop with not a single weed. Four years later, Thorny pronounced the cut-down hoe to be too small. She gave it to a neighbor, and her birthday was complete with a cake and a new hoe—adorned with a red bow. Monte never liked the bow tie anyway.

Thorny folded the maps back into the envelope and walked to the door. She turned, looking down. Her pause, Monte recognized pure thought being stifled or redirected.

She looked up and out the wall of windows as an old Locomobile truck rattled through the intersection. She knew there were shovels and picks in the back bed. The mortician's cemetery truck never changed. Digging graves and mines hadn't changed either. "I need to find Heather."

She turned and left.

08 BURN IN THE NIGHT

T he last heat of the day made Thorny's shirt stick to the sweat on her back. The bag of supplies hung heavy from her left shoulder. The claw held it in place. The red gallon can of kerosene was almost light in her right hand.

She saw the boot first. She stopped and thought for a moment. Six more feet and she would be around the large boulder and whoever the boot belonged to would be as exposed as she was.

"I thought you would be up here before the heat was so intense." The boot shifted, and the other landed next to it. The deputy stepped out of the little shade the boulder provided.

"I was going to come up last week, but then I thought about the moon. Tonight is the first moonless night."

Thorny slumped on her left hip. "Why?"

The man stepped closer and held out his right hand, "Because, in the dark, nobody can see the smoke."

He shook his hand at the bag over her shoulder.

"No. Why did you come?"

His hand dropped a few inches. "Have you ever burned a shack before?" His hand rose and held steady.

She passed him the can of fuel. "Not lately."

He sloshed the can. "First, you don't need this. You go splashing fuel on old dry wood, and you won't have a fire— you'll have an explosion."

"And the second …?"

"You're going to need a deputy. An explosion like that will swoop down this canyon, and even the people watching Fred and Ginger dancing at the Bijou will hear it. Then, as the rest of the camp gets lit up, they won't see the smoke, but the fire will light up the mountainside. Passable road or no, they will be here within the hour."

Thorny looked over the top of her green glasses. "And the good deputy will be here to greet them."

"Better if the good deputy shows you how to burn the shack so nobody finds out."

"It will still be a large bond fire."

Pete hefted the can. "But, without this, it will be smaller."

Thorny chuckled. "Good because the fuel is for starting fires in the wood stove. But dip a stick in kerosene, light it, and toss it into the shack. It's all you need."

His voice was small with chagrin. "Oh."

"Where did you grow up?"

"Salt Lake City."

She gave him a side glance. "Hmm, city boy."

He blushed. "Somewhat."

As they walked past the boulder, he leaned over and picked up a small rucksack and thermos. Thorny noticed him tighten the top before sticking the cylinder in the bag.

"Been waiting long?"

He gave her a sideways glance—looking for any malicious intent. There was none.

He swallowed and looked up the canyon. "Since sunrise."

They walked in silence. Thorny wasn't sure it was out of reverence for what they were about to do or just nothing to say. Either way, she was grateful.

The late afternoon sun turned much of the canyon into an oven. An old ore car, once used on long-gone tracks, lay in the struggling weeds growing in the old tailings. The waves of air above it testified to the heat of rusted black iron in the desert sun. Thorny wondered if the hot iron could cook a pot of stew in the afternoon.

At least reheating some stew would avoid her having to make a fire in the wood stove. Breakfast in the desert was different. A small fire in the early morning chill of the shadowed canyon made for a welcomed comfort.

She looked at the remaining dozen structures. Most were in a slow rigor mortis of falling. In the desert, structures didn't succumb to their weight on rot. The dryness preserved the wood, and the wind worked on the joints as it desiccated the fibers.

There was more than a lifetime of fuel for the small wood stove, even if she lived up here like Ulysses. The shallow shelter leaning against the last parts of the stamping mill showed marks of being the man's woodpile. His final woodpile would burn faster.

The two sat in the dark. The boulders were at the far end of the tailing pile. Even then, the heat from the fire lighting the night felt like too many blankets or quilts on a bed. They both knew the other side of the rocks would be cooler and shielded.

Neither moved.

The fire swayed a mesmerizing dance in the four eyes. They started the fire on one side. The fire burned hot with the weathered wood. There was little smoke from the hot flames. As the fire crept around the building, the two retreated from the heat. Even the chilly night air washing down from the still snow-capped mountain did nothing to temper the heat.

Thorny wrapped her arms around her knees.

She smiled as the one side gave way and the burning shack fell in on itself. "Clever idea."

"The wall...?"

She nodded. "At first, I was irritated about the intrusion, but I guess you got to know Ulysses as well. So thanks for coming up."

The flames flickered in his eyes. He thought about the first time he met Ulysses. The man was tying his mule to a car door handle. The mule was standing on the sidewalk. The new deputy asked the crusty old desert rat if he had ever received a ticket for his animal defecating on a public walkway. Ulysses had turned and looked the deputy, in his fresh pressed uniform, up and down. Finally, he looked the young man in the eye and said the word defecating was a big word for such a young man and then asked if he knew what it meant.

The new deputy stood with his mouth open.

Ulysses moved closer so he could talk quieter. "Son, when you learn what eschew obfuscation means, come on back and talk to me." He studied the young face and added, "Do I need to write them big words down for you?"

The deputy only shook his head.

Six months later, Peter saw the man again. "Don't let your beast shit on the street."

Ulysses had stopped with a small smile. "You're learning. But you have it all wrong. A cow or horse is a beast. This fine specimen of equine grandeur is a mule. They are called Jenny because they are all ladies, even if they are kicking you in the buttocks. They never piss or shit where they sleep, eat, or will walk again. Much like the much-maligned porcine, they are very picky where they do what they do and who they associate with."

He started to walk off, leaving the mule parked on the side of the street with its lead hanging in the dust. There was nowhere close to tie the animal.

The young deputy pointed at the mule. "You forgot to tie up your mule."

The man turned. "Nope. She don't need it."

"But you tied her to a car the last time I saw you…"

Ulysses thought back. "Nope. Jus' tied doc Bullard's Packard to my mule. I wanted him to know I needed to talk with him." The man turned and walked into the store, leaving the deputy to work out the ways of life.

Peter pulled his knees close and rested his chin on them. His voice was quiet and far away. "He was the best education I ever got."

A soft snort came from between Thorny's knees and crossed arms. "If nothing else, he was an education."

THE STEW THORNY brought went well with the small loaf of hard-crust bread Peter brought. Waking up to a fire in the woodstove felt cozy. Hearing the flames expand the cast iron and the smell caused a dream of her grandfather waking up before her every morning. Anticipating soda biscuits had wakened her to find only a shivering deputy.

She laughed. "The secret is to start the fire, and then climb back under the blankets to stay warm."

He nodded with his eyes. She was wrapped up in all four of the blankets. She couldn't feel pain, but she could feel cold. She had stolen the other blankets in the early morning chill.

She raised two of the blankets—leaving the other two wrapped around her. Her offer was of warmth, and only warmth.

"Are you planning to stay in Bishop?" He tore off a small piece of the loaf. Mopping the rim of the tin bowl, he stuck it all in his mouth.

She nodded.

"Are you this talkative every morning?"

She nodded, and he laughed.

"Now I'm sorry I didn't bring any coffee."

She grumbled around the last bite of stew. "No pot to cook it in."

"You've never had skillet coffee?" His face was more glow than it should have been at the early hour.

"You made that up." She leaned back on the small stool. Her legs bent like a grasshopper. The table was once a powder keg someone had nailed boards onto.

He shook his head. "Do you have a cast iron skillet around here?"

"I didn't look, but I would not be surprised to find at least a dozen of them around the camp. They used to melt down the cinnabar and silver in them. Coat them with mercury, and you can pan gold powder from mine tailings. Catch your husband with a floozy, and you can leave a large dent in his head or backside. They are the most useful invention since the wheel."

"Is that what you did... leave a large dent in Danny's head?"

She looked at him with a stone face.

He rolled his eyes and wiped his mouth with his shirttail. "I'm just saying. I saw how he looked at you the other day. The man is still smitten. What happened between you two?"

"Nothing."

"It didn't look like nothing."

Thorny sighed as she took up the bowls and stood. "He has always looked at me with a goofy face. I think in the second grade, he thought we were an item. When we started high school, he started having fantasies. He'd ask, and I'd point him at some other girl."

"So you never dated...?"

"Good friends, but never anything close to dating. This morning, you were closer than he ever got. And if you ever tell him... you may never speak to me again."

The man passed his fingers over his lips in a zipper motion.

"So who did you date?"

She worked the lever on the water pump. By the fifth pump, she could tell it was bringing water. "Never did."

"No one?"

She looked out the gray smear of a window. The large dark mass of Mt. Tom was starting to glow pink on the tip from the early morning sun on the snow. The first gurgle of water splashed on her thumb. She started and looked back over her shoulder. "No, I never did."

"Can I ask why?"

"No." She shook her head. Filling the tin bowls, she placed them on the stove. She bent down and took a piece of wood from the box with her claw. She hefted the weight a few times and nodded at the secure grip. Stepping to the table, she laid her right hand down with the palm up. The deputy looked at it and then her with a frown.

She nodded at her hand. As he looked, she began beating her hand with the piece of wood. He leaped up and grabbed the hand and stick.

"What are you doing?"

She took the stick back from him. Turning, she grabbed the hot handle of the stove and opened the door. Throwing the wood in, she calmly closed the door. She turned back and motioned him to sit back down.

She pulled her stool around and sat down. "Oh, good gravy, sit down. I'm not going to beat you."

"What the hell was that all about?" He cautiously took back his seat.

"You seem like a smart guy. My guess is you're even educated."

He nodded. "University of Utah."

She shrugged with a slight smile. "I would have guessed more Provo."

He snorted softly as his eyes drooped in memory. "More Jack than Mormon and the folks needed me around the place."

"Did you take any psychology courses?"

He shrugged, and his head weighed to the left. "A few... what's your point?" He pointed at the makeshift table.

Her jaw pushed out. "Do you know what a sociopath is?"

He started to speak, and then closed his mouth to think. "They are conniving and have no remorse for using other people for their gains. They don't have any understanding of right from wrong, and are incapable of empathy," he looked up, "or of feeling any emotions."

She smiled loosely. "Somewhat there, but you mixed in a little bit of psychopath, as well. Where the psychopath knows how to mimic emotions, they only do so as a form of fitting in with everyone else. The sociopath might know how, but doesn't, because it serves them no purpose—they don't care about blending in. Neither one has much capacity to feel, even physically. Emotionally, the feelings come from being able to physically feel. Like a hug. You feel the other person, their touch, their smell, their closeness. This translates into a sense of intimacy. If it's your mother, you feel love and closeness to her. If it's someone you are dating, there might also be feelings of lust."

He shifted uncomfortably. "But your hand...?"

"My hand. I can feel, just not pain." She raised her left hand. "When I was a baby, my mother had..." She bit her lower lip. "There was a fire, and my mother died." Thorny unbuttoned her sleeve and drew up the shirt's arm, exposing the skin. "A neighbor pulled me out, but not before I was burned. I lost the index finger and the pinky. This scarring runs up to my body."

She pushed the sleeve down and cinched the button. "Maybe I was born a sociopath, and maybe I wasn't—but they think the burn damaged my nerve receptors, and now I can't feel pain. I like the feel of fine silk, the softness of a kitten or bunny, but the pain from stepping on a tack or cutting myself—it's not there." She wet her lips. "My... emotions... aren't the same as yours. I have respect for people, or maybe concern for their well-being, but I don't love them or care about them like other people."

He sat with his elbow resting on his crossed leg. His index finger hid his thin mustache. His head turned, more in a grinding way, until he looked far out the open door. His breathing was slow.

"So... if we go to dinner sometime at the Kettle, it would be out of mutual respect and concern for our well-being—"

"Not a date. No." She didn't move. What had taken Danny years to understand or accept, this man got in minutes.

His eyes turned back. She saw a mischievous twinkle. "What if I want to pay the bill?"

Her lower lip pushed out as she shrugged. "It's always your prerogative... as I don't have a job yet."

He frowned. "What are you going to do for work?"

She glanced at the bowls now steaming. She stood. "I have a job or work. It just doesn't look like what a lawyer usually does." She took up the bowls with her bare hands and placed them in the sink. Swishing the hot water around, she cleaned the bowls. Working the pump, she rinsed them and turned them upside down on the sideboard with the spoons.

"Ulysses asked if I would do some discovery work."

"But he was long dead before you got in town."

She stopped and thought. Nodding, she looked at him as she straightened the few items. "Let's just say he wrote me a letter."

Peter realized they were leaving, and he put the few items back in his rucksack and drew it over his shoulder. "What sort of discovery work?"

She looked at him for the span of a few heartbeats. "Finding a killer."

Deputy Pitchess swallowed.

09 STICK A PIN IN IT

The view of the valley from lower Buttermilk stretched from the hazy tan of the north toward the Nevada border and down the patchwork of gray, tan, and green to the south. Just around the last hill to the south was the next town of Big Pine.

As she sipped warm coffee from the lid of her thermos, Thorny watched the fanciful progress of the unique train known as the Slim Princess. To freeze out competition, the owners bought a European-made engine and cars. The tracks were only a mere inch or two closer together than all the other trains in the United States. They paid little for the train, as it was a wood burner, and all of Europe was switching to the new oil. The great forests can only regenerate so fast, and Europe was running out of wood to burn.

From her perch on the giant balanced flat rock, she could look down into the small dry canyon. Ulysses always called it the Schielkaskin Valley. He spun out a long yarn to a young Thorny about the original Schielkaskin Mountains. The raiders were fierce warriors who even the Mongols, Romans, and the

Visigoths feared. Much later, the Visigoths, led by King Alaric—a child of Visigoth and Schielkaskin parents—would overrun and sack Rome.

At college, Thorny could never find a mention of the Schielkaskin people or the valley, but she cherished the stories Ulysses could spin. The large flat rock sat above all else. The length and width was the size of a large hay wagon. Even in the late winter, the sun would heat the dark boulder, making it a comforting picnic spot.

Movement down the narrow gorge caught her eye. The bird was large and darker than the shadows along the vertical south wall. Spreading its large wings, the eagle caught the updraft at the end of the gorge and lifted high into the blue sky. She knew it would now be hunting the rabbits unique to the greater Owens Valley. In the mid-1800s, the early settlers brought a few dozen large bunnies to the valley and let them go. The large meaty domestic rabbits bred with the scrawny jackrabbits. The result was a fast rabbit with hind legs worth eating. The white fluff of a tail made them cute, but also easy to spot running away.

She took one last sip and slid the thermos into the rucksack. Shouldering the small pack, she made her way down and then back up along the canyon. At the shallow west end, she crossed and walked across the desert of sand and bitterbrush. A small animal slithered from one bush, under another, and squeezed into the crack under a large flat rock. She could hear Ulysses teasing the small girl about it being her little brother—another thorny toad. Years later, she would find it was neither thorny or a toad. The protrusions were horns, and the reptile was in the lizard family. But her nickname stuck and followed her into adulthood. She glanced at her left hand. She came to accept both as a part of who she was.

After her grandfather had passed, only Ulysses knew she had gone to see a judge and changed her name.

She opened the door of the old Ford and got in. The road up ahead was only a few miles, but it would take most of the afternoon. There was no pain, but she would feel the tiredness of the muscles being tossed about by the rough wagon-rutted road—barely better than a mule deer track.

She parked the car in a dry turnout. The river hadn't been robust enough to come close to the gravel patch since Los Angeles dammed the canyon and started the water down the mountain in a wooden pipe. The hard black locust saplings around it had long withered and died. The dark gray and black stand camouflaged the old car.

She only took a few glances at the piece of the map to remember where she was going. The hills, ridges, draws, and the shape of the valley was all flooding back and filling her memory. She hoped the small pond of warm water was still there. Shouldering the pack, she started up the draw. In the still of the evening, she could hear the small animals. The rustic static of the desert crickets gave way to smaller wet crickets with a slower, softer pulse. As the green increased and deepened, she could hear the deep thunder of the tiny tree frog.

She smiled at the memory of once telling an old friend she was going to become a lawyer. The wise old Indian scratched at his face. "You will become like the tiny tree frog, small in body, but giant in voice."

She didn't know if her voice sounded as sweet as the frogs around her, but she hoped the old man was still alive. As the tribal chief, his wisdom went far beyond his meager schooling.

Thorny had fallen asleep many nights up this canyon listening to Ulysses and Tom Brown argue over politics of the valley, the right way to make a fire, and even how to trap a woman.

As two old bachelors, Thorny had asked at their wisdom and knowledge. They both laughed and explained how they were talking about a woman trap instead of a mantrap—and how to bait such a dead-fall trap. The men were pragmatists and were talking about physically trapping or killing another human being. Obviously, to them, there were subtle differences between trapping a man and trapping a woman. Thorny took refuge in sleep.

The two men brought their protégés to the campsite to learn the ways of the forest. In the later years, Thorny and the grandson of the chief just figured the men came for the hot water and brought the kids along as an excuse. Excuse or not, Thorny and Charlie were a friendship of equals in the forest but strained or separated in town. The Paiute children were kept in the back rows of seats. Thorny was not allowed to sit in the back. Because of her clawed hand, many of the teachers believed she was also hard of hearing and maybe slow in her mind. By the first tests, she would prove them wrong on both counts. The racial fear or prejudice she could do nothing about. But walking home with her friend, they reviewed lessons. At his grandfather's house, they would study and do paperwork. Charlie graduated two points below Thorny. Both threw some last-minute tests to force Phillip Partridge into the position of Valedictorian.

Thorny didn't want to give a speech with little meaning and that no one would remember. Charlie was Paiute. The speech would be given only by a white child—preferably male.

The graduation melted away in the warm water. The campsite had changed. The pool was deeper, and the dam was now a stone and concrete wall instead of just stacked rocks. Thorny skated her feet in the deep sand. The pond used to have more mud than sand. She leaned against a reclined wall of smooth concrete. A roll of smoothed concrete nestled the neck and supported her head. She didn't know who would have made this much effort but was thankful.

The water rippled. Thorny's eyes cracked, and she took in the large hulking figure. The moon wouldn't be up for another hour, but even then, it would only be a sliver. Good illumination would take another week.

The figure groaned softly as it let down into the warm water. Thorny closed her eyes and relaxed. Her nakedness wasn't even a thought.

Her lips cracked, and she licked them smooth. Her voice was soft and quiet but carried across the pool. "You are getting sloppy. I heard you crashing down the north draw a half hour ago."

Charlie lay his head back. "Wasn't me. I came over the crest from North Lake. It must have been hungry bear looking for white meat who glows in starlight."

A third voice croaked from a short distance away in the small grove of Aspen. "No bear. I am embarrassed to say, I have a son who raised his son to not know how to walk like a Paiute. You better have brought those fish you caught this morning when you slipped in the falls. A noise I heard while I was snoring. You very noisy, child Chauncey."

Thorny chuckled as she could feel the larger ripples coming from the silently laughing, large man. "Never lie, little one, when your grandfather will call you a liar."

The willowy shadow crouched at the edge and then stepped in. "You're in my seat."

Thorny shifted to her right and found another dished-out area in the concrete. She guessed it would have been the chief's best friend. By inheritance, it was now hers. Wrapping his long braid around his shoulders and neck, the old man softly swirled into his seat and settled. "Thank you, mother, for the gift you give so freely."

The silence of the night was a symphony of tree frogs, water rippling down rocks as it flowed out of the pool, and a gentle tin rustle of the Aspen trees. Thorny closed her eyes and let herself be only ten again. In her mind, she could sense her grandfather, Pops, mostly lying in the water. Ulysses would have been with his head toward the north. The chief and Charlie with their heads toward the reservation. The chief and Ulysses were always the first to grouse about the pool being too cold or too shallow. Pops would point out the thermal dynamics of deeper water bringing more mass for longer sustained heat. The frogs, water, and Aspens were the same. She missed Pop's simple, straightforward way of looking at the world. There were facts or a story. Stick to the facts, and you wouldn't have to spin a story.

She rolled her head in the direction of the darker shadow of the chief. "The depth makes it warmer." She knew he wouldn't want a thank-you. The acknowledgment was enough.

"This isn't warm. This is barely what the sun blessed the sand with." He shifted, and his head raised. "Littlest of tree frogs, make yourself useful and open the little dam so we get some heat for these old bones."

As a shadow more the size of a large bear moved across the

pond, Thorny snorted at the old nickname for her friend. "You might need to revise his name to at least bullfrog."

The chief snorted loudly. "His gas sounds like a bullfrog in mating spring."

The quiet settled on the pond as Thorny could feel the surge of warmer water bringing the pond up to a good warm bath. The heat felt good, but she knew it was going to become too much when the large shadow rose from the depth and sat on a rock at the edge.

"Is this just a visit or are you planning to come home?" The voice could have passed for the deep rumble of thunder of a distant storm.

The chief choked on his laugh. "My little boy is pining for his old playmate. I tell him you are now an adult and have work in the big city... but he still hopes."

Ignoring Charlie, she played to his grandfather. "Does he still run in circles and cry at the moon?"

"Only when mother moon is full and shines bright. Other times he lays in his bed and makes a terrible noise. It scares the dog, and he asks to be allowed to sleep in the yard."

"You two are terrible."

Thorny laughed and beat the old man to his tribal saying. "It is the way of nature, little one." Then three laughed at old times. It would be the closest to remembering the men who were gone.

Thorny pushed with her arms behind her. She wetly sat on the flat behind the dished-out headrest. "After I passed the bar exam, I got a job at the District Attorney's office. They wouldn't let me litigate because I'm a woman."

The old man still in the hot water mused. "Women don't fight fair. Only boys are raised to fight fair, but women fighters don't take prisoners—they only leave bodies."

"Sounds like the right way to fight the war in Europe. In the Pacific, they are fighting by bombing and shelling islands. There is no way to take prisoners."

The man hummed in the water. "But if you leave one hundred wounded, it takes five hundred to tend to them. This is six hundred you do not have to fight."

Thorny splashed some water up on her face. "The war is why I'm home. When they started rounding up the Japanese in southern California, the work of processing them fell on our office. There were two legal clerks and me. We were the only women in the office. As the only lawyer, I had to read every single file. There were people in those files who had grandparents born in California before it was a state. They are now grandparents themselves. Right down the road from here is a camp full of Americans who have been charged with a crime they didn't commit. They have been imprisoned, but they received no trial. They were assumed to be guilty. Yet, they have been denied due process." She started coughing as the spit and stomach acid met at her lungs.

The chief rose out of the water and sat beside her. His arm found her shoulder and his hand gently slapped against her back. "Calm yourself, little cricket in the field. You are among friends. This is not one of your white man's courtrooms."

Her breathing slowed, and she softly leaned in against his chest and shoulder. It felt smaller than she remembered but no less comforting. "I'm sorry... I just get worked up."

The soft roll of Charlie's deep voice rumbled across the pool. "But it is not why you are here."

She shook her head. "No, it is exactly why I'm here. Going to work each day, living in a house with no lock on the door, walking down the street a free woman..." She sighed. "It tore at me. They were no less American, but they were in a camp, and I was free. I had to leave."

Charlie slid back into the water. He washed his face with the hotter water. "This is not what I meant. I was not asking why you returned to Bishop, but why you are here, at the pool, in the night."

She slumped.

The chief chuckled. "It is chilly, and my bones are old." He squeezed her shoulder and then reclaimed his seat in the water.

She sighed and slipped back in the water. "Does it have to be this hot?"

The large shadow moved in the night. "Come over here. The cooler water will come along this wall first."

The small sliver of moon peeked above the White Mountains as Charlie showed her the boards which made the dams to control the temperature in the pool. The cold mountain creek and the hot water spring, when blended correctly, made a very comfortable soak.

"About Thanksgiving, I got the last letter from Ulysses. By Christmas, I figured he was dead. With Pops gone, I didn't have anyone I could think of to go up Silver Canyon to check on him."

The chief grunted. "We saw the light in the canyon three nights ago."

Charlie sensed his old friend stiffen. "It's okay. We were out on the ridge from Coyote Flats and could see across. The mountain was black, but the canyon was a warm yellow. There was very little smoke, but lots of fireplaces in Bishop, so nobody would know. We heard you were in town, so we thought it might be you."

"It was the way he wanted it. He left a letter for me. I

brought up the new deputy because I thought I could trust him. He made out the official death certificate, and I'll go down to Independence one of these days and file the paperwork."

The old man's voice was stronger. "He left the mine to you?"

She nodded. "The mine, the canyon, and a few other places. This is one of them, but I don't know how or why."

Charlie looked down into the water. "Probably because of the mine."

"There's a mine here? Where?"

The two Indians laughed. "You're sitting in it."

The chief splashed water across the pool. "For years, we panned a little gold out of the streams, but even more came out of the old pool here. In the spring, the hard water rushes down and carries much sand. In the pool, it calmed, long enough to drop the gold. While Ulysses was making the pool deeper, he was panning the sand. Stopping to pan was slow. We thought about making a dredge or something. Instead, he built a long sluice-box and kept throwing the sand in. He lined the bottom with skins from bummer lambs. The wool was about a baby's finger thickness, but it trapped the gold, and the sand washed on."

"How did he get the gold out?"

Charlie chortled with a smile. "He put the skins in the big black iron cauldron up at the mine and lit them on fire with a roaring fire underneath. The skins burned up, and the gold melted."

Thorny smiled at the simplicity of the process. It was pure Ulysses. "It must have been how he sent me to college."

Charlie's large smile glowed in the night. "Me too."

Thorny frowned. "Where?"

"Arizona State. Eventually, I will be chief one day, so I studied business and water."

Thorny looked over at the current chief. Thorny's face was a dim glow in the moonlight cast by the thinnest of slivers. The old man shrugged. "At least he passed."

She looked back at her friend. "You were a good student... What was your standing?"

He held up four fingers and smiled.

Thorny shrugged with a smile. "Fourth in your class is a lot better than just passing."

The chief growled. "From the bottom."

She stopped with a gaping mouth. Her stun gradually morphed into a frown and one eye half closed. She growled. "How many in the class?"

The old chief laughed as he held up a full hand and a single finger.

Thorny realized she had been away for eight years, but nothing had changed.

10 MORNING LIGHT

Thorny left her blanket draped over her shoulders. There were two ways to get warm from the early morning desert chill. Charlie was predictable and was back in the water. Thorny joined the old chief at the small fire. The flat stone on the one side reflected the heat back toward the wall of stone where the two sat.

The bony hand held the piece of map up to the light. The pinhole was exactly where they were sitting. There was a symmetry about the mark on the map and their presence. "There are those who would say our meeting here was fate. Others would call it serendipity." The paper and hand softly joined the two piles. The man looked out at the fresh rising sun across the valley.

"But you would call it...?"

He took in a large slow breath as his eyes closed. "The world turns slowly as a child. Each day is a patchwork of adventures. As we age, the patchworks take longer." His eyes opened. His head softly ground around at the nature of where they were.

Landing on Thorny, he softly let out his breath. "I just accept. We came down from fishing the Brook Trout our good friend Norman Clyde planted in the high country. They have grown fat. They will now become good jerky. We will go back up and fetch them in a couple of weeks. If a raccoon has found some, they have been fed. If a bear was hungry, they too might have eaten. We will not starve. Little tree frog in hot water most certainly not starve."

The offended grandson spouted a stream of water in the air. The giant body was more muscle than blubber, but his imitation of a whale was perfect.

"We arrive. We are looking forward to soaking in the warm waters. A friend is here already. This is just a good thing on top of a good thing. There is no mystical word for it other than *friend*." His head hung as he reached out with a stick to stoke at the fire. "I have lost too many of them lately."

Thorny leaned forward and pushed a few small broken branches onto the fire. "And the judge?"

The dark finger waved back and forth. "You two were just children then. The news tore at the people of the valley. The church ladies were all shocked. He was a good man and well liked. I'm sure the Methodist church by the school still hasn't recovered."

Thorny leaned back against the large boulder. "Do you think he did it?"

The man looked at her through the side of his eye. "As opposed to being killed?"

She nodded.

The thinning lips curled as he thought. "I've thought on it many times. Every year, something comes up, and I think back about Harold. The man was gentle and kind. Even when he was a lawyer and had to prosecute someone, he tried to find a way for the accused to make amends and reach redemption. He would rather seek a sentence which kept a man near his family. There were a few... he found work on the highway, instead of sending them down to Tulare or Tehachapi. There, it would have been a hardship for the family to come visit." He cleared his throat. The frog was wet but no less large. "He just wasn't the type of man to take his own life. But I don't want to believe he was the kind of person who someone would kill."

She reached out to his knee. "Pops drilled into me the truth of matters. There are the facts, and everything else is just a story people tell themselves or others. It's not always a lie, but close." She considered his damp eyes. "This is what I'm here for... to find the truth. Otherwise, everybody is just telling stories." She stuck the stick of jerky in her mouth. Snarling, she tore off a bite. She forgot how much she hated fish jerky.

The sun had started to warm the camp as they ate the pancakes Thorny had brought the fixings for. Some of her cherished memories of the upper Buttermilk were breakfasts of pancakes at the hot springs camp. Most of the time, it had only been Ulysses and her. Other times, Pop would come along. Rare but welcome were the chief and Charlie. It was always a camp of men and Thorny. She was never treated different or even like a girl. She never saw herself as different—except for her claw and burn scars.

She looked over at one of the guiding figures in her life. The man was sorting the maps.

"What do you see?"

He looked up. "I'm not sure, but this pile, I'm guessing you have some paperwork on."

She glanced through the stack. "I'll be filing the deeds in Independence on Wednesday."

"How are you getting down there?" The man looked up with concern.

"I'll take the morning bus down and wait at Austin's until the courthouse opens. After, I thought maybe just hitchhike. The northbound bus won't come through until about one."

He looked over at Charlie. "Do you have Red Leaf's Chevrolet Supreme running again?"

The man bobbed his head. His lower lip pushed out. "Last week. The new Lincoln motor makes it run a lot faster."

The older watched the younger as he rocked gently back and forth. "You might need it." He turned back to Thorny. "Frog will drive you. If there is any problem, he is big, but he can drive better than anyone else in the valley."

She looked at the man who was twice her size. "Why would there be any trouble?"

Charlie growled around a wad of jerky. "Because you're going to be filing on five to seven sources of water to the valley. It wouldn't be the first time Los Angeles has killed or at least threatened people over water."

"What about the gold?"

The chief swallowed. "They are like a thirsty wolf. They don't care about the fish in the stream, but they will kill you to get at the water. Back in 1924, a group of farmers went down to Lone Pine and blew up one of the control gates above Lake Owens. The water ran into the lake for almost a month until the engineers from the city turned off the new control. Shortly after, one of the policemen from Bishop died in his sleep, and one of the farmers slipped and drowned in his own outhouse."

Thorny squinted. "How do you get through the hole to—?"

Charlie harrumphed and finished for his grandfather. "Someone pulled the outhouse back about ten feet. But the farmer hit the back of his head on something when he fell into the four feet of poop."

The chief sipped on his coffee as he drew his hand down his long braid. "They weren't the only sudden deaths of the group. One whole family just suddenly up and disappeared one day. The food was in the dishes on the dinner table. The front door just swung in the breeze. The neighbor saw their calf standing in the field of turned dirt. He could tell the animal was dehydrated and starved."

"Did they ever find them?"

He shook his head. "Not so's I ever heard."

Thorny shredded her last small piece of jerky. Sticking a tiny sliver in her mouth, she sucked it over into her right cheek to juice it up. "But this is 1942. Do you think they would be as ruthless today?"

"More so. Back then, there was almost a million people in their county. Last census, they said the Los Angeles County was now close to four million. That's many water glasses to fill. But if you think about it, they grew four times in only twenty years. How much water are they going to need in another twenty years?"

Thorny sipped on her tin cup. Grimacing, she swirled the cold liquid and watched the reef of grounds stick up the sides. She swirled the coffee and splashed it out on the still warm embers of the campfire. "In court, we call that a whole lot of motive." She stood and stepped to the hot water coming out of the small spring. Rinsing her cup, she looked at the boulder, but her mind was elsewhere. "How is Bishop set for water?"

The chief looked up at his grandson. Thorny noticed and turned around.

Charlie squinted with only one eye. "They have three large commercial wells and a few smaller ones. They'll be fine for water. The reservation has been sinking a few test wells to try to find the same underground river. They draw mostly from one well because it hit one of the artesian rivers which produce the three artesian wells down near the Owens River. Los Angeles can't control the water we pull out of the ground on our land or Bishop on their land. One day, we will have the free-flowing artesian well on the reservation and can grow more food."

The chief explained. "Charlie is one of the Inyo county water engineers. All the wells must be mapped to see where the water level is. As the years go on, it will become even more important to know where the water table is and see what damage Los Angeles is doing to the whole valley."

Charlie stood and washed his coffee cup in the hot water. "The hunters, both Paiute and white, have noticed over the years how the deer are coming down later and later. The water and better feed are keeping them higher. They used to stay low until about May, but they are already up here in Buttermilk and over on the top of Coyote Flats as early as late March going into April."

"What about the Tule Elk? They don't migrate up the mountain, but stay on the valley floor?"

"They are starting to become a problem. The graze is drying up, so they are mowing down some of the rancher's fields of alfalfa. Many have taken to putting up barbed wire, but even a five-string fence can disappear in the night when a herd of thousand-pound elk walks through it because there is tender green feed on the other side."

Thorny thought about their earlier discussion as they stored the cooking gear in the small cave. "Do you think maybe Judge Hodgins was a victim of the water war?"

The chief handed the 30-30 rifle to the larger man to carry. Charlie already shouldered the large pack with supplies and the previous month's jerky.

"Harold was pretty outspoken about the water. One of the first big trials to come before him was the banker and his brother Wilford, and Mark Watterson. The two saw the way things were going and started skimming money from the bank at the farmer's and rancher's expense. The funny part about them two was they were some of the loudest rabble-rousers for blowing up the aqueduct. Nobody ever thought they would be stealing from their neighbors."

"How much?"

"Close to a million dollars."

They started down the trail. The small bird noises replaced the night's tree frogs. The light through the Aspen leaves seemed to quiet the rustle. The lower down the mountain they walked, the quieter the air became. As they cleared the tree line, the air took on a cooked or stagnate texture.

As they reached the old Ford, the chief snapped his fingers. "If you are looking at old records, look up a case old Jess Hession filed against a bunch of farmers back around '27. The case didn't go anywhere, and it finally got dropped in the early spring of '28. It was just a brief time later they found Harold."

He reached his hand out for Thorny's shoulder. "I don't know if anything is there, but it's worth looking at if you're looking."

"I'll look." She waved her finger at the two and the old two-seater car. "You sure I can't give you a lift down to the reservation?"

The old man's face split into a large laugh. "If we had some rope, we could tie the frog over the front bumper like a deer."

11 SINGLE FILE

The county clerk reminded Thorny of one of the actors from the silent era. The man only needed a straw boater hat and to be slapped real hard so his eyes would stick in the wide-open position—the same position they hit when the tall white woman in pants and boots walked in with an oversized Paiute with long braids.

When Thorny put down the stack of documents to file and have conformed, his eyes hit the mark again. She wondered if it was maybe his first week on the job when his Adam's apple first disappeared and then slammed into the man's jaw.

When he asked who the filing attorney was, he went for the record when she told him who she was and who she was filing the claims for. The Adam's apple became a basketball which never came near the hoop.

The man carefully looked through all the documents. Thorny was familiar with the court clerks in the big city making sure everything was filled out and complete before they stamped the forms and accepted the check. She had never watched one read all the documents... for every case. She knew things could be slow and boring in a one-elk town with four blocks of paved Main Street, but this was something new.

She crossed her arms and turned her back as the man took the motions back to his desk. The older woman typing at another desk paused, watched him, and shrugged as she resumed typing.

Thorny leaned back against the high counter. She watched the impassive face of her friend. "What's he doing now?" Her lips didn't move.

She never even saw his lips crack open. "Making a phone call." She wondered if Charlie could whisper through his nose.

Her eyes closed gently as she turned her head in boredom and watched the typist. Charlie continued to report. "He's scared. He just covered the mouthpiece and turned away."

Their wait wasn't long. The man hung up as his Adam's apple made the fight between Max Baer and Cinderella Man Jim Braddock look like a game of patty-cake. The man sat with his eyes closed and worked on controlling his breathing.

"He's coming back." Charlie sighed and rolled his head to the side. He was the quintessential statue of bored.

Thorny turned as the man got to the counter. His eyes opened wide again. "We have to do some research about the authenticity of the claims—"

"No, you don't." Thorny grabbed the papers from the man's hands before he could think about withholding them. "The conformed copy of the original deed is article two. The letter of clearance of the title is article three. The quitclaim, county surveyor's documents, plot map, and my certifications are articles four, five, six, seven, and eight through twelve. Everything for you to intake, certify, and conform these motions are right here." She leaned in as the man swallowed harder. "But if you want to be a fall guy for someone else, I'll march these over to the Sheriff and let him come have you stamp these with handcuffs on."

Her eyes were hard as granite as she saw the man swallow and his bluster turn to sand. Thorny could feel the heat coming off Charlie's chest as it hovered an inch from her back. Even at her height, she knew his head was floating above hers.

The man opened his ink pad and checked the date on his stamp. Carefully watching Thorny's face the entire time, he stamped the conforming copies and filed motions. He handed back the shortened stack of papers and held his hand out.

Thorny pushed the cashier's check into the man's hand as she leaned in and growled. "Next time, we will do this without you calling your boss."

"I am the county clerk." His huffiness was false bravado.

Thorny leaned in. "I meant the person who pays you more than your paycheck. The one you are willing to break the law for. The one who doesn't belong here."

The Adam's apple was bouncing between his bow tie and jaw like a trip-hammer. She held his stare for a slow count of five. She could tell the man would be lost in some of the backstreets where she had learned the real law of the land.

As Charlie and Thorny walked down the two marble steps of the courthouse, a tan Cord quietly motored past. The men didn't look like farmers, and the nickel details were polished as if someone's life or livelihood depended on it. The two stood on the sidewalk watching the car reach the end of the paved street and turn east.

Charlie shrugged. "I guess this means we won't be getting a chocolate malt at Austin's."

Thorny brushed the stack of papers across his chest. "Come on. I'll buy you dinner at the Kettle."

They turned toward the black Chevrolet sedan. Charlie cocked his head as he listened for the sound of the Cord's multi-barreled exhaust from one block over. "I hope we make it there."

The large black sedan shot from the curb as the tan coupe fishtailed around the corner ahead. The driver was obviously used to driving on paved city streets and was having a tough time with the dusty dirt streets of the small town. As he straightened out, the left arm came out the window—holding something.

Charlie growled about not playing fair and mashed down the gas pedal as he let up the clutch on third gear. The large Lincoln engine pulled hard on the sedan as the pavement began to run out. The two cars were now closing like a couple of runaway trains.

As they neared, Charlie flicked the wheel, and the larger sedan feinted the babied coupe. The driver reacted to the threat and pulled to his right. The tires bit into the dust, and the slight pull became oversteer as the passenger threw up his arms. The right tires bounced up onto the wooden sidewalk as the Cord ran along the front of the feed store.

The Chevrolet raced past the endangered thugs and their city car. Thorny could see the panic on the drivers face as he fought to keep from crashing. Charlie downshifted and drifted the rear end in the soft dust of the street. Pulling the car through the right turn, he upshifted and mashed the gas pedal back down. The last house on the east end of the tiny town flew past as Thorny frowned at the road leading out of town.

"I thought we were going back to Bishop?"

"We are. We just aren't taking the highway. My guess is there is another bunch of guys coming this way from Big Pine and maybe from Bishop. If these two clowns missed us, the next two would have a shot at us in twenty minutes or so. But we haven't lost these two... yet. So now they know where we're headed."

Thorny looked back through the rear window. The dust obscured the view. "I don't see them."

"Their car is good, so they're there. They just aren't as close as they had wanted." Charlie glanced over with a large smirk. "It's just like Halloween when we were kids."

Thorny snorted. "Maybe you—I was never a kid."

Charlie laughed. "Yeah, it was someone else tipping over those outhouses with me."

Thorny smiled at the memory of the two riding bareback on horses they had borrowed. The middle of the night pranks were basically harmless, but some had a meaner intent, but never anything causing serious harm.

Charlie threw his head back toward the rear. "Jump back there and lift the seat."

Thorny crawled over the seat and settled in the large legroom between the seats. She lifted the rear seat. The base was a large box affair. She smiled at the wood crates.

"I've got twelve gallons of moonshine, a squirrel gun, and some rope."

"Don't drink the moonshine, it hasn't been cut yet. I'm not sure the rifle is loaded, but I'm not about to shoot anyone. Mobsters are out of season, but pull out the rope and rifle."

She pulled out the large hank of prickly rope. "It looks like we have about fifty feet of it."

"See if you can open the hatch door on my side."

She moved the crates of liquid. There was a small hinged door in the floor. She pried with her fingernail. The door creaked with a little rust but opened. She looked through to the dirt road racing by under them. "It's open."

"Half-hitch the middle of the rope around the rifle, and then feed the ends of the rope out the hatch."

Finding the center, she made the loop and fed the weapon through. Pulling it tight, she pushed the two ends through the small door. As the rope fed out along the road, the dirt pulled the rest through. The gun banged tight to the floor.

"Done."

The car bounced over a wood bridge. Thorny looked out and saw the bridge was crossing the Owens River, but there were no guardrails. She wondered if the following car would hit the center of the bridge.

The car slowed and slewed left. The road now ran along the eastern side of the river. Charlie slowed as the tan car came into view—headed for the river bridge. The dust cloud was thinning, and they knew the thugs would make the bridge. Charlie watched with his door open.

As he closed the door, he laughed and smiled at Thorny. "Now the party can start."

He slammed the car into first, and they shot away. Keeping the speed at close to twenty, he kept watching the dust cloud.

"What's wrong?" Thorny kept turning and looking back out the rear window. "Why are you driving so slow?"

Charlie grinned and almost glowed. "I don't want to lose them." He glanced over at her. "Climb in the back and watch. I want them about a hundred feet behind us. Just so you can make out the shadow of a car in the cloud."

"Why?"

"Because then I know they can barely see me. But we need to sneak them up to a faster speed."

Thorny knelt on the seat and watched the dust cloud. She could feel the car moving faster every time she called out seeing the car in the dust.

"Grab ahold to something or get on the floor. I have a sharp right turn up here."

She felt the car surge. The cloud blossomed largely, and the following car disappeared. She grabbed the back of the seat and spun around to brace her feet against the left side of the car. The car slewed right, and she was compressed against the wall.

Through the window, she saw where the river had suddenly cut a new trace. The road ran straight out into the river. Charlie guided the Chevrolet into the sagebrush and made a large circle.

Thorny watched as the large shadow in the dust cloud kept going straight. And then—dropped.

Charlie laughed maniacally as he circled into the disappearing cloud.

Opening his door, he stepped out. He opened the back door to let Thorny out.

They stood on the bank of the river watching the two men flounder out of their car. The one made motions like he was reaching for his wallet. The gun came up and slipped outward from his hand. The splash was quiet, barely louder than the word coming from the man's mouth.

Charlie ducked back in the car for a moment. In the doorway, he tore at his shirt. Stuffing it in the mouth of the bottle, he tipped the bottle until he could see it getting damp. Handing the lighter to Thorny, he held the bottle, ready to throw.

The flame was transparent from the almost pure alcohol. The bottle shattered on the rear bumper of the car sticking up out of the river at an angle. The contents of flaming liquid engulfed the car sticking out of the water. The two men foundered about in the shallow water. Obviously, neither had tried to stand up. Charlie and Thorny could tell the front end was stuck in the sticky clay mud—covered by less than four feet of water

Still laughing, they drove through the stunted sagebrush and picked up the river road again. The little-used road was slower than taking the highway, but a lot safer.

"What happened to the road back there?"

Charlie smirked. "There was a deep pool just upriver from there. The trout would get huge. There was a tree hanging over the river, and people hung old ham bones and steer legs from the tree. The flies would land, lay eggs, and the maggots would get fat and fall off."

Thorny chuckled at the old ways. "Chumming the pool."

"Well, the new Fish and Game guy didn't like it. So he pushed a detonator into a box of eighty percent dynamite, and threw it in the pool."

"Eighty percent? Was he crazy or just stupid with a death wish? How far away was he with the plunger?"

"Nobody ever found out if he wanted to die or not. They found the plunger about a quarter mile away. There were about thirty feet of wire attached. About twenty feet of the bank disappeared, and the river cut a new loop across the road."

"Does the rest of this go all the way?"

"It should. Or at least it used to. This was how the miners got the silver up to Big Pine. From there, we can take the old trace road. Our friends from the big city graded it smooth last year. I think they want to put a new pipeline in along the edge of the White Mountains."

Thorny ran her claw through her hair to get the dust out. "Why would they do that?"

The big Indian shrugged. "I don't know. Maybe it has something to do with the pipes along the Sierra side." He looked over at her with a serious face and then smiled. "For some reason, they keep getting blown up."

LATER, as they parked in front of the Copper Kettle, two men in a tan Desoto coupe drove past. The looks were stone and cold. Thorny knew she hadn't made any new friends that day. For some reason, the corned beef seemed sweeter somehow.

12 NEW WHORE IN TOWN

Thorny snuggled in the hay. Sometime during the night, the pregnant mare started rubbing against the wall of her stall. The old dried boards in their sockets were loose. The noise was soft, but it woke Thorny. Thorny had felt her. The colt was still probably many hours after sunrise away. She had rubbed down the mare until she calmed, but the young mare was calmed more by Thorny's presence than the brushing.

Thorny pitched in a large pile of hay and snuggled in. The smells were as comforting to her as her to the horse. Her last thought before drifting off was of the ewe who had thrown twins in the same stall the winter Thorny was six. The young girl had woken in the morning cuddling one of the lambs. The ewe could only take care of one. The other became Thorny's.

SHE SAT up and looked over at the mare munching on the feed in her box. Mr. Ferguson was quiet, or Thorny was tired. Either way, she had slept deeply. She watched the mare, and as she scratched her hair and pulled out pieces of straw, she thought about Fluff, her first lamb.

As Fluff grew, she knew, even as a small girl, the lamb was future food. She asked Pops when they would make Fluff into dinner. The concept of 'farmyard to table' wasn't clear at age six, but dinner was. Pops had asked her why she wanted to know and if she would miss her lamb. It was the first solid indication of her lacking deep feelings. The term sociopath would come later.

Every year, Thorny had a new lamb. Every summer, they had lamb for dinner.

Thorny frowned one eye as she stood. She stretched and knew she wasn't going to make a habit of baby-sitting mares.

"Pitchfork is by the door... if you want to make your bed."

She laughed. Taking the fork, she cleaned the stall. Tying the mare outside the stall, she raked and shoveled it clean. Forking a fresh thickness in, she made a better bed for the expectant mother. The foal would arrive in the world on the softest of terms. There was war in the world, but on her farm, there was at least compassion.

The man stood in the gateway as he stroked the horse's neck. "You looked so natural there. I didn't want to wake you."

Thorny poured a couple of handfuls of oats in the box. She knew the mare wouldn't want it now, but after giving birth, she would appreciate the sweeter taste. Looking at the man, she gently grabbed two-handed at her small belt buckle. "I think she'll show a woman's prerogative and drop about the time you're having supper."

The man smiled softly as he ran his left hand back along the belly. "More like while you're having breakfast. She's already starting her contractions."

Thorny looked at the large brown eyes. They were staring at a distance. The mare was peaceful and ready. "How many she had before?"

"Three. You go get some breakfast, and I'll take care of Buttermilk."

Thorny hadn't known the horse's name. She smiled as she passed the two. Calling back over her shoulder, "I have an early appointment in town. I'll eat at the Bib."

"Suit yourself. But no reason to spend a ration stamp for food when we have it here. Oh, and the nice gal down the road... her husband is a bus driver. She stopped by looking for you."

Thorny stepped back out of the tack room. She was frowning in confusion. "What did she want?"

"She wanted you to know you can stop by anytime. She said to tell you she would like a visit. I think she's feeling a little cabin fever with her husband on the highway and all."

Her eyebrows raised. "I'll stop by and have a talk with her."

The woman she needed to talk to wasn't the bus driver's wife. The one Thorny was searching for was everyone's lover and nobody's wife.

THORNY STOOD AT THE DOOR, looking at a woman who was no older than she was. Her hair was in a scarf of diaphanous silk. The dressing robe was embroidered with Chinese dragons with intertwining gold and red. Thorny's small smile strengthened her softening eyes as she removed her green glasses. The woman was barefoot.

"I wasn't expecting you for another hour." The woman stepped back into the parlor.

Thorny stepped forward into the darkened apartment. Although there were three other apartments on the second floor above the police station, Thorny knew the others were part of the same business. "I took the car home. I was hoping to catch you before you had breakfast. I wanted to offer to take you to the Bib." She looked shyly at the woman but rushed to assure her. "I have plenty of ration stamps left, and it's the end of the month."

Bertha looked squarely at the woman. The pink scared claw had not missed her evaluation. "Nobody takes the town whore out to a public restaurant. There might be decent folk about—whom would talk." The statement was delivered flat, but no less of a challenge.

Thorny mirrored the woman's face. "Those puritans have wagged their tongues all of our lives, which is the problem. All they have done is talk. If they had done anything productive, this town would be different, but I would suppose it is exactly their talking which produces your business. The more they wag those tongues, the more their husbands take refuge..." she waved her open palm about the parlor, "here."

Thorny took a step forward. "Look, you don't know anything about me. I could walk back out the door, and your life won't change an iota. I didn't come here to be friends or to change things. I also didn't come back to Bishop to hide from wagging tongues. So if you want to come to the Bib with me for breakfast, I can sit here and wait."

"Why did you come to Bishop?"

"I grew up here. I inherited my grandfather's farm. I have a few friends here..." She thought about laying in the warm pool of water. The warm turned to hay, and the sense of the mare becoming calm just because she was there. "Because... it's home."

She shifted the weight onto her other hip. "Look, you know there are wonderful things here in the valley. There are even a few decent people. There are also bad parts and people. You can keep watching the bad, and live with your face turned around looking over your shoulder, or you can look for the good. This morning I woke up in a pile of hay. During the night, our pregnant mare was antsy. I got up and rubbed her down until she was calm. I forked in some more hay and slept there. She could have walked out of the stall. She could have continued to knock up against the walls. But she was calm, and I was there with her. It was enough for her, and I slept like I did when I was a kid. Tonight, she will have a foal. I'll probably sleep out there again. Nothing smells like a foal when they are less than a day old. The smell is their mother, and yet, it's about the new life."

The woman's hand unhurriedly slid the scarf from her head. "I've never seen a baby horse before."

"If you want, after breakfast, we can go see if she's dropped yet."

BY THE TIME they finished the long breakfast, the foal had dropped. The little stallion was anything but the nature of a stallion. The legs were wobbling as it gently made its way to the two women. Thorny stood back watching the other woman make the first contact.

She closed her hands on each side of the long face. His nose sniffed at her nose. His body still shook as it slowly became used to standing. The foal stepped into the hands as the woman slid them along the neck and onto the shoulders. She buried her nose in the neck.

Turning, she held on to the foal. "You're right. This smell is like nothing else I've smelled. We had dogs when I was growing up. But dogs don't smell like this. And he's so soft." Her hands continued to stroke and pet.

Thorny knelt. "He's never been out of this stall. Nothing of the world has touched him. This is as pure as he will ever be. His mother licked the placenta off his body, and he stood up in the fresh hay." She leaned over and forced her face into the depression between the neck and shoulder. Her voice was muffled. "This is what a good spring morning smells like."

The two women lounged against the stall wall—watching the foal gather his strength and coordination as he nuzzled for his mother's milk. The small tail thrashed back and forth and then in a propeller. The women laughed about his hindquarters taking off.

As the foal settled down, the conversation over breakfast resumed. Thorny looked sideways at Bertha staring at the tiny horse. "So, you do know where she is…"

Bertha didn't blink. She had been ridden, cajoled, questioned, beaten, and prodded by far more intimidating people than the woman next to her. But she liked this woman. She licked her lower lip. "I'll reach out to her. But it is all up to her whether she will talk to you."

"I understand. I'm only trying to put a—"

The prostitute's head snapped around. "No, you don't understand." Her voice backed down. "Sorry, but you don't. When one of us goes into hiding, there is a good reason. I'm sure she will be afraid for her life. You want to know about a death. But that knowledge may lead to her death. You or I don't know what this could start. You said some men tried to stop you down in Independence, and there are more up here." She picked at the hay and threw a few straws toward the colt. She bit her lower lip. Turning, her voice lowered, "Your world is about nice people doing nice things and living nice lives. Us girls... we're part of the otherworld. Whether we like it or not, those guys have probably sat in my parlor."

Thorny thought about the woman's world. Even if it was located over the local police station. She nodded her head gently. "Okay. Whatever she says, I'll live with it."

Bertha leaned back and slumped down. "It's pleasant here." She snickered at the foal's ungraceful drop into the hay. It rolled over on its side and was fast asleep with a full tummy of milk. The mare folded her legs and settled next to her baby, her nose checking the entire length of the tiny body.

Thorny speared a long piece of hay toward the two horses. "You're welcome to come out any time. The Fergusons are here all the time. They send Felix into town for the supplies. Mr. Ferguson doesn't like to drive anymore, and his wife never learned."

The blonde twisted her finger in her curls as she thought about the offer. "Thanks." She looked over. "I'd truly like that."

Thorny snorted softly. "I'll teach you how to shovel the manure."

The woman smirked. "Shoveling shit will be a change. Usually, I'm taking the shit."

13 HOW DARE YOU

Thorny could hear the pounding on the house door all the way out in the barn. The bed of hay worked its magic again. She had been sound asleep.

The yelling was the final galvanizing trigger to her being fully awake. She looked about for her boots and then waved at the air as she marched out of the barn. She knew she was a rumpled mess with as much hay sticking out of her head as there was hair.

The man pounding on the door to the house was large, fat, and sloppy. The tan uniform shirt, half pulled from his pants, clung darkened with sweat stains. The starch in the shirt kept the sweat wrinkles bunched halfway up his back. A swathe of thin white undershirt laced the bottom. The weight of the holstered pistol drooped the belt meant to hold up his pants. At least to a degree of decency. Thorny tried not to look at the fat-teats of his butt cheeks. The cleavage created a few inches of dark line.

"Hey," she barked.

The man startled and spun around. His face didn't create a

better view. She almost wanted him to turn back around. The man's face and form was a topography of lumpy fat. His face was beyond piggish. It was a striking view, considering the previous decade of starvation the nation had been through. This much fat didn't occur overnight.

Her right eye lowered as she passed through the cocked gate of the picket fence. "This is Sunday. Have some respect." She knew Mr. Ferguson would be out in the fields, and his wife would never answer the door to violence.

He dismissed her and her charge. His voice was no less corpulent than a wet passing of gas. "I'm looking for Elizabeth Wallace."

"And what makes you think Miss Wallace wants to talk to you at the break of day?"

"Because I'm the chief of police for the City of Bishop, and I have business with her." The man stepped off the single-step stoop. "Is that you?" His demeanor was no less threatening.

"Hmm, the chief of police... way out here in county sheriff territory. And on private property too. Which means I can shoot you, bury you, and forget you, and nobody would care, and if I were caught, it would be self-defense and protecting my property against a hostile intruder." She stepped into his face. She regretted it immediately as she struggled to control her urge to throw up. Beyond the man's lack of hygiene, his breath reeked of coffee, garlic, and onions. The memory of walking through a city dump with burning garbage oozed through her.

The man blinked.

"You're poking your nose in places you best stay away from." His growl might have caused others to comply. "We don't stand for outsiders coming into our town and stirring up our business and folks." His hint of a southern accent squirmed on his vowels.

Thorny smirked. "Outsiders such as yourself? You didn't even grow up here."

"That's not the point. You are—"

She cut him off. "But it is the point. You're not here because the good citizens of Bishop asked you to come. You're here to look after the interests of certain people down in the city who want to steal more of what isn't theirs." She poked his chest with her finger. With each poke, she could feel her finger sink into the flabby chest up to her second knuckle. It was pure fluffy fat, but she could tell from his wince it still hurt.

She leaned into the putrid storm of his breath and body. "I filed papers. I will be checking on the disposition of those papers in Sacramento. If any of the paperwork is delayed or lost, I will be having a conversation with the Attorney General of California."

He snorted as he rubbed his chest. "Hah. What do you think you are... a lawyer?"

"As a matter of fact, I am." Her left hand wiped a few stalks of hay from her hair. She saw the recognition of her hand in his eyes. She pushed. "And I work for Michael Vance, the District Attorney of the Greater Los Angeles. So you can tell your bosses I am here on official business."

The man saddled sideways around her. "You'd best go back to your desk where you belong. This isn't over." He waddled hurriedly to his car with a couple of looks back. His left hand, in an iron grip, kept his pants from slipping lower.

Thorny stood near the house stoop as she watched the boil of dust follow the rapidly retreating Desoto sedan. The white door was almost as dark gray from dirt as the black body of the vehicle was lightened. The man's laziness surrounded him. She turned at the soft click behind her.

Mr. Ferguson stood at the corner of the house. His thumb was still on the hammer of the old double-barreled shotgun. His smile was thin as he too watched the dust. "Just so you know, breakfast is almost ready, and I have a burn pit out behind the old ice shed."

Thorny wondered if the man knew the shotgun hadn't worked in her lifetime. As she studied his face, she wondered if the man had fixed the weapon from the previous century.

The door opened slowly. The almost empty dress of Mrs. Ferguson stood in the half shadow. "I would have brained the old poop if I hadn't already started the bacon in the cast iron skillet."

Thorny smiled as the scent of a farm breakfast filled the air. The eggs wouldn't be as old as for yesterday's laying. The ham and bacon would be part of the three hogs hanging in the cool shed.

14 WHO IS WHO

I f Amelia Earhart had shown up at Monte's door, slouching in boots, jodhpurs, and white blouse with rolled up sleeves, he would have asked her if she wanted the usual.

The replica was lacking the boots and jodhpurs.

Thorny was barefoot with dungarees.

"There better be some coffee." She stepped into his small living room.

"Well, good morning, Monte. How are you this fine morning, Monte? I'm fine, Thorny. Would you like some coffee, Thorny? I just brewed some. Why, how considerate of you to ask, Monte. Well then, come right on in, Thorny, and make yourself at home." The sarcasm dripped from his words but did not affect the woman. She disappeared around the corner into the small kitchen. The man snickered and closed the door. His slippers shuffled softly as he followed her.

The disconnected voice floated out. "What do you know about your police chief?"

He stopped—stunned. He started again, rounding the corner. The full cup of coffee met his chest.

"If you are referring to the large blob of pork rendering who leaves a trail reeking like rotted casting... not a whole hell of a lot."

She looked at him with one eye as she sipped on the hot coffee. Lowering the mug, she straightened her head. "Just the fact of your swearing tells me most of what I wanted to know."

"Hell, for your edification, those words weren't swearing." He leaned against the wall as she sipped the coffee and thought. "The other words I would use to describe him—those are swearing."

"Who put him in office and when?" They moved to the table and sat.

The man thought. His hands picked at his bathrobe and pajamas. The motions didn't escape Thorny. She slid her hand across the table and gripped his at the lapel of his bathrobe.

"I'm sorry, Monte. Some days I just have no sense of propriety. It's Sunday, I walked seven miles, and I never once stopped to think you would still be in your bedclothes. Go get dressed."

He rose, thought a moment, and then turned toward the back of the house. Turning at the hall entrance, his forehead furrowed. "Where's the car?"

Thorny paused with the mug almost to her lips. "Someone siphoned the gas out of it yesterday evening. So I left it in the lot last night."

He shrugged as he turned. "Rationing."

Thorny muttered at her coffee. "Or something else."

MONTE LEANED over the table and whispered. "You have to stop throwing ration stamps around. You keep using them like you have a printing press. You didn't have to bring me here. I have food at home."

Thorny snorted. "Oh, yes, I saw the three eggs and a half stick of butter in the cold-box. You are down to five cans of Mrs. Campbell's and have you ever used the yellowing pill in your margarine?" She looked around the Bib. They were the only ones in the room. "Look, last month the Fergusons and I ended with most of our ration books still full. The only thing getting rationed is the water, and I'm tempted to call someone to come drop a larger well. I'm sure somebody would like to make some money during this war."

She leaned back as the owner came with more coffee. She looked up at the woman with only a touch of gray at her temples.

"Tell me, May, do you prefer I pay with money or stamps?"

The woman's eyebrows rose in having heard it all before. "Thorny, we went over this when you first came back to town. You can pay me any way you want. If you give me stamps, I'll spread them around to those who need them. If you pay me with money, I'll do the same. If you don't pay me, it doesn't matter."

Monte choked on his sip of coffee. "Why?"

May looked from the man to Thorny. Thorny pointed with her eyes and tossed her head back toward him. Her lips mouthed it was okay to tell.

The woman put the pot on the table. "The year Thorny became a real lawyer, she was looking for work. Our Danial got into some trouble, and we needed a lawyer for him down in the city. We knew she was studying and hoped she might be working for a lawyer or could recommend one. She took his case, took it to court even. Danial told us she talked an hour when it was her first turn. He was very impressed. More importantly, so was the prosecuting attorney. They asked the judge for some time to talk to her. They offered her a job, and Danial got only a year probation. She even got them to transfer the probation up to here. We have him home and away from trouble."

Monte looked at the young woman staring intently at her coffee. "And...?"

Thorny looked up. "And what? It was the opening argument. Maybe if I had been better, they would have dropped the charges."

"And you charged them how much?" The lowered eyelid was pure avuncular.

"She didn't."

Thorny picked up the small menu. Her voice was distracted with the hope of the subject being dismissed. "It was only an hour of work."

Monte leaned back as he looked down his nose. "How much time to prepare?"

"On the city bus while I was going to court."

The man was getting irritated at having to pull information from the same petulant child he had known since she was three.

"How many miles did the bus travel while you worked on his case?"

Thorny scowled as she lowered the menu she already knew by heart. "Sixty-seven blocks. My shoes were new, they didn't fit right, and my feet hurt. The bus took longer than I could have walked in bare feet, but I couldn't appear in court without shoes." The glower around her eyes darkened. "Are we done here? It's Sunday, and this is my favorite place to eat, and I wish my favorite living uncle would please show up—I'm tired of the grumpy inquisitor."

She turned to look at the proprietress in her blue gingham apron.

Thorny snapped one last glare at Monte and turned a beaming smile to May. "I'll take the usual, please. If you have any old cold gruel, the other side of the table can eat also."

Monte glared at Thorny as his voice was gentle. "I'll just have what she's having."

May barked a spare laugh. "Not on your life, Mr. Geronimo. You're having yesterday's leftover gruel as ordered."

He looked up in shock to find he was being teased and laughed at. He was the only male. He was never going to win at this table.

Later, as they both pushed fresh homemade bread about their plates, the last of the orange egg yolks disappeared. Monte didn't ask but guessed the eggs came from a certain farm sitting seven miles from the city line. He knew, even with isinglass to preserve the eggs, the three could only use so much. The henhouse was built by Pop to accommodate an even gross of chickens.

As May came to remove the plates, Monte looked up. "Do you remember when Reseda became the chief?"

The plates hovered a moment and then lowered to the table. "I remember there was something going on at the time..." Her voiced drifted off.

Thorny put down her mug and shifted in her seat. "Maybe the judge hanging himself?"

May's eyes widened. "I'd forgotten about Judge Hudgins. But no, before then... it was something up Bishop Creek. Something to do with the new dam they were building."

Monte ran his finger out along the tablecloth in thought. "If it's the one near South Lake, someone died up there. I don't remember hearing of it ever being looked into. They found the body in among the rocks below, and that was that."

May sat and rested her arm on the table. "It was in the spring. Some thought he was washed down by a surge of water or something. Building those dams wasn't safe, even on a good day." She drew out her towel and rubbed at a spot on the table. "I think it was close to Thanksgiving the same year the new officer was made chief. There were grumblings, but they simmered down as Christmas settled in."

Monte considered the information. "If it's the year I'm thinking, we had a deep white Christmas."

May snorted. "Extremely deep. The kids were mad because school was already out for the holiday. Even Main Street was closed for five days. Jeb Jensen brought his team of mules in and marched them up and down the street until at least a Model A could make it from Short Street, to the highway Six cut-off."

Thorny refocused. "It must have been the year the snow was over my hips. Pops had to break a trail so I could get out and collect the eggs." She scratched the side of her jaw. "I was about eight.

Monte chuckled. "If you had made it into town, we could have had fun tossing you into some of the snowdrifts. Some of the ones on the east side of Main were higher than a man and big enough to have buried a wagon."

"So, if I was eight, it would have been sixteen years ago. How fat was the chief then?"

Monte looked at May. She looked out the window. "He wasn't. In fact, he was a dashing cut of a man. I knew a few women who would have loved to be arrested by him—but then he changed."

Monte agreed. "He got mean as well. When he was just an officer, he used to stroll along Main Street. He even stopped and knelt for children. Even though he wasn't from around here, he seemed to just fit in. Then he became the chief and everything changed."

May's head drooped. "Bishop changed. The whole valley changed."

"What changed?"

May looked at Thorny. "You were just a child, but Bishop changed. The prohibition was about four or five years in. Small stills in the valley kept most of the valley happy for the hard liquor. There were a few barn brewers, and of course, we have always had our share of the Greeks and Italians making use of the grapes. But it's also when the dude ranch grew from a few buildings, almost looking like a ranch, to the complex it is today. There were days when the chilly air swept down from Bishop Creek and blew the smell of the stills into town."

Thorny frowned. "But the Dude Ranch is out in sheriff territory. How would the ranch affect the chief and Bishop, or vice versa?"

Monte tapped and then circled his finger on the white tablecloth. "In the early days, the sheriff down in Independence didn't have enough money to pay for deputies up here. Even though half the population of Inyo County lives within twelve miles of Bishop, the county seat is down there—forty-five miles away. So it fell on the city police to take care of any problems arising up around here."

The three-fingered claw ran through the short curls of brown hair. "So... where do you think the case files are on judge

Hudgins death? Do you think they would be here or down in Independence?" Thorny frowned slightly. "Where did he live?"

"You know Phillip Brockman, the driver for Greyhound?"

She nodded at Monte with a puckered brow. "He was the driver when I came up from Los Angeles."

"He married a girl named Debbie." Thorny's forehead furrowed harder as she listened to Monte. "Ten years ago. They have two girls..."

May finished for Monte. "Debbie Hudgins... Harold Hudgins's niece. The judge owned the small house out on the corner of the ranch there at Brockman Lane and Highway Six. He rented the eighty acres to the Brockman ranch for growing their alfalfa. When Harold..." Her voice drifted.

Monte finished. "Debbie got the land and house. It was in trust until she was twenty-one. When they got married, she was only eighteen, but they released the trust to her husband."

Thorny slumped. Her head ground back and forth.

"What's wrong?"

She looked up at the man who could have been one of her uncles for all the strange relationship of her life. There were things she could tell Monte, but nobody else. He knew when she became a young woman and helped her buy what she needed. When she grew out of undershirts, it was Monte to the rescue— along with the help of the corsetiere at Katherine's Closet.

"The day I got home. Phil invited me to Sunday dinner. He said Debbie would be happy to see me." She looked at May and then continued. "He said she would be happy to see a friendly face..."

"But...?"

"I told him I'd stop by and make sure she was fine with me coming for a Sunday dinner... but I never did."

Monte tried not to smile, but May got a sudden coughing fit and covered her face with her apron. Her eyes twinkled above. Monte glared at her as he spoke to the younger woman. "It looks like you have some crow to eat while you make nice to the young mother."

Thinking about the police chief, who wasn't from around here, she added her musing. "I also need to write some letters. I need answers, and they aren't coming from Bishop."

Monte's eyebrows took on a small twist of curiosity. It used to make the girl Thorny laugh. Now she knew it was his asking, but to be told later.

As they strolled back to the barbershop, Monte only waited a block.

Thorny cleared her throat as she looked down the street at the retreating car. "No officer of the law in the state of California can become an officer without a background review. All the reviews get filed in Sacramento. But... the District Attorney of Los Angeles County can ask for a copy or, at a minimum, a brief or extract of the information."

"And you think he would do this for you?"

"The District Attorney? No. But my old boss would."

"Why?" Monte's look was one of a parent looking for the errant child to lie.

"You remember May's son?" He nodded. "The job I was offered wasn't for the District Attorney's office. I didn't get that job for another month."

"What job did the man offer you?"

"His daughter had been rounded up for prostitution—for the third time. Only, this time, she was also running a speakeasy with other girls."

Monte was laughing. "And...?"

Thorny was chuckling as she remembered. "The first detective in the place showed her identification of being a city health inspector. When the uniformed police broke down the door, he was drunk, naked, and in bed with a Saint Bernard dressed in garter and stockings. When I approached the bench with a handful of large photographs to enter as evidence, the man screamed to stop the trial. The prosecution's entire case rested on this man's testimony. So they dropped the case."

When Thorny could talk again, she continued. "Barbara now works in her father's office. She's working as a law clerk, but I think she has also moved up to a better clientele with her evenings." She smiled as she glanced over at Monte. "I know she will read my letter first, as I'll provide a cover letter and address it to her personally."

15 YOUR UNCLE

Thorny stood at the corner of the alfalfa field. The smell was intoxicating in the morning sun. She leaned against the old post as she closed her eyes. The heat on her back, the warm dirt between her toes, and the intense smell of green vegetation were the touchstones of her childhood she had missed in the big city of Los Angeles.

The concrete gets too hot to walk on. The asphalt is no reprieve. The pale ocher of the stucco houses with the white-wash intensified the heat. The sticky humidity would mop her shirts from the outside as it sweat-drenched them from the inside. She hadn't come home—she had left the irritation of the city. Noise, people, heat, sweat, and all the other assaults on her mind and body.

In Bishop, her claw was no more than her curls and sand-colored hair. The scars on her arm and body had only been an issue in the girl's locker room the first year of high school. Everyone she saw every day had grown up with her or had watched her grow. The city was a never-ending string of fresh faces struggling with horror, revulsion, or trying to hide the reaction.

She had taken to keeping her claw in the pocket of her slacks. Even the slacks on a woman startled some until she took to having her hair cut to match the woman she resembled. Meeting Miss Earhart shortly before she disappeared had solidified Thorny's affection for the look. After 1937, she had noticed many startled looks. Only a few people had questioned whether she was Amelia or not.

A raven in a distant tree raked the still morning with their rusted rasp. Thorny's face pulled back on one side as she opened eyes behind the green glasses. The grain-eating birds were sometimes confused with the carrion-eating crows. The appearances were similar, but to Thorny, their calls were as different as Ford and Desoto horns. She had missed the Ravens of the Owens Valley. The dry-land wheat, oats, and barley kept them in the valley and the crows in the city.

A battered yellow Mack pickup rattled to a stop. The man leaned slightly out of the opening of the doorless truck. Thorny smiled. Jessup Perkins was the first farmer in the valley to buy an automobile to haul his produce to town. The truck ran the ten miles to the market. Jessup had never driven the truck east of his farm, south of town, or turned north out to Round Valley.

"Do you need a ride, Thorny?"

"No, thank you, Mr. Perkins. I was just enjoying the smell of the alfalfa with the last of the morning dew. But I appreciate the offer."

"What neighbors are for. I heard you were back. You stayin' this time?"

"Yes, sir. This is it. I'm done with the city."

"Where the Fergusons going?"

Thorny chuckled. She was sure the man was the occasional recipient of Mrs. Ferguson's baking. "They'll stay. I'm in the old groom's room in the barn." She hung her head to the side. "It suits me better than a house."

The man eased down on the clutch and put the truck in gear. "I heard about the new colt." The truck gently rattled off.

Thorny harrumphed. The man had never been long on greetings or departures. She thought on the man's courtship and the spare woman his wife had been. She could imagine the original conversation had been the proposal of marriage. Pops had always commented on how Jessup was the talkative one of the two.

Turning, she looked down the long road toward town, and then across the field. The squat home lay low to the field. The low pitch of the tin covered roof was built more for shade from the brutal long sunny summers than any occasional snow. The low-lying two-story was the newer thinking than the post-Victorian, three-storied, saltbox farmhouses. The wrap around porch was the same, only deeper. But where all the construction was above ground with the saltboxes, the bungalow would also have a full basement for storing food and cooler sleeping during the hot summer.

The bungalow, probably built in the last century, still had good bones. The roofline was straight with no sag. As she ambled along the front walk, her eyes followed the twin wires, bare in spots, that ran from glass knob to glass knob. Pops called the electrical system a *drunk killer*. There were many drunks who came home in the middle of the night and stumbled up against the two electrical wires. There was enough amperage in the two thin wires to guarantee a burial the next morning.

Thorny stepped lightly onto the deep porch. She could see the main door was open behind the screen door. A young girl stood looking through the screen. Her blonde braids hung down both shoulders over her dress. The brand of the small local flour mill was faded on the front of her dress.

"Good morning." Thorny stood with only her one foot on the porch. Her claw was in her pocket.

She had been trying to remember who Phillip had married. Between the local and boarding student body, the high school held over two hundred youths. There had been more than one Debbie.

"Honey, who is it?" the voice called from deep in the house. The echo nature told Thorny it was from the kitchen.

The small girl turned and ran back into the dark. "Mommy, it's a man."

Thorny sighed. It wasn't the first time the short hair and pants confused a child. She stepped across the porch. "It's Elizabeth Wallace, Mrs. Brockman."

A light body formed out of the gloom. She walked as she washed her hands in her apron. "Thorny?"

Recognition was completed as the woman pushed open the screen door. All their lives, they both were recognized by their markings. Thorny's claw was no less distinctive than the splash of red wine and purple across one side of the woman's face. The long braids, which hung past the girl's waist in school, were woven across the top of the woman's head in a traditional Dutch bun. The flour marked her face in patches where she had touched. She had become her mother.

Thorny took the young woman's hand. "All the way over here, I was trying to remember which Debbie Phil had married. I feel such the fool now."

"Don't be. You wouldn't have known. When you and Phil graduated, we weren't dating. By the end of summer, you were gone. Phil asked me to dance at the street dance in September. We talked some, but he didn't ask me out until Christmas Mass."

Remembering, Thorny flushed. "I'm sorry about the Sunday dinner."

"Sunday dinner?"

"The day I got back, Phil asked me to come over for Sunday dinner. I told him I'd stop by and make sure it was all right with you. I—"

The woman laughed low and light. "He probably meant any Sunday dinner. One is as good as the next. Phil told me you were in town. But I'm so glad you stopped by." She turned and pointed to the kitchen. "I'm kneading bread, but I'm almost done. I have some coffee I can make." She reached behind her. Thorny could see the small hands as they reached around to grab the front of the long dress.

"Water."

"What?"

"Water is just fine. I'm not much of a coffee drinker. But well water is what I can't get enough of. Ten years of city water has me parched." She knew the rationing made for commodities like coffee scarce.

"Mama, who is he?" The small voice was muffled in the back of the woman's dress.

Debbie rolled her eyes and knelt as she turned. "Honey, Thorny is an old friend of your daddy's and mine. She and I went to school together when we were your age."

The small face shied into the tiny chest and then moved to the protection of her mother's shoulder. "Why does... if she... she looks like a man."

The blonde glanced sheepishly at Thorny. "She just has short hair, that's all." The woman picked at the end of the girl's braid. "Just like your braids are shorter than mine. Her hair is shorter than yours."

"But why is she wearing dungarees like daddy?"

"Honey, those are called slacks. They are what some women wear in the city." She glanced back into the house. "Why don't you go play with your sister while Thorny and I have a chat. Can you do that for mommy, honey?"

"Okay." She turned and then turned back for a hug. Releasing, she ran into the other room.

Debbie watched and then rose slowly. She turned. The sigh was deeper than just the past few minutes.

Thorny stalled. "You look like you have your hands full. I can come back another time."

Debbie reached out and lightly grabbed her arm. Pulling her toward the kitchen, she sighed a tired laugh. "My hands are full all day every day. Come today, come tomorrow, come any day— it's all the same."

"Don't they go to school?"

The woman turned at the large table in the middle of the kitchen. "The schools are godless. I teach the girls what they need to know here. We want our girls morally armored before they have to deal with the sins of the world."

Thorny's mouth opened. She started to ask about how the woman had grown up in the public school... but then thought better. "Oh, I see."

Thorny leaned over and smelt at the large wooden bowl filled with risen dough. "What kind of bread?"

"I grow herbs. This batch has rosemary, marjoram, and tarragon. Do you bake?"

Thorny thought about the rolls she had tried to make when she was twelve. "No, I never learned. We weren't much for cooking anything that took longer than frying up steaks or chopped plant stock." She looked up at the woman's shocked face. "My grandfather was a widower before I was born. You either have time to farm, raise a little girl, or cook. He chose the first two. But we survived, and I think I'm actually healthy."

The woman stared at Thorny and then shook herself. "Well, my daughters will know how to clean house and cook their husbands a proper meal."

Looking out the small window over the sink, Thorny thought before she spoke. "How much do you know about your uncle?"

She could feel the chill from the woman's frozen body. Even the air seemed to lose its heat. "He passed away when I was very young. We never speak of him." It was everything Thorny needed to know. She and the woman would never be friends. The woman had concrete beliefs about her, her daughters, and her husband's place in the world. The woman even had a concrete belief about the world itself. And, like concrete, it was all mixed up and set for life.

A few minutes later, as Thorny once again felt the warm dirt between her toes, she thought about the two girls and the plans their mother had for them. She glanced back at the small house. "I wonder if I could appreciate a wife who cleaned and cooked me a proper meal?" When she reached the city limit sign, she was wondering what a proper meal looked like.

As she walked past the commercial fuel station, the numbers on the sign tugged at another thought. Phil and Thorny had only graduated ten years before. And yet, Phil said they'd married ten years before, which would match their girls' ages, but Debbie was insistent of their not even dating at graduation...

A truck went by and honked at Thorny. She stepped to the side path as the forming thought about who the children's father was faded with the dust.

The older officer looked only vaguely familiar. The razor marks on his neck and face looked self-inflicted. The tanned sidewalk around the top of his ears made the wings resemble one of the pictures

Thorny had seen of an Indian elephant—the size wasn't too far off. The sunken eyes were a liquid powder-blue as if bleached out by the sun yet set in cavities of coal. The man looked like he regularly stood in a weeklong soup line but only the door was slammed in his face.

The startled look when he heard Thorny's question didn't help.

"Well?" Thorny asked again. "Are the records here or would they be in Independence?"

The man shook slightly as if waking up from a daydream. "Why would there be any records of a person shooting another person's chickens?"

Thorny leaned in on the tall counter. Her hand felt the telltale markings of boredom—carved into the softwood top.

"Because in the state of California, if a person shoots, runs over, or causes to be dead another person's property, then they can be arrested, and a police report is filled out. Poultry is livestock and comes under the heading of personal property."

The man sucked on the four lower teeth he no longer had. "You sound like one of them city lawyers. Are you a lawyer from down in the city?"

Thorny pulled her left hand out of her pocket and drew off her green glasses. "Officer Watson, I am the kind of lawyer from the city who makes your worst nightmares seem like a baby kitten's breath. Now, I will ask you only one more time—"

The man pointed at Thorny's claw and began to chuckle. "Ah, hellfire. You're Titus Wallace's kid."

"Eustis. My grandfather's name was Eustis."

He waved his hand in dismissal. His soft rubbery lower lip tugged at one side. "Pft. When we was at the Academy, he was just Wally. Heck, so how is the old cuss?"

"Dead." Her face was now stone.

The man's shock was carnal. "Dead? When?" He straightened and his voice softened.

For a small town, his innocence surprised her. "Six years or so. He fell and broke his neck. The cattle got out and ran rampant through Laws. It took the police, sheriff deputies, and ranchers about a week to get them all rounded up. There should be a report about it in your files also." She didn't flinch.

Suddenly the man burst out laughing again. "Pfft, now you're just funnin' me. Ol' Wally never done had more than a dozen or so head." The man sobered. "Seriously... he's dead?"

She nodded. "Passed in his sleep. The Ferguson's had been living with him since the crash. The missus found him. They buried him out on the north forty and sent me a letter. You wouldn't have a report or a record. The death certificate was filed down in Independence." She cleared her throat. "So, what about the chickens?"

"That's sheriff territory out that away. The officer would have been helping as a fill-in deputy so it would have gone down on the bus or on the Slim Princess at the end of the quarter. Most of the time, they would have jus' put the stuff in a mailbag and throw it on the swing arm. The train comed along and off it went. In Independence, they just throw it out to the platform."

"Same would happen if someone shot someone else or they hung themselves?"

The man stopped. His eyes twitched back and forth between her eyes. He palmed his mouth and wiped slow and hard. Glancing back at the rear offices, he leaned in. His voice was barely more than someone walking past outside. "There were only two shootings in the last thirty years. One was on the reservation, and the other was out toward the Dude Ranch. The second was one of them whores shot a guy with his own pistol. He was showing off his new gun, and she didn't know it was loaded. Winged him in the left thigh. As for the one and only hanging..."

Thorny tipped her head back. Her eyes slowly drooped closed. "There never was a report—" She looked over her glasses at the man.

His face was putty and stone. "Not one that...um... made it into the mailbag on the Princess." His face never moved.

She studied his eyes. There was no malice nor weakness. She lowered her head.

"The Indian church is never locked. In the front office is an old roll-up desk. If you roll the front down and lift on the top from the back, there is a space down the back just big enough for a large atlas book or a thick file. I'll probably want to go to church this Sunday. But I get bored easily and might want something to read. What's in there next Wednesday I probably won't care."

He thought about what she had said. "How long are you back for?"

She sighed as she lowered her green glasses. "There's a shady spot out in the north stretch next to Eustis. I don't care how my remains get there."

"You are persona non grata down in the city?"

She snorted softly. "Los Angeles is persona non grata to me." She stopped at the door but didn't look back. "I'll be seeing you... Officer Watson." Her head bobbed slightly as she stepped out. She knew it could go one of two ways. Either she got a look at the file on Sunday or the man would tell his boss, and the fertilizer would be in her bed.

Looking down at her shadow, she considered the smaller shadow on the east side of her feet. Realizing she was barefoot, she thought about the Bib. As she walked, she wondered if Monte ever hung a sign saying he was closed for lunch.

She shouldn't have wondered. The sign had stopped swinging long before they reached the Bib, a pair of dusty blocks away. The salad was spinach, kale, dandelions, chard, and any other greens May could harvest in the close blocks. The whole was tossed with balsamic vinegar and honey with caramelized black walnuts.

"So, what do you think my chances are at seeing the report on Sunday?"

Monte opened his mouth as he thought.

May poured some more lemonade. "I wasn't eavesdropping,

but I would say your chances are somewhere between great and guaranteed."

Monte leaned back in his chair to look up. "How so?"

May ran her palm along his shoulder as she pushed the chair's front two legs back down. "I can't afford new chairs, and John Watson can't afford to make my sister angry. But she isn't the all of it. This town is small. If you are an outsider, like the chief, you never know who you may have crossed. The chief wanted to buy a house. The house he liked wasn't for sale... until a tax lien was levied against it for five years of unpaid taxes. The widow who owned the house couldn't afford the taxes and so was evicted, and the chief bought the house for the cost of the back taxes."

Monte's mouth twisted into a tight purse, but his brown-black eyes sparkled with the stars of mirth. "And the widow would be...?"

"The widow of John's uncle—she now lives with her sister out on Barlow Lane."

Thorny mussed as she sipped on the lemonade. "The true power of a small town is knowing and understanding who family is."

Monte's laughter rumbled. "And who their friends are." May rubbed her hand along his shoulder as they shared smiles.

Monte lowered one eyelid as he looked at Thorny. "Need a date for church?"

Thorny smiled mischievously. "I was thinking I might talk a certain grandson of the chief into escorting me. After all, it's their church."

May's eyebrow notched upward. "He's a fine looking young man."

Monte's eyes mirrored Thorny's as they made a foursome of eyes rolling.

Later, as the two walked back to the barbershop, the talk was soft but personal. "At twenty-eight, I understand why people are trying to match make me. They think I will soon slip into being an old maid and no man will want me. What they never stop to consider is I may not want to date or get married."

"You never thought about having a child?"

She snorted rudely. "To what... carry on my name?" She glanced at the man. The black curls were edged with silver. She knew the man was at least seventy, but she wasn't sure. He never seemed to age. She glanced down at his left hand. There had never been a ring on any of the fingers.

He felt the scrutiny and glanced over. "What?"

"Did people try to ever get you married?" She stopped and braced his arm with her hand. "Wait... were you ever married?"

His face was as solid as the elm tree next to them. His eyes were steady. "No."

Thorny felt there was more to the conversation than just the single word. She took the lighter way out. "Did people try to push eligible young women at you?"

He turned to continue walking. "No."

"Why?"

He peeked at her out of the side of his eyes. "I'm Apache."

"But you could pass for Greek or Italian or any number of—"

He stopped her with a loud laughing snort. "Being any bloodline isn't why. I was too fast." He took her hand and kissed it lightly as he walked. His fingers entwined with hers.

"When I was young, some tried. But then there was the war, and we were gone. When we came back, the four of us pretty much kept to ourselves. We started sorting out our lives, even in

Cuba. By the time we came back, I had cut almost every head in the troop—especially the big dandy himself."

"Roosevelt."

He nodded. "I touched up his mustache and around his ears every Saturday night. He would engage in a few rounds of bare-fisted boxing and maybe wrestling, cool off in the river or the ocean, and then come see me before dinner. He believed one should dress proper when partaking in dinner."

Thorny snickered softly at his voice taking on a gruff snooty air as he looked down his nose. Monte softly squeezed her hand.

"I remember one night we were down to the end of our supplies. One of the men found a goat in the brush on the hill we had worked over during the day. Every man was portioned out about two spoonsful of rice and beans, and a sliver of the cabree. The goat was old and tough. The fire dried it out worse. It was almost near jerky, but we just chewed and sucked until one could swallow it with a large amount of water. The next day, there was nothing to eat. We got back from patrolling a little village. We thought about looking for food but realized the people in the village hadn't eaten as much as we had the night before."

When they got to the corner of Main and Line, he didn't turn to enter his shop. He drew her along as they crossed the street.

"When we got back to camp. Teddy stripped to the waist and asked for volunteers. All of us knew we were no match for the bear of a man, but to the man, we stood. For a brief time, we knew our minds and body would be occupied. Every man's mind was on the hundred or so horses let out to graze." Monte and Thorny waved as a truck blew its horn as it passed. "Teddy fought five men to the ground, washed up in a pan of water, and then dressed for dinner. Without a word, we all did the same."

Thorny sighed with realization. "But there was no food."

"None." Monte curled the side of his mouth. "We stood around. Teddy asked the powder boy for his best memory of a Christmas dinner. The boy was a guttersnipe Teddy rescued from the streets of New York."

"Do you remember what the boy said?"

"Of course. It shook us all to the bone. The boy was from one of our greatest cities. Our country was proud of the city. We built large beautiful edifices to our prosperity. And there in front of us was the representation of our greatest city telling us about the most glorious of his holiday dinners."

Sensing the train running off the rails, Thorny stopped the man and stepped in front of him. She pushed her green glasses up into her curls.

Monte wet his lips with the tip of his tongue. "He and his friends had found a cat that froze to death overnight. They climbed down into the steam tunnels and snuck into the service basement of one of the large buildings. They filleted the carcass and cooked the meat on the sides of the boiler. The building's superintendent didn't discover them until he came back the next day. They ate and slept in the heat for Christmas."

Thorny's mouth hung as she examined the man's eyes for any mirth or duplicity. It was as if he were a statue.

"I think Roosevelt had heard the story before. He never flinched at the rawness."

"When did you finally get supplies?"

"Three days later, we found a cache of rice and beans. We were starved, but each man only took his campaign cup level full. The muleskinner grabbed the powder monkey and made him stand there with his plate out. Every man dolloped a half spoonful onto his plate. The cook upended a full cup. We wanted him to know how we felt about him, and we would make sure he never starved again."

"So you had supplies after then?"

His cheeks fluttered with his one fart of a laugh. "Oh, hell no. Starvation was as regular as dysentery, foot rot, and men dying. But, until he died, the lad knew we cared."

Thorny broke the silence they had sunk into. She looked up and down Line Street. Across were a dentist office and the office of a land lawyer. "Why are we here?"

Monte pointed behind her.

The tower was built in the middle of a small open field. Under the modest tower was a small building. Thorny recognized the stylized "CD" painted in blue on the white round field. She had seen a few of the white-helmeted Civil Defense officers near the port of Los Angeles, and she knew officers worked at the airports.

Sliding her glasses back onto her face, she looked up. Monte shaded his eyes with his hand. "Hey, Bill. Anything to report?"

A man came to the side of the tower and looked down. The large binoculars hung from a wide strap about his neck. Thorny couldn't tell if the white patch on the man's face was a mustache or whitewash paint.

The man waved. "A Spad passed over shortly before ten this morning. But other than the frog, it has been a rather quiet week, sir. What do you hear from the north?"

"Quiet there too, Bill. Keep up the excellent work." He saluted the man. The man saluted back and turned back to the south. The white helmet disappeared from sight.

Thorny thought about the exchange as they retraced their

path. "Isn't a Spad... or should I say, wasn't a Spad a plane flown in the first war?"

Monte nodded as they walked. "It was a terrible plane the French flew. They were known to shoot their own propellers in half."

Thorny glanced back.

"Bill's Spad could have been a crow, an eagle, an airplane, or just one nip too many from the flask in his hip pocket. It doesn't matter. We're the last place the Germans or the Japanese are coming to bomb. Besides, what he hasn't figured out yet is there is no siren on the tower. Nobody checks on him, and he comes and goes by a schedule thumbtacked to the walls of his mind."

"But he's not—"

Monte spun her around. "Are you going back there to tell the man the best he can hope for is cuts of dead cat toasted on the side of a boiler? Are you going to tell the man the kind woman he rents a room from is his wife?" He pointed at her pants. "These are challenging times, and yes, sometimes, these times don't make sense. You can't buy any butter without using one of the stamps in your pocket. I get ten gallons of gasoline a month I don't really need. You own a farm, so you get the first hundred, and then have to prove a need for more—but more often, you walk the seven miles." He looked down to confirm. "In your bare feet, no less."

He turned them around and resumed walking. "About a year ago, someone found him standing on top of the roof of the school—watching for enemy bombers. Nobody cared if he was living in France, The Great War to End All Wars, or Bishop, California, in 1942. It didn't matter. A group of the men got some lumber and built the tower. No spotter tower has a shade roof on it. But ours does. Nobody wants Bill to get sunstroke.

But it gives meaning to his life. Me, I cut hair, and it grows back."

"So, the people of Bishop care." She smiled sadly. She squeezed his hand back.

"At least some of them do."

17 OLD PAPER

The scent of juniper was strong as Thorny leaned her head against the window. The building built in the shape of a Mission fort could cause much to be said, but unclean was not one of them. Someone lovingly kept the windows sparkling and the woodwork clean and polished. The roughhewn floor, with gaps between the wide boards, made her want to take off her boots. She remembered the cool air seeming to only rise above the floorboards the height of a child's foot.

The first year she came to the Indian Church, she was only six. In school, there was a large but quiet boy in her class. She saw him as the kind of large that's not fat like an old sow, but more like the kind of thick a calf gets as they become a steer. The meat isn't defined, just thick. She had sat next to him under a tree as they ate their lunches from their pails. Nothing else stood out about him, other than his two braids were longer than Mary Jane Taylor's. The differences were hers were yellow, and his was charcoal black. Her mother tied blue yarn bows in the top of her braids, and Charles had leather tied at the ends.

Thorny never mentioned the braids until they were in high school.

The first day of class, the boy had no braids. She had never seen him wear a hat before, and yet he sat in class wearing a straw field-hat. Drawn to the anomaly of her friend, and as he appeared in two other classes of hers, she found her attention welded to the strange hat.

After school, as they were walking to the library, he lifted the hat to let his braids fall over his shoulders and back.

"Why are you hiding your braids under a straw hat?"

"The rules say they will cut my braids off. If I hide them under the hat, they will leave them. I don't want to be scalped."

The next day, she marched into the principal's office. She was alone but knew the picture hanging on the wall was all the help she would need.

"Is it true you will cut Charles's braids off if he doesn't wear a hat?"

The man blinked at this slip of a girl who, by the second, was becoming as much of a woman as his mother. "Those are the rules. I didn't make them, but it is my job to enforce them." His hands were flat on the desk. Thorny wondered if he was about to push off and jump through the window to get away from her.

She pointed at the print of a painting. The man wore a long dress. The light brown beard was of a youngish man, and the hair flowed down to his shoulders. "If he was a student here, would you be doing your job and cut his hair and shave his face?"

"That's not the point."

"What about the dress he's wearing?"

"It's a little unusual, but I see you are also wearing dungarees instead of a dress."

Thorny leaned her spread claw on the man's desk. She continued to point at the painting. "His hair is longer than many girls. But you don't seem to have a problem with it."

The man eased back an inch. "He lived a long time ago, and in those days, they wore that dress—"

"And the long hair because of their religion. Yes, I've sat in church. I've heard those stories. So as long as the man's religion is the same as yours, his dress and hair are okay. But because Charles Brown's Paiute traditions are *not* the same as yours, you will insist on scalping him if his braids hang down."

The man blanched. His voice was only air. "We do not scalp people."

She stood. "No, no you don't. But you do allow your Paiute students to live in fear of being scalped, just for being the person they are. I suggest you consider making a change to the rules before someone decides to go on the warpath." She held his eyes with hers for a few seconds and then left.

A week later, the board of education decided to come into the twentieth century and removed the rule. There had been a quiet celebration on the Reservation. Thorny had sat on the log next to Charles. She wore the straw hat pushed back to the back of her head. Later, in the dark, they took a knife and cut a small slit down their thumbs then pushed them together.

Charles had stumbled with the idea of her being female but every bit the warrior. "This makes us blood… um… something."

She rested her claw on his shoulder. "It makes us blood."

He giggled. "I always wanted a little sister."

"Shut your mouth. I'm two months older than you." She looked up at him and patted the top of his head. "Little brother."

Their relationship never changed.

"I've seen more substance in a recipe for scrambled eggs."

Thorny pulled her head from the window and looked at her friend. Charles sat on the piano bench across from the desk. He used the one end as a small desk. The church prayed for one day to have a piano to complement the lone bench.

John Watson sat on the small stool at the desk—the only other furniture in the large, stark room. Thorny looked at the floor. Even a large rug would help fill the emptiness.

The man rumpled himself as if he were shifting information or loyalties within the bag of his body. "He wasn't a well-liked person within law enforcement." He cleared the croakiness in his voice. "The swells down the valley didn't much care for him, either."

Thorny's eyes paused as she looked at her memory behind closed eyes. There were no pinholes of light coming through to lend an understanding. "When you say down the valley, how far are we talking?" Her eyes opened and took in the slight slump of his shoulders. He knew he had been caught but was in friendly territory.

"Mulholland's Empire." Charles looked back through the papers. "According to this, the man cleaned his house until it shined. Did his laundry and neatly put it all away. The pantry was fully stocked, and the icebox was full." He looked up at the other two. "If I were going to go hang myself, I don't think I would care if I had enough soup and beans to last the winter." He harrumphed. "And I damn sure wouldn't wash any dirty clothes. Wait…" He scanned his finger over another page. "Says here in the inventory, the car was clean, and the gas tank was showing full." His finger continued down the page. "The yard was freshly weeded and mowed." His hand and the report gently floated to his lap.

"He was as meticulous in his death as he was in his life."

The three turned at the new voice at the door. The young man stood leaning his shoulder against the doorjamb. An older woman with a small veiled hat stood quietly behind him.

Thorny smirked warmly. "Hello, Danny. What brings you slumming?"

He shrugged his shoulder off the jamb and stepped into the room. "Rumor has it you're looking into the death of Hank Hudgins. I saw the chief's car and thought I would stop and offer my help." He glanced at John, silently sitting on the stool. "Hello, John. Good to see you out and about." The man watched him but didn't say a word.

Thorny didn't move from the window. She rolled her body around until her back was to the light. Her attention wasn't on Danny but the woman still standing in the doorway. She never moved. Her hands protectively held her small cream-colored clutch. The fact of it matching her shoes and the unneeded belt at her waist didn't pass Thorny's notice.

As the man stopped a few feet in front of her, Thorny's eyes moved to his face. "Who's the woman, Danny?"

"Her name is Inez."

"She looks a little old for you."

The man was quiet. Thorny had known him to do this before. He was slow counting to ten. His face never showed it. He never got angry. But, at the count of ten, she had seen him break a few noses when they were in high school. He once told her about it. His uncle had taught him how to calm down. If you speak or fight in anger—you have lost.

"She wants to talk with you."

Thorny's count only went to five. "Okay, I'll bite, why?"

"Because you are looking for the woman known as Violet. Her real name was—"

"Ethel. I know." She leaned slightly, looking around his head. "So, who is this?"

He didn't move. "I told you. Her name is Inez. You want information, then you need to talk to her."

"How do I know I can trust what she has to say?"

Danny took a deep breath and turned. "Is that the police report, chief?"

Charles softly closed the folder and held it out. Danny took it and held it out toward the woman. The woman's head moved, and Thorny could tell she was now the subject of observation. She nodded at the folder, and the woman stepped into the room.

Taking the folder, she stood next to Danny as she read through the report. She turned over pages, and then scanned back.

Thorny allowed her eyes to drift closed as she turned and leaned her forehead against the glass. The juniper carried some of the heat now. Wisps of barefoot summers drifted by. Lunches on blankets and the smell of pinion pine trees and their seeds notched on her memory stick. Pops, the chief, and Charles. Occasionally, they were joined by Monte. Sherwin Pass was still another hour up the hill. But the gold in the dark nutshells made the long drive from town worth the day.

Thorny's eyes fluttered open as the woman stepped over to her. She held the folder out to Thorny. "Excuse my French, but it is pure mule droppings. You could fertilize the entire valley with those seven pages."

Thorny smoothed her mouth with the thumb and second finger of her claw. The woman's face was as motionless as the building they stood in. "Anything in the report true?"

"The date and time they found him. I'm sure the address is accurate. But anything about him—pure bullshit."

Thorny looked down at the folder in her hand. She held it up and bumped it into the air at John. The officer stood, took it, and then walked out.

Thorny watched the man leave. She looked at Danny for a few seconds. The man was showing none of his cards. Her eyes softly blinked as she turned to face the woman. "When do you want to talk, Violet?"

The tiny flinch was only in the woman's eyes. "This is my day off."

"Can I buy you lunch?"

"How private?"

"How about the back porch of the Bib?"

The woman turned and held out her hand. "Danny, you're walking home."

The man looked at Thorny. The small smile only crept up one side of his face. His hand came out with the key to his car.

Thorny squeezed the shoulder of the large Paiute as she walked by. The low grunt was all he needed to say. Thorny knew he would be watching her leave. She rolled her shoulders and stretched her arms as the two women walked out. Since their youth, their conversations were as many silent gestures as they were words. As they walked, Thorny massaged her right shoulder with her claw. The left hand was known as a South Paw.

The conversation in the night would continue in the closest warm water—south of town. Thorny needed the mineral water to soothe her scars. Even if the water wasn't so hot and the creek little more than a muddy ditch, the view on a moonless night couldn't be beaten. Up above, an enterprising endeavor had real bathtubs and even private rooms. The water was cleaner and hotter. But, by some, the quiet of the night and the muddy creek were the preferred refuge.

"How much do you know about Harold?" Violet's hands floated and relaxed in her lap.

Thorny picked at the yard salad. She knew tomatoes were already red and splitting in the Victory gardens of Los Angeles. She had tilled and weeded the large plot at UCLA for the right to come pick produce grown as part of the war effort. She had stepped onto the bus to Bishop having only enjoyed some of the early lettuce.

"I was eight when he died. I remember reading about it in the paper. My grandfather..." She looked up with a slight wrinkle above her eyes. "I think they were friends."

Violet studied the young face. With the dark green glass of her glasses, the young woman could pass for any of the pictures of Amelia Earhart preparing to fly. The bright light of the valley had her wishing she had some darker glasses, but the filtered shade under the large elm tree was cooling and inviting.

The privacy of the hedge surrounding the back porch was a bonus.

A soft smile played on the older woman's face. "Eustis. Yes, they were. It was Eustis who talked him into coming to the Owens Valley. He would talk endlessly about the valley when they were all in Cuba. The jungles were the exact opposite of the open fields and grasses of the valley."

She looked through the last houses toward the river a mile away. Her face soured.

"When the water dried up, and the big city bought all the land, the desert started." She looked back at Thorny. "It was a prohibition of the land. As the beer and whiskey dried up, the land withered and died.

"When I first came here as a young girl, there were huge orchards. Truck farms had so much produce, Taylor's market was only a dry goods. The rest was almost free. There were always stacks of empty Ball canning jars lining the front wall. People used to help pick for the right to glean the imperfect fruit and vegetables. There were root cellars in most everyone's backyards, and even a few of the nicer homes were built with basements."

The woman drifted off in her memories of Bishop's better times.

Thorny sipped on her iced tea. The woman was due her privacy. The times would never return. Where the thirsty metropolis smashed its footprint—nothing but rabbit brush would ever grow again. The valley which was once the second most productive breadbasket in California was now considered High Desert. Other than the random ranch or farm, the scorched earth of sand without water was complete.

True to the nature of families producing more families, the large city would only get thirstier. The desert would only become a concrete way of life.

Returning from the toilet, Thorney found her glass of tea

full again, and May was standing with Violet, looking up into the large overhanging elm.

"Squirrels?" the two women started. They turned with only one of them showing any guilt as they smiled.

May's face turned into a short scowl. "No. Crows. Noisy, dirty crows."

Thorny's face was blank as she watched Violet's face flush. She heard nothing but a few smaller birds. Violet cleared her throat softly as Thorny retook her seat.

May topped off the other woman's glass. "I'll just leave you two to talk." Taking up the plates, she left.

Thorny looked over her glasses. "Crows..."

The woman sat silent and then leaned forward onto her elbows with a soft chuckle. "As a young girl, May had high hopes about being asked to the big dance by Harry. It was I who had to intercede for him."

Thorny's head cranked sideways in tiny jerks. "Big dance?"

The woman's smile only raised on one side. More reflective than humor. "The dance of life, of marriage..."

"May and the judge?"

"She wasn't alone. Several young women were smitten by the dashing man with the thin mustache. His hair was jet-black, and he would pomade the sides back over his ears. The thick top and back you just knew were made for your fingers to slide through. The man performed his regimen of exercise every morning before he dressed. Rain or shine, the man walked to the court from his home on Brockman Lane. He said the three-mile walk was to get his blood flowing before he had to sit the day away."

Thorny hesitated, but asked. "He was a..."

"Customer?" The woman laughed lightly. "If he had the

interest, I would have never charged him. The closest we ever came to sex was giving each other a massage." She smiled and leaned in. "I even tried to give him some oral or hand sex... nothing."

"So, you were just friends?"

"Is that so strange?"

Thorny sat thinking. She thought through the few people she considered to be friends. Almost all were male. "Not from my perspective, no. But I was... well, he was a judge, and you..."

"A whore? It's a profession, not an insult. It was who I was—the town whore or madam. But when I wasn't working, I was also a person." She leaned her head over on her right fist. "When the doctor finishes his day, is it wrong for him to have friends? What about you?"

"What about me? Do I have friends? Yes..." Thorny took her glasses off and cleaned them on her napkin as she thought. "I never thought about how people have friends or don't have friends. But I guess it would be natural, given the proximity of the court and your residence upstairs." She folded the glasses onto the tablecloth. "If you weren't... involved... was anybody?"

"Not anybody who was female." The woman's face was stone. Waiting.

Thorny's mind raced. The one bit of information twisted out and became a rope connecting so much. The woman sat back patiently as she watched the younger eyes bounce about the table—searching.

Finally, Thorny turned her chair sideways and looked down the hot street. The waves of heat shimmered from the black car. A cat and a dog laid in one of the yards as if they were in a stopped chase. No cars moved down the long street. No breeze disturbed the leaves of the trees.

Her voice was small but deep. "Oh, my..."

Her head turned to look at the woman who probably held most of the secrets of the town. The woman's head bobbed once gently.

Thorny's eyes were still searching. "Ulysses never married..."

"None of them did."

The implications roared in Thorny's mind. Her vision constricted. "Monte...?"

"Or Eustis."

Thorny's head jolted. "Pops? But he had a daughter..."

The woman's face was placid but unmoving. Her eyes were soft. There was no evil or duplicity in her face. Her mouth made the word, but no sound. "No."

"But... my mother..."

The hair sparkled with tiny flashes of white as the woman's head moved gently side to side. The eyes softened. The woman understood the pain of losing what one thought was their life.

"Then it was a lie..."

Violet sighed. "Some... yes. But only to ease what was complicated."

"Then who am I?"

The woman opened her clutch and drew out her handkerchief. Softly blowing her nose was her only admission to emotion. She pulled the information into order.

"You were born in Los Cruxes, New Mexico. I think your real grandfather served in Cuba with the boys. You were barely walking when Eustis brought the two of you home. The war in Europe was going, but the United States hadn't entered yet."

"I was born in October of 1914... or at least that's what Eustis told me."

Violet put her hand out on Thorny's claw. "He would only have told you the truth. Maybe he didn't tell you everything, but you can keep in your heart everything he did tell you."

Thorny hiccupped quietly as she muttered the words he would have said. "There are only facts. Everything else is just a story."

Violet's laugh was more of alfalfa moving in the breeze than a girly tinkle. "You sound just like him."

"I don't think a day went by without him reminding me. I think it may have been why I became a lawyer." She sipped her tea. "Do you think it's true about my mother? About her dying in a house fire?" She held up her claw.

"You two lived with Eustis. What burned was the cooling shed. It never had electricity, and the lantern fell over and shattered on the cutting table. The burning oil splashed on the two of you and in the hay.

"You were strapped papoose style to your mother. Your mother saved you by pushing you out the door, but her dress was already burning up. There was nothing Eustis could have done." She took a deep breath as if a weight was lifted. "I do know any of the four could have been your grandfather, or uncle, as it were. They all loved you as much as any could."

"I don't remember the judge, but Monte and Ulysses were always there. I just didn't realize they were as close to each other as they were. I don't remember them ever out to the farm."

Violet's lips rolled as her eyes looked down the street. "If they came out, it would have been discrete. There are some things society doesn't like."

"Like whores and homosexuals."

The woman's eyes slid back. Her blink was slow as the heat of the day. "Just like."

"Were you friends with the others?"

Violet dipped her head. "It was a safe place for them to meet. It wasn't always about sex, and I do miss playing gin with them." She snickered. "A little hooch, a deck of cards, and I could see the boys who went to Cuba."

The two drifted in their thoughts. The heat played in the leaves, scenting the air. The buzzing of crickets lent to the stupor as the afternoon settled in.

"Do you think his being homosexual had anything to do with him being killed?"

"Harry? Killed? I thought it was suicide."

"According to the police report..." Thorny sat back with her arm hitched over the corner of the chair.

The woman's eyes twitched back and forth across the table. There were no answers to see. She was rapidly reaching a loop of evidence dissolving into vapor in the sun.

Thorny could sense the woman never considered an alternative to the accepted story.

The woman sighed as her voice was more breath than sound. "I never saw... I mean, nobody but the police saw anything."

Thorny took up her glasses and put them on. "That's what I'm afraid of."

As they pulled into the driveway of the Dude Ranch, Danny stepped down from the porch. Part of the newspaper from the city was in his hand. He opened the door for Violet. Thorny walked around, glancing at the paper.

"Anything interesting in the Times?"

He flapped the paper in the air. "More war. We've started using our bombers. Maybe the boys will be home by Christmas, but I doubt it. The Japs did something up in Oregon, but they think a plane crashed. It started a fire in the forest, but the rains put it out."

"We could use some of those rains here."

He nudged his chin at the retreating Violet. As the front door closed, his voice lowered. "Any answers?"

Thorny nodded as her mouth twitched sideways. "Some, but also more questions."

She removed her glasses. Her eyes locked on his. "Would any of your father's friends have any reason to kill the judge?"

His head shook loosely. "I remember when the news came. Dad was stunned. I think he was friends with the judge. As strange as it may seem, they had a lot in common. I remember them having arguments with a lot of the books from dad's library on the table. Both were deep thinkers."

"But none of the men from down the city way?"

"No... but it does remind me someone mentioned a couple of mookes going swimming the other day down in Independence. You might want to lay low for a while."

Thorny raised an eyebrow. "A couple of fellas in a tan Desoto drove past the Kettle later the same afternoon."

Danny's eyes turned hard under his furrowed brow. "Are you sure it was a Desoto?"

"I can ask Charlie, but I think I know the difference between a Desoto and a Cord with a flaming trunk sticking out of the Owens River. Why... friends of yours?"

"More like old associates of my father's. Not anyone I would want to be associated with, and they were never friends of anyone in this valley." He reached out and placed his hand on her shoulder. "All the more reason to watch your back."

She wiggled her eyebrows as she put her glasses back on. "Let me give you a lift back into town."

She pushed her lower lip out. "I'm fine. I need to walk and think. As we passed the church, I saw Charlie's car. Either he is still there, or he left it for me, but thanks anyway."

"What are you doing for a car anyway?"

She shrugged. "I like to walk, and most of the time, I use Monte's Ford."

He thought about it. "If you change your mind, I can probably find you a car to use."

She laughed. "I bet you can. It would just need new license plates, the bullet holes plugged or time to cool down."

He shook his head as he chuckled. "I was talking about one of mine from here at the ranch."

She poked his chest as she turned to walk away. "So was I."

19 HORNET'S NEST

The knock was nimble on the door's window. The light in the kitchen shown out on the crude cement stoop. The lit window's reflection glowed in all four polished shoes.

The two men watched as the older man in striped boxers and sleeveless undershirt with a thumb-sized hole near his ribs came into the light of the kitchen.

Mr. Ferguson squinted at the door. Danny waved. The man scowled and squinted again. He put his hands to his eyes and then silently swore. He held up his finger and disappeared into the dark of the house. Moments later, wearing his glasses, he opened the door.

"You do know it's the middle of the night, Danny." The man was making a statement, not asking a question. He stood with only his boxers, shirt, and glasses, but it was his house.

Danny smiled as he jerked his thumb over his shoulder. "Thorny wasn't in the barn." Danny knew the light in the kitchen at four in the morning was about the man starting work. It was the start of the man's long day of moving water about the farm.

"She came home last Sunday about supper time. Gathered some stores and left. We ain't seen her since." He started to close the door.

Danny stuck his foot out to stop the door. "Did she have a car with her?"

The man scowled at the foot. "Why?"

"Well, if she packed some food in a car, she could be going farther than if say she had a mule or was walking."

"She had a truck."

Danny blinked. He tried to think of what truck she could have borrowed. "What kind?"

"What do you mean what kind? The kind with four wheels and a carry bed on it. Now move your foot."

Surprised at the short nature, Danny gave ground. He turned and stepped off the stoop with the other man. "Come on. We need to get you different clothes."

As the sun rose over the White Mountains, the two men stood next to the car. Danny looked at the dusty road. In the dust, dirt, and rock of the track, he looked for impressions or of rocks twisted out of their place.

He knelt and picked up a golf ball sized rock. He extended his middle finger and drew an 'X' in the dirt. Looking along the track, he drew another. Soon, there were two more. He stood and stepped back.

"What are we looking at?"

Danny turned with a quirk in his smile. "That's my line. Those X's I drew are tire tracks. They are moving up the canyon."

"Four tires? It must be a heavy truck."

Danny looked up the canyon. "Exactly… and she's still up there." He started walking.

"You're going to walk? How far?"

Danny half turned to look at the man from the big city. The man was a bit soft in the middle. Judging by the color of his skin, he hadn't been out of his office in years. Danny turned and continued walking. "It will do you some good. It will remind you what air feels like in your lungs."

The men started walking. As the summer sun rose, the shadows became slivers. Even the rattlesnakes would hide by digging into the north rim of shade. The man's handkerchief was almost ready to wring out when he stopped for the ninth time. Walking up a dirt road in the high desert wasn't the same as strolling to lunch down Wilshire Boulevard in the big city.

One thing that felt the same as the big city was the barrel of a gun in the small of your back.

The man froze.

Panic set in as he looked up the empty road.

Danny had disappeared at least a half an hour before. He was alone with only city legs and a butt for sitting at a desk. The closest he ever came to danger was shaving with his grandfather's straight razor or letting the barber do the same. Guns were something he knew about, but he hoped were not part of his job.

The hand patted him down around his belt and under his arms. Even though his white shirt was almost see-through with sweat, the hand was taking no chances. There was a pause, and then the man felt his ankles being probed.

"What are you doing here?" The whisper was next to his ear. Little more than a slight hot breeze along his cheek.

He was more afraid he might embarrass himself, but he whispered back. "I'm with Danny."

"He's dead." The voice let the information soak in. "Now, you have three seconds to tell me what you are doing here. I already know you aren't with the Bureau of Mines and Minerals."

"We... I'm looking for..." The man realized he was alone. His information could be the death of him.

The gun probed. "Looking for who?"

"Miss Wallace," the man blurted. His chin and lower lip began to quiver.

The whisper in his ear turned to gravel. "Why?"

The quivering reflected in his voice. "Because she's in danger."

The voice carried down from the turn in the road. "Do you treat all of your visitors this way or is it just because it's Sunday?"

Thorny stepped around the small quivering man. "Only when you disrupt my breakfast, Danny." She eased the hammer back down on the 30-30.

As she moved past the taller man, he assessed the rifle—the bare feet were a given. "Flapjack's rifle?"

"Eustis's. It was in the barn. I figured I might need it up here. Ulysses only had an old open port squirrel gun. The bolt was rusted shut long before I went on down to UCLA." She looked back. "Get your dog or the rattler near his right leg will."

Danny looked back as his eyes closed with a sigh. "Come along, Leonard, before the animals get you." He turned and passed Thorny. "Coffee on?"

"I can heat some." She took the rifle by the barrel in her claw. The lever rested on her shoulder with the stock weighting the whole over her back as she scratched at her neck with the hammer. "What are you doing up here?"

"Looking for you. Larry drove up last night. Obviously, you have stirred up a hornet's nest."

"Here or there?"

"Both."

"Guess I need to get some new loads for the rifle."

The man frowned in confusion. "Why? Nobody would find you up here."

They walked around the back of an old Diamond Rio flatbed truck. The wood deck was loaded with large rocks tied down with a net made out of wire cable. Before Danny could ask, he had his answer. Attached to the front was a plow blade. The up and down adjusting cable ran to a pulley on the roof of the cab. He noticed the large lever hanging down into the cab and knew it was so a single man could manage the jerry-rigged snowplow.

Thorny leaned the rifle against the building near the door. "You found me." She noticed him looking back at the truck. "It was up at South Lake. They won't need it before the snow comes."

They stepped into the gloom of the shack. "I found you because I know you, and I've been here before. Charles would find you, and if Pete were to think about it for a few minutes, this is where he would look, too."

Thorny reached into the back of a cupboard and drew out a small box. She slid out the tray of shells. Stepping to the door, she took up the rifle. The man outside put up his hands. His breathing was labored. She ignored him and turned inside. She pointed the rifle to one side and started pumping the lever. The shells ejected as a surprised Danny held up hands to catch them at his belly.

Empty, Thorny began to reload through the side port. Danny held up the crimped over single-use shell. "Birdshot?"

"Varmint. The rats are about the size of large house cats."

"Are they destructive?" He looked around the interior of the shack at what rats could chew on and damage.

Thorny noticed the short man was now standing in the doorway. "Not really, but they are tasty." She held out some jerky.

The reaction was exactly what she expected from both men. Danny took the offered meat, and the other rushed outside.

Thorny, laying the loaded rifle on the table, bent to light the oil cup under the coffeepot. "It seems like he has a delicate nature, for someone who is willing to drive all the way up here in the dark of night."

Danny smirked at the poke toward the city man. He remembered what kind of dark night flooded his backyard for the last few nights. The full moon was over, but there was still a few more nights to see by. The last night's moon would have provided more light than the blackout slit-covers on the headlights. "And when did you do all the work on the road?"

Thorny smiled as she turned around. "High noon, of course."

She put two more enameled mugs on the table as she sat. "So what's so important a desk rat would scurry up here."

Danny turned and called out. The man appeared in the door. What little breakfast he had in his gut was now gone.

Thorny pointed. "There's a pump on the side. Wash the stench off you before you come into my untarnished house."

Danny snickered as the man disappeared to where he had been directed. "You're brutal."

"I don't want to hear it from someone I don't know. So tell me what's going on."

Danny jerked his thumb toward the door. "He's the only one who knows. He told me you had everyone screaming for your blood, and we came to find you."

"Who is he?"

"You might say he is the one who looks at records and books and then makes the suggestions about how to fix them."

Thorny slid the metal plate over the canister of fire. She poured the two mugs full. Pushing one at Danny, she moved the other toward the only other seat. "So he would be the one hiring to have me killed?"

"Think of him more as an accountant. But when he worked for my father, yes, he would be the one recommending—not the hiring, but the recommending. He would weigh the gains versus the losses."

Thorny's eyes narrowed. "If he doesn't work for your father's thugs, who does he work for now?"

Danny paused with the mug halfway to his lips. "A much larger and more ruthless gang."

"I work for the Los Angeles Department of Water and Power." The man stepped lightly into the room. He waited for his eyes to adjust. "You might say, I work for William Mulholland's old gang."

Thorny indicated the empty seat and mug. "There's coffee if you want it."

The man smiled meekly as he sat. "Is it made from the well water out there?"

Thorny nodded. She knew how crisp the water tasted.

As the shadows lengthened, the man talked. With each revelation, he had explanations about the viewed implications. He explained what it meant to her, and what it meant to the water district. Evidently, Ulysses had been more of a water engineer than he had let on.

"But I don't think I own the stream or the land."

It astounded both Thorny and Danny. The man's memory of

maps and the logistics of how things under the earth worked kept flowing. "No, you're correct. The stream is below your property. The spring on your property gushes at over a thousand cubic feet a minute. If you have been up there, the fountain supposedly throws a stream as thick as a man's middle, and over his height in the air. Forty yards downstream, it disappears in a large crack in the rock. A mile later, it exits the mountain on Los Angeles's Department of Water and Power's land. Nobody thought to look higher in 1917."

Thorny leaned back, looking at Danny. "So, this is all about water?"

Both men nodded. Leonard wiped his head with his handkerchief. "Since 1905, it always has been. Until they turned off the water to everyone and the land, people up here didn't know or think about it. The water flowed, they moved it about where they needed it, and the crops grew. It was Mulholland who looked at the hundred-thousand people of Los Angeles and saw a million thirsty Angelinos."

"You thought the thugs staying at the ranch were bad." Danny clenched his furled lips. "And several were. But compared with Mulholland and his gang, they were stealing rotten apples from the trash cart. When it comes to protecting what they stole, this gang will stop at nothing, Thorny."

Thorny stood and grabbed the coffeepot. She stepped to the door and threw the water and grounds out onto the dirt. "How do I make them go away?"

"I don't think you can." The man looked up. "Who are your heirs?"

Thorny froze with the lid halfway to the pot. "What do you mean?"

"I mean, when they kill you, who do they kill next?"

Thorny put the pot on the dry board and turned to Danny. The gangster's son was rocking his head. He had heard this kind of talk and thinking before. He had grown up with it. She could tell by his face that he didn't think it would ever come to the valley, but he was also not pleased how it did.

"How long are you here, Leonard?"

"I need some food and to drive back tonight. I have a meeting at nine-thirty in the morning. I've gone over the general figures, and I'll play catch up as the meeting progresses, but I don't dare miss it."

Danny stood. "Who else knows you're up here?"

"I'm having a tryst with a woman friend down in Laguna Beach. Her uncle has a beach house in Crystal Cove he lets us use."

Thorny stopped at the door and turned. "If I have some maps, do you think you can explain what's important and why?"

"Are they road maps or topographic?"

"Topos."

He nodded. "Sure. Do you know where your holdings are?"

She smiled at Danny. "With pinpoint accuracy."

As Thorny drove them down the hill in the truck, Danny was quiet. "You sure are talking a lot this evening, Danny."

He looked out the window at the now smooth road. "I was thinking about the Kettle and Leonard."

"I wasn't taking him into town."

Danny leaned forward and looked across the other man. "We can't risk him at the ranch or even out at your place. You just don't know who might be watching these days."

Thorny snorted and smirked. Her glance was pure mischief. "Have you ever tried to sneak up to an Indian's house?"

The man in the middle blanched. "What sort of Indian?"

Thorny snuffed as she upshifted and let the truck roll. "Paiute. Generally passive and fun. But the nine dogs will tear you apart by your third heartbeat."

The breaks squealed with dust as she slowed to a stop by the car.

"Stay close. I'm sure they haven't fed any of the elk to the dogs yet."

Danny laughed as he opened the door. "Stop. You're scaring the help. Besides, his wife breeds vicious dogs."

Thorny looked at the man. "What kind?"

The man flushed as he scooted toward the open door. "Pomeranians."

20 READ CAREFULLY

"**D**id you go by the bank?"

Thorny looked up from the maps. "The bank?"

Monte dug his thumbnail into the letter and showed it to her. "He said to go talk to Elijah Jacobs down at the bank."

She shrugged. "No, I didn't. I guess I missed that part."

Monte started laughing softly. "But you fully understood the part of stirring up a storm when you filed them papers."

She rolled her eyes with a cocked open smile. "Well, it wasn't exactly what I was expecting..."

"Good thing you took Charlie."

The tip of her tongue peeked out of her furled lips as she stared at the one swirl in the linoleum floor. The blink was slow and thoughtful. Her voice was barely more than a mutter. "You know, Danny said those two thugs were not part of his father's..." She looked up. "Bank. Elijah Jacobs." She stood and was out the door.

Monte's eyebrows rose as he started picking up the maps and paperwork. "No, don't mind me, Thorny. I've got work to do here... like picking up all this paper."

The small drawer only held extra razors, scissors, and combs. The back of the drawer kept it all to the front. Monte's hand drew the drawer out to the stop. His right hand worked a small latch as the left pulled the drawer past the stop. He laid the paperwork in the hidden compartment as he heard a footstep in the door. His hands brought back some tools as he closed the drawer

He turned with a salesman's smile. "And how may I be of service to you gentlemen?" He studied the two faces. Both had received hot towels and shaves within the last day, and their haircuts were only a week old. The bulges under their arms weren't their lunches, either.

His hands found the lower pockets on his smock. Both hands held straight razors on each side. Stropping wasn't needed for how he would be using them.

The smaller of the two men stepped forward. "You're Monte Garcia or something. The fella they call the nigra."

Monte didn't care if the insults were intended or from ignorance. He took the two steps to close the gap. He could see the move unnerved the man. "The name is Geronimo. The same as my great-uncle. And the word is pronounced Negros, like egg rolls. It means dark or black heart in Spanish."

His nose was less than two feet from the taller man, but six inches higher than the other man. Monte volleyed, and the ball was now actively in the men's court.

His voice was only slightly less threatening. "We're looking for Elizabeth Wallace."

"There is a dive bar on First and Spring Streets in Los Angeles. I hear she spends most of her time there these days. Why don't you two go back to Los Angeles, and go see if she's there."

The man flared and moved a few inches tighter. "Why you greasy little spit wad. I ought to—"

Monte closed the final gap. His left hand was at the man's throat. His right hand was in the man's crotch. "I would suggest returning to Los Angeles. It would be far better for your health. For, you see, the straight razor at your throat, I stropped this morning. It is resting on your carotid artery, which will bleed out in only ten seconds. But my other hand is holding the almost rusty razor at your femoral artery. If I slice there, your friend might get you back to your car. But you will be dead before he can start to take the keys out of his pocket.

"So, if you value your health, I suggest you go have a little chat with your boss about how things are up here in the wild west. If he wants to find out how things are himself, tell him the crazed, bloodthirsty Apache named Geronimo is here to explain what's what."

Thorny stood next to the door as the two men in suits and Fedoras backed out of the shop. They didn't even tip their hats as they turned and stepped back into the black sedan.

Monte stepped out next to Thorny as they watched the two make a U-turn on Main and drive south out of town. The dust from the end of the pavement rose higher than the second story above the police station. They both knew the tires were turning faster than the stated sign of twenty-five.

Monte hummed as his head wagged back and forth. "Some days, you just wonder about people. How in the world can two grown men be so lost as to drive three hundred miles out of their way before they stop and ask for directions?" He smiled and turned to take in Thorny. "How did it go with Elijah?"

She turned inward and drew her hand out of her pocket. "I

think I need you to come back with me and go through many papers. The box was a small footlocker." She turned her hand out as he watched.

In her palm was a skeleton of a hand only slightly smaller than hers was, each part held to the next with fine wire. The casting was as perfect as any fine jewelry. The whole gleamed of gold.

"Is it solid?" His voice was hushed.

She shrugged her eyes. Her voice was barely a sound. "It's heavy enough." She put it back in her pocket as she looked up into the closeness they now stood. "I was hoping you could tell me where it came from."

His eyes went wild and wide. "I suppose..." His body slumped. "I have no idea. Let me see it again." They stared at it as Monte carefully turned it over.

Thorny mussed. "It wouldn't be the first time Ulysses surprised me, but I don't think he had the skill to cast something like this. I mean, where do you get the bones to take casts from?"

Monte left the hand in hers. He looked up with a dark look. "I'm not sure I want to know... but a miner, maybe? There was nothing there saying anything?"

"I told you. There is a footlocker's worth of papers, maps, small books, and I don't know what all. We will need a couple of suitcases to take it all at once. But then, if it was safe to be out here, why would he feel the need to keep it there?"

Monte turned his sign. "Let's go take a fast peek. Mr. Taylor won't be here for his shave and haircut until three."

The heat seared the street. Even under the awnings along the street, the two wiped their brows as they walked. The last of the shoppers scurried here and there before the noontime meal and, for some, the only meal of the day.

"I heard you met Violet."

The five small words hung heavy in the air. Not for the first time, Thorny wondered if there was anything in the valley that Monte didn't know about by the end of the day. Drop your milk bottle in the early morning, Monte can tell you where the last piece of glass is hiding by noon. Thorny sniffed at the memory of the bummer lamb when she was twelve.

The ewe died during birth in the middle of the night. Pops dried off the armful of lamb and tucked her under the quilt covering the sleeping Thorny. The early morning woke Thorny with a small mouth sucking on her chin. Pops had milk in a small bag with pinholes at the one corner.

The next morning, Thorny walked into town. As she climbed into the chair for her haircut, Monte had asked her how the new lamb was doing. It took the young Thorny years to figure out how Monte had smelled the lamb on her.

She snuck a glance at the man. His head was always held high with his chin out, challenging the world. He was quiet, but like a large rock in a stream. Life washed around him, and he was always there. She smiled softly. His being there provided her with a solid grounding.

"Do you want to talk about the four of you?"

Monte opened the door to the bank. "In due time."

They stared at the largest safe-deposit drawer the bank had. It had come from the bottom row of eight. The low groan of the banker lifting it onto the table did not escape them.

Elijah pointed at the tin box. "This is the last time I'm willing to pull it out and lift it for today. When you're done… you put it back. I'm getting old, and the back is getting weak."

The two nodded as the banker left them alone in the vault. He wasn't about to carry the drawer into the privacy room.

Monte opened the top to find the box filled with a collection of thick folders—each tied with string to hold them together. Only on a few was the string missing.

"What in tarnation is all of this?"

Thorny picked up a thin envelope, drew out a paper, and handed it to Monte. "You tell me."

Monte frowned as he unfolded the letter and began to read.

My dearest Ulysses,

If you are reading this, my body is cold in the ground. I pray my soul is warm, but not seared like the summer in Cuba. How we survived with only a mild touch of malaria, I will never know. But, without the days of wild, at the hands of Teddy, I would have never known the greatest friendships a man can be allowed to have. I have no regrets and only fond memories.

You are reading this because you have opened a rather large box being held by another good friend of mine. Over the years, we have kept each other's secrets. The box has no record of ownership. It is best this way.

The workings of the valley have changed since we returned. I have secured the water rights and freed the land for Eustis. The city can do no more troubling to him and the young child. Monte is now the owner of the land and his building. We have all done well, but I fear the big city is hungry and my time may be closing soon.

What this box contains are case files of events which have gone unsolved for years. For some—decades. These are the mysteries of the Owens Valley. Much of it doesn't matter to anyone living today. It is only the matter of curiosity for history's sake. If you can solve any of these, maybe a ghost can find peace and final rest. The value is for naught now.

There is one curiosity, though. Inscribed in very small detail on the metacarpals of the gold hand are petroglyph symbols, which I believe to be Paiute. Possibly your friends in the tribe may prove some assistance.

The skeleton was in a hidden drawer of the rolltop desk I bought. I have carefully taken the desk apart and found no other hiding spaces. If it is of tribal interest, for my part and thought, I say let them have it.

The mine in Silver Canyon, as well as the other sights in the valley, is now in your name. Silver Canyon needs only show some improvement or signs of being actively mined to hold the claim for another eighty years. I don't know why you like it up there, as I find it hot and extremely dusty. But you never were one for order and cleanliness. I guess those traits are the opposite of what I was always drawn to. I never could be such a willow wisp, but it suits you as you wander back and forth across this heaven of a valley. Thank you all for convincing me to come here.

In the red folder are the findings of the hydrologist from San Francisco. He thinks you could drill a side-bank well to drain off at least half of the spring above the old hot spring camp. It wouldn't be stealing water from the city claim down the mountain, as they can never prove the ownership of the water until it reaches their land. Good luck with the new creek.

Your loving friend,
Harry

Monte pensively turned to sit on the edge of the table. He wiped his face with the back of his hand holding the letter. His body was slumped as if drained. He looked over.

Thorny dipped her head. "I read it. Nothing here helps my investigation, but it has value. If nothing more, it has the value Harold saw in solving the mysteries for solving sake."

Monte carefully tipped his hand and lowered the letter into his lap. His furrowed brow was soft with age, but he was waiting for the answer.

"The man has reached out from the grave, which is almost twenty years old. He saw the worst this valley produced, but in looking down into those depths, he also saw the potential for good. He wanted someone to continue what he had started." She rested her hand on the box. "In a small valley like Owens, this box represents an awful lot of work."

She sat down next to Monte. Putting her arm around his shoulders, she continued. "I never questioned why none of you even dated. I never thought about not seeing a photo of my grandmother. There isn't even a photo of my mother. I had Pops, Ulysses, and you to raise me up. I don't think you three did such a bad job. Even if my mother had been around, I still think I would have preferred to walk barefooted and wear men's pants. It's just how I am. Just like you four. You found each other—it was enough. Now through one, another has asked for help. I think Harold would be fine with Ulysses asking you and me to continue the work.

"I need to find a job soon, but I think I also will have time to maybe figure out where some of the bones in this valley are buried."

His eyes were wet. She noticed the lower lids hung deeper than she had thought of him. All of his friend's deaths were finally catching up with him. He leaned into her.

"I'd like to help. I think, if they could hear how you turned out, it would have meant a lot to them."

She leaned her head on the top of his. They sat in the heat of the afternoon. The dull brass of the little doors was like gold, hiding secrets. Thorny's eyes danced over the rows. Tiny boxes holding large secrets. Each of the empty ones—ready to hide more.

21 SIDE OF THE ROAD

The morning had a bite to it. The summer was losing the battle as the chill would begin to creep down the mountainsides. In the valleys with water, the Aspen trees would begin to lose their green for the last yellows and golds of fall. In Silver Canyon, it was the dust in the road. There was no more heat stored in the ground to last through the night. Thorny knew her days of walking barefoot would soon give way to the pinch of shoes.

As she stepped from the dry sand under the rabbitbrush, the harsh grass prickled at her feet. She clicked her cheek as the small knapsack slid from her shoulder. Reaching the old fallen cottonwood, she sunk onto the smooth gray where the bark had fallen away—probably before she was born.

She watched the river lazily move like a mirror made of mud. The color never changed. In the spring, the mirror was just below the overhanging green grass. At the end of summer, the moving mirror was feet below the longer translucent tan of the dead grass. The ripple guided her eyes to the darker shadow. She could tell by the calm in the middle of the torpid swirl that the catfish was large enough to swallow at least one if not two of the small cooters. The larger mallards were only small enough in the early spring.

Her hand absentmindedly reached into the sack. She withdrew a handful of carrots with their greens still on. The apples had a worm here or there, and more than a few bruises from where they hit the ground, but still good tasting.

The soft step crunched on the last of the desert sand and turned to dull pressure drumbeats. The mule was still wary, but the fruit and vegetables were too tempting. Thorny could feel the hot fetted breath from the delicate nose. She resisted the temptation to reach back and pet. "Hello, Heather. I figured you could use something sweet."

The nose smelled around the back of her neck. She smelled like the nice person who brought food the last couple of months... so she might be okay again this time. The nose and mouth moved to the offered foods along the log.

Thorny talked to the mule as it slowly ate its way along the log. Thorny's hand would stroke along the neck as the mouth took another piece of food. And then, it would rest in her lap. Another piece of food, a pet, and then rest with talk. It was a process. She smiled as she thought about being a little girl standing near Maybell. She had never seen a halter or reins on the mule, and yet it was never further than a few yards behind Ulysses. She asked him how he trained his mules. He looked stunned. He never trained them—they just liked being around him.

By the end of summer, she could feed Maybell or even pet the mule. But if Ulysses walked away down the trail, the beast was walking after the man with its tail wagging like a big dog.

At her high school graduation, she hadn't seen Maybell. She

looked about and finally found Ulysses sitting at the end of one row, but no mule. Thorny walked up to Ulysses standing with Pops and Monte. The three were beaming.

"Where is Maybell?"

The nose of the mule shoved her in the small of the back. She had been standing behind the grandstand for the sixty-eight students. The joke was on Thorny. The mule snorted, shook its head and leaned into the young woman for a rough scratching.

Thorny stood and reached out to rub gently between Heather's ears. "I'll bring you some more in a few days."

As she trod the dusty road, she wondered how much longer she could wander around barefoot. The dust was just dust— soft, but not warm. She looked down, and then to her left into the cemetery. The granite headstones and markers she knew were still cold. Even with the all-day sun, she knew the stone would never get warm. The grass under the spreading elm out in the east forty covered Pops. Ulysses was now the dust and ashes he wanted to be.

The Ford sedan eased to a stop next to Thorny. The driver's elbow was cocked out of the window. Thorny guessed the band on the man's fedora probably matched his belt, shoes, and socks. The kerchief in his jacket pocket was silk, but red. Thorny waited. She was sure there was nobody in Bishop who was stupid enough to wear a black sharkskin suit in the summer heat. Her feet reminded her the real summer was over. This was just the warm Indian summer to offset the chill turning the trees gold and orange.

The man considered the woman standing barefoot in the middle of the road. The green glasses and hair were only the finishing touch to a package who could pass for the pilot's twin.

"They told me if I wanted to talk to you, I would have to

come up here and find you. You're not easy to find." He changed the toothpick from his right cheek to his left. "Not so hard to find either."

She stood silent. Her hands hung in only the top of her pants pockets.

The man looked straight ahead down the road. The gentle grade was only a small hill, but enough to let the car roll and it would almost roll the entire way to the river. His sigh was deep and expressive, but not from boredom or frustration. Thorny could tell the man had played many waiting games with many results for many years. This was nothing new for him.

Thorny studied the silver brushstroke at the man's temples. The extension curled to behind his ear. The sunshine sliced along the line in his darkened glasses. Bifocals in darkened glasses would be expensive. She was sure there wasn't a ration coupon for such an item. This wasn't one of the low-level thugs sent to send a message. This was the message itself.

She turned toward town. "You're wasting your time."

The man looked over at the cemetery. "There are alternatives."

Thorny stopped. She looked toward town, and then toward the north. Nine miles away, the five-wire fence started her property. The walk would take her across the new airfield. The walk was one she had done many times before. There were many ways to get somewhere or to get something done.

She turned and stepped to the car door. Her face was inches from the man's as he turned. "When did your mother die?"

The man thought. It was not a question he expected. "She's still alive."

Thorny's eyes watched the man's face. "When was the last time she slapped you for not saying please or being polite?"

The man could feel his grip on the upper hand was rapidly slipping. He wasn't sure how to get a fresh grip with this woman. His voice lowered to a growl. "What's your point?"

"Go sit down with her. Tell her you drove eleven hours to insult a woman who was standing barefoot in the middle of a dirt road. Tell her it's high time she slapped you again and remind you about simple manners." Thorny turned and walked away. Town was only thirty minutes away.

The second street into town and one block from Main Street, the car eased alongside. Thorny almost smiled. It had taken the man a long time to think through his approach or figuring out what he would do now. She never thought he would have a gun in his hand.

The morning sun glinted off the polished nickel-plated barrel.

"Excuse me, miss, but have you had breakfast yet?"

"Do you always ask women for a date when you have a .38 hog-leg pointed at them?"

"It's more productive to ask nicely when you have a gun in your hand." His smile became toothy.

Thorny never broke her stride. "You have some salad green on one of your teeth."

The car stopped, and the man leaned up to look in the rearview mirror. When he looked back, she was gone. He whipped around looking for her. She was nowhere on the street. It was as if she had never been there.

"Damn it." His hands pounded on the large Bakelite steering wheel.

Looking around one more time, he pushed the car into gear and drove off. As he crossed Main Street, he noticed the dark barber sweeping the sidewalk. In the rearview mirror, he could see the man waving at him. He wasn't sure what it was about.

Sitting on the large back bumper, Thorny smiled and waved back at Monte. She figured the man would eat breakfast where he was comfortable. The food at the Dude Ranch was just as good as anywhere else. But if she needed him, it would be good to have Danny near.

AS THE CAR slowed to a stop in the curved driveway, Thorny stood and walked to the driver's door. Opening it, she stood with the post slightly obscuring the view of her. The man only noticed the white shirt and someone tending to his needs. He nodded to the young man in the white shirt, black vest and bow tie standing near a podium. The front door also opened as he approached.

Thorny smiled at the valet as she followed the man past Danny. Stopping once inside, she muttered out of the side of her mouth. Her eyes never leaving the man's backside. "Is this one of your father's or one of the city's?"

Danny blinked. He turned with his eyebrows arched. "He's not one of my father's associates, but I've also never seen him before. Who is he?"

Thorny moved forward. "Well, let's find out. I believe he asked me to join him for breakfast."

Danny caught up. "Where do you want to sit?"

"Somewhere we can have a talk, but I'd like you nearby." She glanced over. "Is that okay with you?"

Danny motioned to one of the waiters. The man removed his vest and clip-on tie. Danny leaned over and whispered as he motioned at the man standing to be seated, and Thorny. The young man nodded and cut off the host.

Danny watched the man's surprise. Thorny was right behind him. Recovering, they were seated at a discrete table, but near the water station for the waiters. Danny smiled as he walked over with the pitcher of water. He knew the type of man. They never paid attention to the people who served them.

The conversation chilled the air around them. Danny didn't see any weapons, but the man had his jacket on, and Danny knew Thorny's tongue all too well.

"You filed the documents for land trust transfers. Six of the nine have free-flowing springs on them. We want to know what you intend to do with those springs." The man's voice was even and low—but not threatening.

"Who is we?"

His manicured hand held the butter knife loosely, but in a fashion that Thorny only equated with the Europeans she knew. He spread the butter away from him with the flat of the knife. "*Who* is none of your concern."

She braced her hands on the table as she scooted the chair back and began to rise.

The knife clattered to the plate as the man reached out. Gripping her arm firmly, he forced it not to leave the table. His voice was through gritted teeth. "Sit. Down. These are desperate times, and we need to talk."

Thorny leaned into his face. "If... you value your hand... you will let go. I know where bodies are buried in this valley. I also know even better hiding places for new ones." She stood from his relaxed grip. "You can trot on back to your Mister Mulholland and tell him I'm not interested in anything he has to say, offer, or threaten. Good day."

The man's face fell open. "Mulholland? I'm not with the Department of Water and Power."

The man was unaware of Danny standing behind him. Thorny could see Danny's wrist disappearing under the black apron. She leaned on her right hand as her face neared the man. "Then let's start fresh. Who are you and who do you represent?"

"My name is Stan Manly, and… I'm not at liberty to say who I work for."

The barrel of the .38 Special nestled in the hollow of his neck. His eyes only blinked at the new knowledge and circumstance. "Even if you knew, it wouldn't matter. It only matters if I keep my job and we keep doing what is needed in this valley to protect people. You saw my white fedora. I'm one of the good guys."

"So you say." Thorny reached for the man's jacket and felt for his wallet.

He gently rose on his left leg. She felt around for a gun. Finding none, she fished in his back pocket. The wallet was thin. There were only a photo identification and a badge.

Her one eyelid drooped. "Not much here. How did you plan to pay for breakfast?"

The man stiffened. Danny prodded him in the neck. He sighed and rolled onto his right leg. The new wallet proved more productive. Thorny exchanged the FBI wallet with Danny and sat down with the other.

"It must be nice in San Pedro this time of the year. Fishing fleet coming in with a fresh catch and the sea breeze cooling off the day's heat." Thorny continued to take out each piece of information as Danny refilled the coffee. Turning the third cup over, he filled it and then sat across from Stan.

Thorny pulled the seventeen dollars out of the wallet and

placed them on the table. "You must not have planned to stay long." She found the business cards of Stan and two others. "Either a day run, or you were planning on bunking in with Elmer here." She tapped the business cards on the table.

"So why is the FBI interested in my land?"

The tip of the tongue smoothed along, wetting the lips as he thought. He studied Danny. Her having someone who would back her up changed things. He lifted the cup to his mouth. "It's not the land." He sipped and put the cup down. Patting his mouth, he leaned forward slightly.

Danny nodded. "It's the water. It's always about the water."

Stan Manly's look was cool but calculating. "You're almost there. Yes, it is about the water, but not just the water."

The farmer in Thorny sat her back in the chair. "It's what the water can raise."

The man's face changed as his eyes locked on hers. "How... what makes you say that?"

"You." She smirked at Danny and looked back. "My grandfather used to say, the only thing is facts, everything else is a story."

Leaning forward, she continued. "You have four guys up here. People think they belong to either the DWP..." She thumbed at Danny. "Or are his father's stooges." Her index finger bounced and then slid along the tablecloth. "One problem."

"Which is?"

Thorny smiled as she glanced at Danny. "Nobody pays attention to a flat-chested girl with curly hair running around barefoot in bib overalls. The girl can go anywhere, see anything, and get to recognize everyone else..."

Stan smiled now. "Because nobody sees the kid who's always there."

She nodded. "Stooges paid big money, bags of money, to his father. They had worked hard and risked a lot to get that money. Because they wanted to collect stacks of money? No. They wanted what the money could buy them. In Danny's father's case, it bought booze, girls, and a quiet place to hide out. It still does, but the booze is legal now, there are girls elsewhere, and well, your thugs don't want the quiet this ranch provides."

"And... your point is?"

Curious, Danny leaned in also.

"I asked around. The two guys in Bishop drive up every morning from Independence. There used to be a small farm down there on the east side near the river. The family had seven children, a housekeeper, and a cook. There used to be an outbuilding for about six workers, but it was burned to the ground. People believed the cholera was in the bunkhouse. Nobody wanted to believe the farmer might be to blame. They had gone down to Arizona to some religious gathering. They never came back." She watched the color drain from the man's face. "The house has stood empty since 1918. I don't think your men are in danger."

"So what do my men have to do—"

"They don't. And yet, they are the lie. They are here but never explaining themselves. They snoop around, but everyone thinks they are here from the city or thugs. They never set anyone straight. So they perpetuate the lie."

Stan put his cup down on the saucer with only a slight ring of the fine china. "And the water?"

"Round Valley."

"What about Round Valley?"

Thorny squinted with one eye halfway. "I'll bet it is the one place your men in suits never go."

"Why?" Danny echoed the other man.

"Because there are about twenty thousand acres of prime bottom land there. The problem is there's not enough water for any crops taller than the alfalfa, fescue, and bunch grass they feed the cattle and sheep on., but if you had a constant source of about two-acre feet a year, you could even grow corn."

Stan sighed. The woman figured it all out, except the final what and why. "The season is too short, and the ground stays too mushy for corn. You would never get it to dry, and the combine would mire down halfway through a row."

Thorny turned square to the table and concentrated on her coffee. Danny could see her eyes twitching back and forth. He had watched them when she was studying in high school. When she took a test, the habit returned. She was looking for the answers. It was as if she were rereading the textbooks.

"Thorny…?"

She stuck her hand out. "Shhh…"

The two men waited. Quietly, Danny poured them more coffee.

"Hemp." She sat up.

Stan was going to wait her out. He was feeling like the slapped little kid in school. Everything he thought of as a secure secret, she figured out in minutes.

Danny was lost. "Why hemp? Isn't it just rope? I mean, they can use other stuff these—"

Thorny turned on him. "No. No, they can't." She spun around and pulled her green glasses up to the top of her head. She spoke as if she were reading the writing on the man's face. "They don't need rope. They get plenty of hemp rope from the south and Cuba. The Cuba hemp grows twice as tall as our hemp here in the United States. Other than cigars, rum, and sugar, hemp rope is one of their major exports."

Stan chuckled as he sat back. "What makes you such an expert on Cuba hemp?"

"My best lasso rope is now slick with age, but my Grandfather brought it back from Cuba, which makes it some forty years old. I would still trust it for a grueling day of roping and branding. I had a Louisiana rope Pops bought me for winning the Gymkhana the summer I was going into the eighth grade. Three summers later, I was in the team roping finals. I was out of the shoot before the calf had cleared the gate and really started to run. I shot the back legs twenty feet from the gate. When my horse pulled back, the rope snapped. Short hemp."

"What was your grandfather doing in Cuba?"

"He was helping a friend."

Danny snorted. "His friend was named Teddy Roosevelt."

The man rocked back his head in realization. "So you know the advantages of long strand hemp. What do you know about short-short or winter hemp?"

She furled her lips and shook her head. "Never heard of it."

"Don't feel bad. Neither had I. In fact, we're not sure if it will work. The only test case was in Minnesota. By roughing the strands in steam, the final wad has the properties of cotton wadding."

Danny held up his finger. His eyes closed, and finally, his face scrunched down hard. "Cannons." His eyes opened. "The packing between the shell and the powder..." He stopped as the other man's smile turned into a smirk.

"You're close. What you are describing is back when they were loading cannons from the muzzle, but a packing now is incorporated in the front of the charge package. As the charge explodes, the packing compresses but expands to seal the charge and push the shell. The hemp fiber compresses less and seals better. But we don't have any growing commercially for the war effort."

Thorny thought about the small spring above Round Valley. The flow was possibly constant, but it didn't produce the water the man was talking about. "I don't think the spring over Mesa Run would produce enough water for what you're talking about doing. I don't think it produces even a tenth of what Rock Creek brings to the Valley, and there is little left of it after watering in the summer."

Stan pointed at his wallet. "May I...?"

She pushed the wallet and contents over to the man.

Fishing through the small pieces of notepaper, he found what he wanted. "There is a hydrography engineer up here who said there is a hidden spring. To tap it, we would have to drill a twenty-four-inch horizontal well about a half mile. DWP would hate the results, but it would give us the feed. We would only need to run the pipeline about six miles to where we needed it."

A snort softly bounced in Thorny's chest. "Who is the hydrographer?"

"A guy by the name of Ulysses."

Danny and Thorny didn't flinch. "But you didn't find him. You only knew when I filed the paperwork the land was transferred.

"Do you know where he is?"

The two nodded. "Ashes."

The man only blinked three times. Thorny was impressed. It was a long leap to go from who you're looking for to cremation.

Thorny moved into the void. "Let me ask you this. We have a police chief who—"

The man's two hands snapped up into the air. "Not ours." He chewed on his lower lip, weighing what to say. He looked at Danny who nodded only slightly.

Thorny leaned back. "If I help you, then he might become a problem."

The agent leaned in. "What kind of problem?"

Thorny and Danny chorused. "LA Water."

22 WATER AND WAR

The man wasn't deaf—yet. But even standing eighty-feet away from the diesel-drilling rig, the man still yelled out of habit.

"We've pushed fourteen-hundred and eighty feet of pipe into the mountain. We're getting a lot of water, but not the kind of flow the hydrologist said there would be, though he did say it would take more like twenty-six hundred or so."

"How much are you getting now?"

"Getting what?" His pitch was climbing past the uncomfortable point.

"Water. How much?" Thorny was losing interest fast.

The man pointed at a small creek running off down the hill. "Joe is our expert. Joe thinks we are getting the oversheet, but it's close to fifty gallons a minute. Fifty isn't bad for a home with a six-inch well, but we are boring a full twenty-four."

Thorny's voice was getting as tired as her ears. "Okay. Keep at it. I'll check in with you next week."

The well driller circled his thumb and finger. Turning, he walked back into the noise.

Thorny stared for a minute and then walked downhill. The work was noisy, but as far as she could tell, nobody in town knew the crew was up here. She had brought the crew in from Nevada under cover of darkness. They were camping on-site, and any supplies came in at night. The same small company who delivered the diesel to the farm also delivered the fuel for the project. And Charlie and his grandfather weren't going to talk.

From the look of their insulated clothes and sturdy tents with woodstoves in them, she could tell they were used to working outside all winter. Drilling the large-bore well through solid granite was proving to be a long, slow process. The crew chief hadn't said anything about the men going home to Nevada for Thanksgiving. This gave Thorny pause to think about what kind of meal she could deliver up to the crew of six.

Her boots crunched on the frost-welded gravel as she stepped around the large boulder. She thought about finding an old chair to bring up and leave sometime. The view cast out north across the entire Round Valley. The matching view, but looking south, was a point in a tiny town named Paradise. Nineteen souls enjoyed the solitude of the village, but it was a long grueling drive for supplies in Bishop.

Thorny leaned against the boulder and thought about what the trip must have been like in 1863 when Jonathan Peele and his brother Timothy built their matching log cabins along the small river where they were successfully panning gold.

Without the stream, the gold would have stayed in the mountain. Without water to drink, cook, and bath in, there would be no camping for the miners. Without the two miners, there would be no Paradise. Everything depended on the water.

Round Valley was the living proof of the provision of water.

Enough water always provided grass for cattle and sheep. Crops, on the other hand, demanded more. A few farmers had enough to raise a couple of cuttings of alfalfa, but even then, it wasn't the best feed. With the extra water, the valley could turn into the much-needed crop producer the war effort needed. The big city people would just have to drink one less glass of day or cut back on their bathing. Thorny knew from experience that telling them to stop watering their lush lawns was futile. Water for grass was their god given right—Reverend Mulholland had told them so. And so, they would continue to fill the pews and aisles of the First Church of Sucking All the Water from the Owens Valley.

A small movement in the sky caught Thorny's eye. She circled her right hand into a tube and watched the bird. She was certain it was one of the few eagles left nesting around the base of Mt. Tom. The valley caused by the two mountain ranges were as diverse as the lush Sierra Nevada Mountains with its abundance of water and the White Mountains with less than a few inches of precipitation. Many storms dumped feet of snow in the Sierras, an inch on Bishop, and it was as if the clouds never reached the Whites. Her favorite memories of snow were when both mountains and the valley between were awash in the white of an overnight dusting of purity.

Thinking of the opposite of purity, she looked down the last of the incline to the Ford parked on the alluvial fan of Lower Buttermilk where it washed out into the bottom of Round Valley. A car parked in the desert was a curiosity. But when it was parked in the middle of wide-open space, it was only a passing curiosity. The sand and gravel crunched under her boots. She thought about things nobody noticed when they were out in the open.

A few days before, she had received a large thick envelope. She had to sign for it at the post office. The letter from her old boss was almost as interesting as the chatty personal letter from his daughter. Both wished she would return to working at the District Attorney's office, but it was the complete photocopy of both the sealed juvenile record and the adult criminal record of one Jefferson Langstone Becicka. There was even a thin note about a break-in at a winter residence of one William Mulholland in Yuma, Arizona. They caught the burglar by private security, but there were no records after that. Three weeks later, a man fitting the same description landed a position with the Bishop Police Department. He filled the position left empty by an officer who suddenly died in his sleep. A powerful convenience.

LOOKING DOWN to where she placed her feet, she missed the spark of white light across the narrows of the valley. The sun reflected off the glass of a large telescope on the top of Chalk Bluffs. The elevations were the same, and it provided a line of sight straight into the pass leading into Upper Buttermilk canyon.

The slender man under the sand-colored campaign hat placed the telescope on the pillow of his jacket. Sitting back on his campstool, he took up the small black journal. He noted the time and who he had seen coming out of Buttermilk Basin.

23 WAR FOR WATER

"You sure you want to do this, Chief?"

The old man had taken to using a cane for the last few months. The fall from his horse a few years before had never healed solid. His face was a grim stone of determination. He stepped toward Thorny and the fuel truck. The cab would be a tight fit with Charlie, Thorny, and now the chief.

The fall of light, fluffy flakes highlighted his hair. His lower eyelids hung wetly as he looked her in the eye. "Did you bring the hand like I asked?"

She slid the skeleton hand of gold out of her pocket. Even in the winter overcast, it now shimmered.

"I need to show you what you need to know about the hand." He started to turn to the truck but then turned back. "But also, about the writing."

"Why can't you just tell me?"

His hand froze on the handle of the door. His one foot rested on the step. "Can you tell me what a peach tastes like?" The man pulled and climbed into the cab. He would ride in the middle.

"Sure. Its texture is like a summer melon, but sweeter like—"

Charlie snorted from behind her. "Don't even try, Thorny. The man has never eaten any fruit other than a tomato."

She turned with a scowl of horror. "But you raise apples, peaches, apricots, grapes, and melons..." Her voice drifted off as she watched his face.

The large man slowly wagged his head. "It's against his religion. We think he ate a bad apple when he was little. He was seriously sick for a week. During his illness, he was delirious and had dreams. In his dreams, his spirit guide came to him and told him to never eat fruit. He has never even picked it since. He will eat squash and onions while he stands in the garden, but no fruit. He can even smell it when we cook or bake with it. He won't come into the house until it has aired and the evil spirits have left."

Thorny mused as she climbed into the cab. "How do you get through the summer without melon?"

The old man smiled simply and shrugged. "The summer is hot and long... but moonshine starts in October."

The three laughed most of the way up to the Buttermilk turnoff. The dirt road was a soft gray in the darker desert with the quarter moon. The blackout shields on the truck did help, but at the slow speed, they didn't hinder, either. The light dusting of snow had only stayed at the higher levels where there was shade from the trees. Even without their leaves, the shadows had been enough.

As they rounded a bend, a large patch of white bisected by car tracks appeared.

"Stop." Thorny leaned forward as the slow truck shuddered to a stop. "Hold up here a minute."

She got out and walked carefully into the light from the

headlights. "Chief?" She could hear both men getting out. "What do you make of these tracks?"

The two Indians bracketed Thorny. She looked at the oldest and best tracker in the tribe. This man had once tracked a man for nine days. The escaped prisoner had beat a man in a bar fight. Nobody knew the two men and neither had any identification. The fight started over a woman who wasn't even in the bar. One man went to the jail while the other to the hospital.

When they fingerprinted the prisoner, he smashed the deputy's face on the desk and then drew his pistol. Forcing the other officer onto the ground, he handcuffed him to a pipe running along the wall. Two days later, someone thought about getting the chief. He tracked the man for over a hundred miles. Finally arriving at the man's house in Fish Lake Valley, he told him he had money in Bishop, but he needed a ride. The next morning, the man hitched up his wagon and carried the chief back to Bishop—and to his arrest for manslaughter. The man he had beaten had died. The twenty-year-old chief drove the wagon back to Fish Lake Valley to fetch the man's wife. It turned out at the trial that the woman was the victim's widow. She had left her husband and moved in with the man on trial… the dead man's brother.

Thorny cleared her throat and shoved her hands harder in the pockets of her coat.

The man looked up and then leaned forward on his cane. He looked at his grandson. "My tracks say the doe is pregnant but came up this way about five hours ago. What do your tracks say, Frog?"

Thorny glowered at the old man who was now smiling. Turning, she hoped for a better answer.

Charlie crouched in the yellow glow from the truck's dim

headlights. "It was a Chevy. Probably a Deluxe. Came up in the afternoon before sunset. The edges have a little melt to them." He pointed along the edges. "That spray is them going up in the almost slush, but it was well after dark when they came back down. They were already crunching on the frozen skin." He pointed at a few places in the tracks. "The track is broken by the hard skin of the snow. The afternoon softened the surface, and then, when the sun went down, it hardened again. The car came up and did something for a couple of hours, and then came back down."

He stood. Shoving his hands in his thick wool coat, his elbows tight to his side. The dark green plaid of the Filson coat looked black in the night. His eyes were crescents of light as he looked east down the road toward Bishop.

"I don't have a good feeling about this."

Forty-minutes later, they arrived at what had once been the well-digging camp. The drilling rig was still a smoldering heap of charred black. The tents and two trucks were smoking heaps of ash. The three poked around carefully—touching nothing.

In the dim moonlight, they counted only three bodies.

The chief made a small torch from a stick, rags, and some diesel fuel. He squatted close to the one body. Holding the hand-sized flame near the head, he looked at the back of the head—it looked like a melon dropped off a truck and then kicked for a few hours. Rolling the man over, he pointed to a finger-sized hole in the forehead. "Carbine. My guess is .30 caliber. Soft lead. Bullet went in, made mush of everything in the skin of the head, but never came out. Not a great shot, but also not from far away." He nodded out toward some large rocks. "Probably find some tracks over that-a-way."

Charlie stood ramrod straight as if he didn't want to see

what was on the ground anymore. "How many were here?" His head ground around. Thorny didn't have to see his eyes to know he was deeply upset.

"There were six the other day. William and his crew of five. None of these is William or the guy named Casey. They were more your size." She pointed to the squashed melon. "There was only one negro, but I never knew his name."

The chief pulled hard on his cane, rising slow and shaky. "If this isn't all of them, where are the others?"

Charlie nudged his chin toward the sliver of moon. "We'll lose the light in an hour. Dawn isn't until seven. What do you want to do?" It was a general question, but he was looking at the chief.

Sighing, the chief looked at the bodies. Blinking slowly, he looked at Charlie. "Like it or not, I need to show Thorny the hole. It's hers now, and she has the right to know about it."

The tall Indian smeared his face as he grimaced. He looked at Thorny as he thought before speaking. "Yeah, I guess. We know her bottom is pink, but she is like family."

Thorny didn't know what was going on, so she slugged Charlie in the arm anyway. The chief stuttered a short laugh, but Charlie just looked at her. It was his way of telling her the matter was serious. She knew from experience, even if she had used all her strength, she could never hurt him. She had already kicked him in the crotch when they were twelve.

She turned. "Lead on, McDuff."

The climb above the soaking pool turned treacherous. The chief hung on to Charlie's long wool coat, his cane hanging hooked on his elbow. The large man's steps shortened and were slower and deliberate. The way was all rocks. There was nothing suggesting a trail. In the last of the moonlight, all the rocks were the same color. Only the cracks between were darker or black. The trail wound around large boulders.

The three rounded a boulder the size of the fuel truck. Charlie stopped. He motioned to Thorny to stand in front of him as the last of the moonlight snuffed out. She turned. Between a few trees and two large formations of the foothills, she could see the few twinkling lights of Bishop.

The words were more of a rumble from his deep chest than actual sound from his lips. "Before the war, people had more lights on. But it still looks to me like a Christmas tree."

Taking her shoulders, he moved her until she stood leaning against the boulder. "Don't move."

She could hear the chief and Charlie moving in the dark, but she couldn't tell what they were doing. The sounds were soft scratching. Occasionally, there was a soft snap of a twig.

A soft glow lit the stack of smaller boulders, two arm-lengths to her left. It was a patina of gold in a world of gray and black.

"You can come in now, little one."

The large stones created an enlargement of a shallow cave. The chief stood at the back wall of the cave. The small campfire danced—no larger than a hand with spread fingers.

The old man motioned toward the small black hole in the rock near his knee.

Charlie stopped her and started removing her coat. "Don't worry. You will be plenty warm." She noted his left hand unbuttoning his coat. The chief was doing the same. "Your arms need to be bare. It is tradition your top also." He studied her face as she lifted her sweater. There was nothing under the thick wool. His eyes closed, remembering her lack of feeling any pain. The prickly rough wool would not be scratchy to her.

Taking the sweater, he ignored her breasts. "Sorry, but we forgot to bring a breechclout." As she pushed her thumbs into the sides of her pants, he shook his head. It would not be necessary.

"Kneel over here." The chief pointed at the hole in the rock face. A loaf of bread might fit, but not a head. The air around the hole wavered.

"Holding the golden hand, put your arm into the wall as far as you can."

Removing the skeleton from her pocket, she leaned over and carefully extended her arm. When her knuckles touched another wall, she was very aware of the heat below. "There is a wall."

The chief crossed his legs in a scissor until he was sitting cross-legged in front of her. His face was stone but softened with caring. "Which way is your hand facing?"

She adjusted her left knee. "Down."

The chief could see the wall was only up past her elbow. "If you feel around with your knuckle, there is another slot. Your hand must be facing down to reach it."

She nodded. "Found it."

"Pull your arm out and hand me the hand."

She placed the skeleton in his two open hands. He didn't move. His eyes slid shut. "Now, reach through both holes. Past the other hole, you will feel it is like a shelf with water. In the water are small stones. Choose one and pull it out."

She looked at the clear crystal she had pulled out. Holding it up to the small fire, she could see it had been tumbled and beaten smooth, but it was still clear enough to see through. She glanced at Charlie sitting by the small fire—focused on feeding it with twigs and pine needles. She looked back at the chief. His eyes were still closed.

"What is it?" His eyes remained closed.

"It's quartz. An old crystal weathered smooth."

His head rocked. "The crystal is clarity of vision. You see truth where others see obscurity. Your vision comes from the past. Place it in your mouth on your tongue. Take the hand and hold it over where you took the stone from the water."

Her face furrowed. "It is hotter now."

The old man rocked softly, or it was only the disturbance of the balmy air. "Open your hand."

She could feel the small splash of the water only an inch or so below her hand as the skeleton hand dropped. The water was hot also.

"Now, reach where you dropped the hand, choose another stone and pull it out."

Her fingers reached down. She expected to feel the skeleton, but there was only a single stone the size of her thumb. She felt around. It was the only stone on the shelf. She pulled it out.

"Put it in your mouth without looking at it."

She could taste the difference. The two were as different as man and woman.

In the firelight, she could see the redness of her right arm. She had known it was hot in the hole, but not how hot. Charlie handed her the sweater. She looked at the chief with his closed eyes—sitting, unmoving.

"He is no longer here. His body stopped on this journey when you stuck your arm in the hole the first time. When you pulled it out and placed the skeleton in his open hands, I knew you could still hear him."

She started to open her mouth to speak. His thumb bridged

her lips. "Do not open your mouth. I am not to see the stones unless we are married. Only you can know what the mountain has given you. You can take them out, but just don't show me."

She turned and palmed the two stones. She faced the dying fire. The light danced across the mineral as pure as the skeleton. The two were distinctive. She closed her hand and looked over at the body of the chief. Her right hand found her pants pocket, and she left the two at the bottom.

Her mind was numb. She had questions but no ideas of words to ask them. She felt the heat of sunshine and her grand-father's words about facts and truth. She turned into Charlie's chest. She wanted to cry, but it was something she had never done. Even as a baby, Pops told her she would fuss, but never cry. She didn't know how.

She leaned against her friend. "What do we do now?"

"We wait for the sunrise."

A short climb away, Charlie showed her an opening in the rocks. The crack was only the width of a man's shoulders. She could smell the taint in the air of the sulfur and arsenic. Charlie poured the chief's body into the hole. "Somewhere down there is much heat. Enough heat to boil the water you reached into and to heat the air to blister your arm. We are one with the mountain, and my grandfather has gone home."

The deep rumble was more than the usual little tremors the valley population was used to feeling every day. There was a jolt and a feeling of the mountain surging. The rifle crack was louder and deeper than any rifle Thorny had heard.

She looked to her friend. Charlie jerked his head. "I don't know. It was down near the drill camp, maybe. I don't know what it was, but it wasn't an earthquake."

Most of the burned-out drilling camp was now washed away

by the geyser. They could see where the first blast of water tore
out the drill camp and the ground around it. Long, broken, and
bent lengths of heavy drill pipe lay scattered over acres of the
upper desert hillside. The fresh unobstructed geyser shot from
the mountainside in an arch as thick as a man and almost half
the distance of a football field. Where it hit was now a gouged
outstretched pond. The water was already cutting a new river,
down the mountainside, toward Round Valley.

Charlie stood with his hands jammed deep in his pockets.
His eyes danced about the scene. One of the trucks had been
pushed around, but the other caught the brunt of the force and
was thrown down the slope. "I'm not a detective, but I think this
crime scene has been tampered with." His voice was light but
shaky.

Thorny was also shaken. The power and devastation, on top
of the brutal murders, took on a surreal bent that had her
wanting to wake up from the nightmare. She looked back at the
base of the geyser.

"What do you think happened? They hadn't struck this
water before... but it suddenly..." She didn't know how to
complete the question or thought.

The tall man stood stiff as he looked up the mountain where
they had spent the night. "Every bit of my college education and
a man of the twentieth century tells me to throw up my hands
and just accept it as one of nature's quirky happenings. Maybe
they drilled just far enough to trigger a small earthquake frac-
turing the last bit needed. Maybe a crack shifted, and the river
changed course. And maybe a butterfly in Africa fluttered its
wings, and the result is this." His flat hand waved at the presentation of the geyser.

"But the Indian in you says...?"

"Two things happened tonight. The ownership of the golden hand transferred to you. In that, the mountain accepted you as... well, let's just say it accepted you."

"But I left the hand in the hole."

His one eyebrow rose. "Did you." It was more of a statement than a question.

Thorny's right hand felt her pants where the pocket was. The one lump was familiar and accompanied the other two smaller ones. Stumbling past what she knew, and what she thought she knew, Thorny looked out across the valley. "What else happened up there?"

He cleared the sticky wet lump in his throat. "The most powerful medicine man and chief the Paiute Nation has ever known has continued his journey but is now back in the mountain. He still has much to do and set right."

"What about the new chief?"

The lower lip was almost white from his bite. His eyes more fluttered than blinked. "He too has much work to do. And like the mountain, the old chief, and the one who asked the mountain for the water to change direction... The new chief also understands how important this water is."

Thorny's stomach churned. There was too much to take in, or even address. She wanted her feet to be on the solid ground of things she knew and understood. "We need to bring Pete up here. But I think we'll have some explaining to do." Thorny shaded her eyes with her hand. She had left her dark glasses in town. The sunlight wasn't summer, but it was still bright.

Charlie squinted across the valley. "We need to find the other drillers too."

They started back down toward the truck. Thorny's right

hand fumbled in her pocket with the two stones and the other familiar shape. "I hope they went home to Nevada."

The new chief raised his chin so his full face took in the sun. "We can drive over after we bring Deputy Pitchess up here."

Thorny leaned against his shoulder and curled her arm around his. "I think I'd like that."

Their footsteps were slow and deliberate, each with their own thoughts about the night's events and what changes were coming to the reservation. Both were thinking about all the explaining they would now have to do.

Thorny liked the smell of his thick coat. Like memories, the wool had collected smells of his life. Smoke and wood dominated, but the smell of his dogs and other animals were there too. She rolled her face so her nose was buried in the wool.

"The writing on the skeleton...?"

The man smiled softly on the side away from her. "Does it matter?"

"I think it does. I think it might help explain what happened last night... and this morning."

There was a rumble deep inside the mountain of a man. Thorny wasn't sure if he was grumbling about telling her or if he was also hungry. "There is no real translation for it... but it has two meanings. If you read the petroglyphs with the palm down, it means you live in the mountain, or you are one with the mountain. If you read them with the palm up, it means the mountain lives in you or the mountain is you."

She looked up at him. "It reads both ways?"

He bobbed his head gently. "It is one of the most powerful spirit bonds. You will need no other spirit guide. I felt you reach in the second time. The mountain gave you two stones. This is all you will ever need."

"I need breakfast."

"We have some leftover goat meat to go with the eggs."

"Can I nap while you cook?"

"No. But we can both nap until Nudge wakes us up."

Thorny hung onto his arm and leaned out. Her face was wary. "Who is Nudge?"

The man smiled, proud of the secret he had kept from one of his best friends. "My wife."

"When did you get married?"

He pushed his lip out. "Been a few years now."

24 THE HILLS ARE ALIVE

Thorny watched Pete look around. His mouth hung slightly unhinged. Over the course of the morning, the pool where the water landed had grown. The burned truck frame had rolled into the pool and sunk out of sight. The water was so agitated by the enormous spew that they couldn't see if the frame was just down there or dredged and buried.

Thorny pulled back and slugged Charlie in the arm—again. The man chuckled and turned to face her. He didn't have to ask.

Thorny spit on the ground. "Married?"

"Might as well be. She's slept in my bed since the first night."

"Not last night. She snuffled her way under my blankets and said you were snoring too loud."

"Huskies speak with forked tongue." He held his wrist to his chin and wiggled his two fingers at her.

Thorny started toward Pete who was distractedly waving a hand. "You're still a horse's ass." She called forward. "What do you have, Pete?" But then she called back over her shoulder, "That dog needs a bath. She smells like she's been rolling in the manure pile."

Pete was looking at the gushing hole in the mountain, and then back at the pond. "Go through this slowly, because I don't see what you're talking about." He pointed at the geyser. "So this isn't natural, but it was drilled?"

"It's a twenty-four-inch horizontal bore. It's a commercial size, the same as the ones for Bishop water. They were drilling about a third or half a mile in to hit an underground river."

"Who hired them?"

"I did."

He winced. Her involvement lent a new complication. "Why... and whose land is this?"

Thorny drew her upper lip in and bit. Her deep intake of breath hadn't gone unnoticed. "It's my land, and I needed the water."

He held her look for an extra second. "How many acres do you own?"

She frowned as she swung around. "This parcel? I think it's about a hectare."

He smirked. He knew she was hoping to buffalo her way through and just maybe he didn't know measurements of land. He looked at the stream and pond. "That's a lot of water for just over two acres. One of which is now under water."

She rubbed the back of her head like she had seen Pop do many times. "Yeah... I might have overestimated my needs."

Pete started to say something but looked over at Charlie who was holding up his hand. The man was looking down the hill where they couldn't see the road. "What do you hear, Charlie?"

"Car coming."

The three stood shoulder to shoulder as the Chevy sedan nosed up around the last turn. Seeing the three, the car stopped.

Pete leaned into Thorny's side. "Think it's one of Danny's friends?"

Her mouth twitched at a smile, but she wasn't sure. Her hand dug deeper into her pants pockets. Her right hand covered the skeleton, as two fingers touched the stones deeper in the pocket.

They heard the driver pull the parking brake and then turn off the car. The door was well maintained and made no noise as it opened. They could see the man adjust his scarf and hat before he stepped out into the cold. He wasn't a local and probably from a warm climate.

The man stood and quietly closed the door. "Did I just land in the last scene of the OK Corral?"

Thorny slumped. "Damn it, Stan. You almost got yourself shot," she whispered out of her almost closed mouth. "He's with me, and he's FBI."

"I didn't hear from you this last wee—" His face fell open. "Holy mother in a basket, what is that?"

Charlie turned and calmly rubbed his finger under his right eye. "My guess is this is the water you asked for."

Pete, not knowing where they stood, but ready to jump in, looked around the man. "I hope you brought a large enough jug?"

The man turned with a gaping mouth. "When?" Leaning back, he looked at the deputy for the first time. "Who the hell are you?"

Thorny took over. "This is Pete, and it was this morning about sun-up. What you see is what you asked for. Twenty-four-inch well, and I'm guessing it's flowing at two-acre-feet an hour. Give it a week, and it will put all of Round Valley under at least two inches of water."

"But… It's too much."

"You're right. What you need to do now is get a crew up here in the next couple of days to cap this. Otherwise, LA is going to send someone up here to find out where their water went. After you cap it, they can run the pipe, bury it, and then connect it. Then you can control what you need and how much water you take out of my mountain and deny Los Angeles theirs."

Charlie harrumphed. "Your mountain?"

Thorny leaned against him. "Don't make me hit you in front of these men."

Special Agent Manly glanced around. "You said you hit the water this morning…?"

Thorny shrugged. "Shortly after sunrise."

"What happened to the drilling crew?"

Pete cleared his throat. Thorny put her hand on his shoulder. "Special Agent Stan Manly, I'd like you to meet Deputy Sheriff Pete Pitchess. Inyo County, meet Mr. FBI, specially attached to the war effort."

Pete half frowned as he extended his hand. "So, you're down in Manzanar at the Japanese internment camp."

The man flushed. "Um, no. I'm, as she said, with the war effort."

Thorny snorted at Pete's confusion. "He wants to learn how to be a farmer."

Stan continued to hold Pete's stare. "The drillers?"

Pete shifted gears. "Right. Well, we were just attempting to figure out what happened up here." Stan turned on Thorny. "I thought you were here when they hit the water?"

"Charlie and I were… um… further up the mountain when it blew, but the crew was killed sometime the night before."

"Killed?" The man was frowning at what he thought was a bad joke.

Thorny put up both palms. "Settle down. We're still trying to figure it all out ourselves."

"But where are the bodies?"

Charlie growled as he pointed at the growing pond. "Last night when we came up here, the camp was still smoldering, and we found three bodies. They had been shot by what we guessed was a 30-30 or similar. The drill rig was still up against the mountain, and there were two burned-out trucks. There was only a small trickle flowing out of the mountain."

Stan glanced over at the scene now. "So, where—"

Thorny cut him off. "We had important business up the mountain. So, we left the bodies and equipment where it was. This morning, we heard and felt what we thought was a cannon or earthquake shock. When we got down here, this is what we found. We looked around, but the original blast and half a mile of heavy pipe wiped away what was left of the campsite." She waved her hand toward the pond. "Maybe there's something in there, or maybe it's down the hill. We don't know, and it wasn't important. But the priorities are clear. You need to cap this off while we figure out who killed our men."

"Where do you start?"

"In Nevada."

"Why there?"

"We only found three bodies last night. There should have been six in the crew." She shrugged. "We're hoping some of them went home for Christmas."

Manly glanced at Pete. "You going to Nevada also?"

"Nope. I'm working the scene."

The federal officer weighed the circumstances. "Care for some help?"

Pete stuck his hand out at the man's voluntary subjugation. "Every bit you can give me. It's Christmas."

THE TRUCK CREPT down the steeper part leading out of upper Buttermilk. Charlie kept it in second gear so he didn't have to ride the brakes. He glanced over at Thorny. Her gloved hands were in her armpits. Her eyes were staring stonily out the windshield. He tried to think if he had ever heard her complain about the heat or cold. Bishop swung to both extremes, but she had never complained.

"Do you feel the cold?"

She frowned and looked over at the gearshift knob. She blinked a couple of times and then looked up. "You mean like, how I don't feel pain?"

"Yeah... I was just wondering. I don't think I've ever heard you complain about being too hot or freezing. So, I was just wondering..."

"Can we take the Chevy over to Nevada?"

He looked over and chuckled. "It would be a lot faster."

"Warmer too."

As they hit the flats, Charlie eased the gears up into third. "You're brooding."

"Thinking about the chief."

The man grunted. At the highway, he turned downhill. Bishop was four miles away, but visible from end to end with two miles from city limit sign to the other.

"Was he really gone when I stuck my arm in the mountain?"

Charlie thought about his grandfather. Sometimes it was hard to explain things the man did or events surrounding the tribe's medicine man. Charlie knew there were things he would never understand or know. He had inherited his title as chief, but medicine man was not something bestowed on you—it was born within you.

"Do you remember me getting up to go get more fuel for the fire?"

"No. You did?"

He nodded gently. "Do you remember sitting after you pulled your arm out the second time and me putting the bear grease on your burned arm and hand?"

She pulled her glove off and looked at her hand. It was redder than usual, but nothing more. Pushing her sleeve up, she stared at the large blister above her wrist. The red around the dollar-sized bubble was angry looking. Not for the first time was she glad she didn't feel pain.

"I started to take the pebbles out of my mouth, but you told me not to show you. You said only if we were married could you see my stones. You held your thumb over my lips."

Charlie shifted into the top gear as they rolled through the sweeping right-hand turn. He glanced over. "I used my thumb to rub bear grease on your lips where you had kissed the hot mountain. I never said a word until we woke up with the dawn. It is the way when someone is on a vision quest with the mountain. Those who are there to attend them never speak. I think even if I had wanted to say something, the mountain kept me silent."

"But you—"

His head, grinding back and forth, cut her off.

As they reached his place, Charlie parked the truck alongside the car. Thorny was still thinking. She looked over.

"Do you want to see the stones?"

"Are you asking me to marry you?"

She sat back and watched the two horses grazing in the small pasture. Even in winter, there were some of the heartiest grasses to crop. "So, it's true."

Charlie pushed open the complaining rusty door. "A-yup."

25 NEVADA

Of the twenty-seven buildings in Dyer, only nineteen were for human habitation. Lynn's Standard Oil was not one of them, but it had the only public phone Thorny knew of.

Charlie and Thorny could see the phone. It hadn't been cleaned or polished since it was screwed to the wall. The grease-thumbed and dirt-smeared map used to write notes on almost covered the ugly square box with a mouthpiece held onto it with what looked to be baling wire. The earpiece looked like it had been rewired a few times in its lifetime. The wire hung inert in a loop to the floor and back.

Thorny stepped back from the window and, once again, looked both ways down the highway. Her tongue worked her lower lip as her upper lip worked against her teeth. Charlie watched as her arms ricocheted from hugging her body to probing her pockets. He had never seen her kick dirt before, but he could tell it might be next.

"The widow done said there be two agitated folks at the station."

The two whipped around at the gravelly whine of a voice. The man stood in knee-high waders, work pants, and a thick green wool vest. His bare arms hung from his thumbs in behind his buckle. The red plaid hunting cap sat low on his head so the earflaps stood straight out. The stubble was more than a week old. Thorny moved to be upwind. This wasn't a Saturday night bather—this was more seasonal. When he was seasoned enough, someone wrestled him into a washtub.

"There taint no electric power at this time of day, so I can't pump you no gasoline."

Charlie stepped back as he was afraid the next punctuation would come with a large load of the man's chewing tobacco.

Resisting the urge to throw up, Thorny pushed on. "I need to borrow your phone to make a call, please."

"Cain't, liken I said, no power."

Thorny rubbed her face in frustration. "Do you know where William Widdon lives?"

"Sure. Everybody knows where Willie lives. His grandfather was the third farmer in the valley. They ain't never moved." The man's face stopped. No more explanation. No chew juice hit the ground.

Thorny muttered. "Like pulling teeth..." She thought of a more direct way to ask. "Could you please tell us where he lives?"

The man waved his hand at the highway. "Sure 'nuff. You done been staring at it."

Thorny pointed across the street at a falling down clapboard house. "The greenhouse..."

The man rolled his eyes, and his head followed. "Course not. That there is the dimwit's house. Willie lives in the soddy up against the hill."

Thorny squinted at the four buildings scattered in her view. Nothing was making sense about what the man was talking about, but she at least had a direction. "Thanks for your help."

She moved toward the car as she poked Charlie in the arm. "Of course, it's the soddy..." The dark green of her glasses hid her eyes rolling to the heaven and back.

Charlie laughed as he nosed the car left off the highway. "You have no idea what the man was talking about, do you?"

She tried to glower at him but started laughing. "Do you?"

The man turned another left and pointed at a low-lying shack. What looked like a hillside eating a house was a house dug into the hillside. "Sure. It's the house made of sod cut from the prairie. In this heat, I'd want to live in the basement too."

As they rolled to a stop, Thorny thought about the cool air from the crawl spaces of houses. In her mind, she could feel the cool on her small feet as they hovered over the cracks in Pop's kitchen.

To the right of the small house was a wall in the hill. The faded red door with white trim opened next to the small window trimmed in the same barn colors. Paul Bunyan's little brother filled the doorway. His morning hair brushed the top of the wood trim. He waved his dinner–plate–sized hand once and then it fell back to his side.

The almost childlike voice was hesitant as Thorny and Charlie approached. "If 'en you're here... it can't be good."

"The good news is you're here, Willie. Who else is here?" Thorny shook his hand.

Shaking Charlie's hand, his face sagged. "Carter and Stern came back with me for Christmas. Come on in and tell me what's what while I pull my boots on."

They sat at the small table as the man got his boots. "We was almost out of drill rod when the mountain took a hiccup. We think it kinked the rod somewhere deep. We shut down the drill and tried to back the rod out, but it would pull. The last resort is to reverse and hope it uncouples deep so we don't lose so much rod."

He sat on the chair Thorny was afraid would break. The joints protested but held. "It was Christmas Eve, and the other three had been home for Thanksgiving, so we came. We'll try to pull the rod and start over when we get back." He sat back in the chair. His eyes searched Thorny's face. "What happened...?"

She took a deep breath and let it out slowly. "There is no sugar coating I can put on this. Someone went up that evening, shot and killed all three, then burned the camp and all the equipment. We think they might have used a 30-30, but when the well broke open in the morning, it washed everything away."

The man's chest flattened as his eyes slid low and looked at the table. His breathing was soft with a chuffing exhale.

"I'm sorry, Willie." She reached out and covered his hand. "I never wanted anything like this to happen. We were careful to try to keep you guys safe with nobody knowing you were up there."

The man looked up with wet eyes. "The only person other than you and Charlie was the dandy from the county land bureau."

Thorny glanced at Charlie. Charlie shrugged. "What did he look like?"

"Tall, but he never got off 'en his horse. Dark hair with one of them mustaches like the movie star who done them pirate movies."

"Errol Flynn, Basil Rathbone, or Douglas Fairbanks?"

The man pointed. "Yeah, that guy."

"Which—"

Charlie stopped Thorny with his knee to hers. "Do you know what kind of horse?"

"Sure. That's what stood out. It was one of them fancy horses. Even though his cropped the mane and tail, a Palomino is still a Palomino."

Thorny's head cocked sideways. "Did you see a brand?"

"It looked like a boat a kid would draw. There was some silver Conchos on the tack. The buckle Concho had the same brand only fancier. There was a half circle rocking on the bottom with a crossed tee on the top like the mast of a boat."

Thorny knew the brand. The current owner was probably kneading out dough for dinner rolls as they spoke. She squirmed in the chair.

"Okay, Willie, we'll look into the guy." She gave Charlie a meaningful look. The man ticked his head sideways in denial.

"You said the water came in…"

She bobbed her head. "Looks like it's throwing full bore about fifty yards. There's a lot of water there. Maybe up to two-acre-feet an hour."

"Throwing that far is probably more like three feet. You need to cap it soon, or you'll have a new Owens River down into Round Valley."

"We told Stan to get it done. He said he'd call up to Carson City and get a crew down today."

The man snorted. "Stuffing a sleeve and cap on it will be like tying a blue ribbon on an angry bull's balls at the state fair. I'm glad I don't have to do it. But what about my boys?"

"Once they cap it, we'll look in the pond, but the sand may have already buried everything."

"I'll tell their families. They were from up Hawthorne way, so I'll go up there later today."

She reached out to his shoulder. "Again, I'm sorry."

Charlie pulled to the side of the road. Thorny had barely even said good-bye to Willie. The next turn would put them on the highway, and they would leave Dyer behind.

"You're awfully quiet." He looked at her staring blankly out the side window. "You haven't said a word since we passed the cow riding on a pig."

Her voice was distant with a dreamy element to it. "Have you ever seriously wondered if you are maybe associating with people who should be in a mental institution?" She looked down the street and suddenly sat up. "Forget the cow and pig crap. You tried that one on me in the ninth grade." She turned and faced him. "When we got gasoline in Hawthorne, how much was it a gallon?"

He smiled at her remembering the pig and cow. "Twenty-six and nine-tenths."

"And the diesel would be, what? Five-cents cheaper? How much is fuel at the commercial station at the junction in Bishop?"

"Last week, it was just over twenty-cents... why?"

"If you are driving a heavy truck with tanks holding two hundred gallons, where would you fill your tanks?"

"Bishop is open until midnight, and it would save me a sawbuck or two."

"Turn around."

As they pulled up to the house, Willie came out. "You forget something?"

Thorny had her elbow out the window. "No, Willie, I didn't

forget. I was working on something and hadn't figured it out yet."

She raised her green glasses onto her head. "We worked real hard to keep your being in Buttermilk a secret, right?"

"Yes 'um, we shore did."

"You fellas never went into town."

"Nope."

"When you left on Christmas Eve morning, where did you get fuel?"

"Right there at the junction. The truck stop has the best price."

"In Bishop?"

"Yes 'um..." His voice petered out as his face drained.

She reached out to his arm. "Willie, it wasn't your fault. I would have done the same. You couldn't know, but I think as long as there was the six of you at the camp, you were safe. I'm guessing when the others came back for Thanksgiving, they came by car."

Willie cleared his throat. "Yes 'um. Charlie here filled them up and topped off the big tank for the drill. Because it has the side push, we use a Ford pony engine out of an old T truck. They run on gasoline and run faster."

"So, they never had to stop for fuel except in Hawthorne."

He thought a moment. "Yes 'um, that would be right."

"Thank you, Willie, I think you've been a tremendous help."

He waved as they left.

Halfway to Hawthorne, Charlie ventured into the silence. Thorny had pulled the blanket around her and was leaning against the doorframe, but he knew she wasn't asleep.

"The evening fuel monkey...?"

She looked over. Pulling her glasses to the top of her head. "He'll lead us to Errol Flynn and who killed the men." She looked back out the side window as she pulled her glasses back down. "Whether it will lead us to whoever killed Judge Hudgins or why he hung himself if he did... I haven't a clue. But finding the killer on the hill is going to be good enough for me right now."

"If you attack them straight on—"

She laughed cutting him off as she looked over. "What? They'll circle the wagons?"

The bear of a man growled as he looked at her with a side-eye. "We never were part of that."

"No, you were delicate and civil..."

He bobbed his head. "Killed them in their sleep." The Paiute, known to few, were the only tribe in the west to fight at night.

Thorny thought about night attacks as the sand and little brush passed. The Nevada desert was true desert. Any water, you had to drill for. Even the horned toad lizard she was nick-named after didn't want to live in these hills. The days would fry you, and the nights would freeze you. People knew about Death Valley, but those in the real know knew about the deadly State of Nevada.

26 HOT WATER

Thorny and Charlie sat on the gray log. Someone at one time thought it might make a pleasant bench to sit on and watch the river. The marks of the large drawknife were still there—if you knew what to look for.

Peter stood, still amazed, feeding what he considered a wild animal. Heather took the carrot and munched contentedly as the man rubbed her along the neck and between the ears. "She knows we mean her no harm…"

Charlie's snort was almost a growl. "Careful, son, your city is showing. That Jenny is no lady. She can kick your head off in a heartbeat. It's you who knows she means you no harm. You feed her and pet her, and she'll be just like your dog."

"I don't have a dog."

Thorny sat up straighter. "You should get one. A big one who slobbers. It's almost like having a wife."

Charlie pushed her.

She took off her glasses and polished the lenses. "So what did you find out?"

"Christmas Eve, Phil was supposed to work, but his sister

said he was home with a temperature of a hundred and three degrees. I asked him who covered for him, but he thought they had closed early for Christmas. So I guess I got nowhere."

Charlie leaned back along the log and cocked up his one knee. "What's the word up the hill?"

Pete fed the last of the carrot to Heather. As he put his arm over her neck, she leaned into him as he rubbed both sides. "The first crew he got down from the Carson City area, took one look at the force of water and ran. They did recommend a crew from Los Angeles. They were a snubber team and went right to work. Stan had told them the size they were dealing with, and I guess they called the guy in Nevada..."

"Willie Widdon?"

"Yes, him. He gave them the specs, so they brought a truck with the right equipment. They had never seen a water well blow out that way, but at least they knew it wouldn't explode or light on fire."

"So the water is stopped now?"

Pete wiped his hands on his pants. "Yes. I nosed around up in the canyon. They mentioned a slowing of the winter water, but it came back, so they figured it was because of the cold or something. The one dam is already spilling extra over the dam so the winter will cover any loss."

Thorny held her glasses up to check the lenses. "Except, someone knows they killed three men up there. They also know what they were doing."

Pete sat on the end of the log near Thorny. "Have you thought about the guy on the horse?"

She pushed the glasses onto her face and hooked the stems around her ears. "I know who owns the horse, but I'm working on the man."

"Wouldn't the man own the horse?"

Charlie groaned as he sat up from lying on the log. "Not if he borrowed the horse. The brand is like a license plate on a car. It will tell you who owns the car, but the driver may be someone who borrowed the car."

Thorny added with a lip push, "Or stole the car. But we're hoping for the former, not the latter."

"So who owns the boat brand?"

She shook her head. "It's not so simple. The brand isn't a boat intrinsically, and we found out it's not registered. But I know where there are cows and another horse with the same brand. I'm just working out who exactly it is and what the brand means. I have my suspicions, but I don't want to go in half-cocked. Mr. Ferguson is asking about a few pairs for the farm."

"Pairs of what?"

Thorny reclined back into Charlie. "He really is from the city."

The Indian smiled. "A pair is a pregnant cow with a four-month-old calf on the ground. The calf means she is proven to give birth, and the one inside is a surprise. You could end up with a steer, a bull, or another cow."

Thorny sat up at the man's obvious confusion. "If it's a boy, but you don't need a bull, you cut his nuts off, and he's only good for meat in six or nine months. If you need a bull, and he looks good, you have a potential of a bull to cover your cows and get them pregnant. He's worth money. And the same goes for a cow. If she drops calves, she will make you money. If she ends up only meat... well, she's only meat." She watched the information settle. "We don't need a bull, but a third isn't bad either. But we could use a couple more cows."

"And these would have the brand on them? Meaning you find out whose brand they are."

Thorny leaned back into Charlie. "He's turning country real fast."

The afternoon shadow from across the valley was lending a chill through the air. Charlie was looking across to the Sierra's toward Buttermilk.

Thorny rocked her head back looking up at his serious face. "What are you thinking?"

"If the water is flowing, we can cool the soaking pond again."

She hummed as she thought. "Peter, do you work tomorrow?"

"I'm off until Thursday."

"How much hot water are you willing to get into?"

"What did you have in mind?"

"We can pack some food. So, at least the three days."

"What should I pack?"

Charlie harrumphed. "When was the last time you went skinny-dipping?"

The man blushed. "My cousin Edna's sixteenth birthday. We snuck out to the beach at night."

Thorny chuckled. "Was she a kissing cousin?"

The man got redder.

27 PIPE DREAM OR DOWN THE TUBES

The two men stood relaxed. They watched a steam shovel grinding in the crust of the still frozen ground. The broken sand helped, but under the thin surface, there were layers of welded volcanic ash called *tuff*. Sometimes it welded in a soft broken sediment, and other layers were hard as concrete. The stench of the poorly burning diesel belching black from the machine washed uphill and burned their eyes. Neither flinched.

Thorny watched the two from the crest. The bear in the green wool coat she had known since the first or second grade. When they entered high school, they had cut their thumbs and held them together to become blood brothers. Their relationship never changed. The FBI agent next to him was growing on her. Him, she knew would never cut his thumb for her, nor she for him, but they would have each other's backs out of respect.

The last three weeks while in Los Angeles, her respect for the man had grown. While researching another matter, she ended behind closed doors with someone who had intimate knowledge about the man—his wife.

She had never thought about the man having another life. As

they talked, Thorny had learned about him as a young man, running off to France to learn how to fly against the Germans. His time with the French Air Corp, as well as his thirteen kills, had helped him move to the American Army Air Corp when the United States entered the war. He added nineteen more kills and rescued a cut-off company in the north of France. The French had decorated his hospital gown, afraid he would die. The Americans waited for four more months and mailed his medals to his wife. Returning her husband had taken a left turn —the intelligence corps recruited the grounded pilot. A year later, they released him to the FBI. Six months later, Ruth was pregnant and on the train to Los Angeles to live with her mother.

They celebrated their twenty-fifth anniversary the night of December sixth. The next evening, two men in a black car disturbed their time relaxing on the beach. The gray suits said everything. Their daughter later apologized for telling the Special Agents where they were.

Mrs. Manly figured, if she couldn't beat them, she might as well join the war effort and work for them. She had been the one who sat across from Thorny and reviewed a criminal file on one Jefferson Lynstrom Becicka, a young man from Texas. Thorny could look over the juvenile file but not take notes. At nineteen, he had moved to Flagstaff, Arizona and partnered with another mistake. The petty theft had turned into a strong-arm robbery and didn't end there. When he finally got his hands on a pistol, he walked in on two other men holding up a small bank. Gunfire followed, and one teller surprised the three with a shotgun. The young Becicka, being the closest to the door —escaped.

His trail was spotty until he was caught by a private security agent. The agent was opening the mansion in Palm Springs for his wealthy employer. The grueling heat was over, and the owner wanted to spend Christmas relaxing in the sun. The agent held the young man locked up in the wine cellar. Six days later, when he arrived at his winter retreat, William Mulholland made the young man an offer he couldn't refuse.

Thorny looked at the man in the wool and leather jacket. She thought about the man's history. The leather jacket he wore today was a favorite of Clark Gable. The man probably liked it because it fit like the jacket he wore when he flew over France.

Thorny sighed. She could smell the green coming in the lower pastures. Spring would be early this year. The pipe to Round Valley was just in time. By the end of the month, six farmers would be turning the soil of their former pastures. Two weeks later, they would be ready to plant.

Thorny's right hand felt along her chest. The small elk hide pouch made only a small lump. She shoved her hands in her jacket pockets and started walking down the gentle slope toward the two men.

Charlie's head eased back as his nose rose in the air. "I hope you used the last of Mrs. Ferguson's winter lye soap. I can smell the dead sheep or is the leather on those moccasins a little fresh?"

Stan looked over at the Indian and frowned. "What are you talking about? There are no dead sheep up here and not even live ones."

"Give it up, Frog. You heard the damn Ford backfire a mile down the road. And for your information, my skin hasn't touched lye soap since we were the same size. The moccasins are the ones your mother made me for graduation. The leather was from the calf you raised for the fair." She stepped between the two men. Turning to Manly, she sniffed and then handed him a thick envelope. "He can't smell soap, but he also can't smell lilacs. Your lovely wife said to tell you happy Easter. She's taking the train up to the Presidio in San Francisco to watch your daughter graduate."

"When did you talk to Ruth?" The man didn't seem surprised at Thorny meeting her.

"She was my briefing officer a few days ago. She's sweet like a little cream and sugar in Turkish coffee. After the war, please bring her up. I'm sure we can find some nice accommodations not entailing a bunch of stinky bachelors. Ruth showed me a photo of your daughter. She is going to break many hearts around the hospital."

The man's mouth opened. He seemed to be chewing air as he thought about what he wanted to know and what he could ask. The war had compartmentalized much information into the tiny boxes of need-to-know—even between spouses. "So how was Los Angeles... in general?"

Thorny squinted and looked out along the scar running down the hill. Where the scar flattened out, she could see men and trucks. The scar of the trench and pipe disappeared into the desert. Soon, every trace of the large steam shovel belching black smoke in front of them would disappear as if it never existed.

"People are tense. The war isn't nearby, but they don't know how far away it really is. Even Hawaii seems as far away as the moon, but every paper has something about rebuilding Pearl Harbor or the Pacific Fleet getting a new ship of one kind or another." She looked down and then over as she licked her lips, thinking about what to say. "We finally had a win at a place called Guadalcanal. I asked a dozen people if they could find it on a map. Only person was your wife—but she just asked if I could give her an atlas and a few hours."

"That's my Ruth. Give her an atlas and a few days, and she can find Shangri-La. She loves maps. In twenty-nine, I had to go back to DC. We made it a family trip on the train. I asked what museums she wanted to go see with our daughter. She only wanted to go to the Library of Congress. They have a map drawn by Christopher Columbus."

He looked up at Charlie. "It seems so surreal, this war. We have rationing, but here, there is food, and nobody cares about the gasoline. They just park the car and walk."

Thorny cocked her head and gave a sideways look at the man. "The last war—you were in the thick of it all. Here, if you don't read the papers, you almost don't know there is a war. But the tension is here too. Just in a separate way. Normal things are different—like the lack of traffic. None of the city folk are coming up to fish or hunt. Even Danny's usual clientele are staying down in the city. Just those differences put people on edge. Knowing there is also a war—and many of the young men are gone—is brutally stressful on a small town like Bishop. The population sign says two thousand. I think it's wrong. I think over a hundred men are missing. While some are gone, their wives moved home with family, wherever that is. I walk past houses these days, which are just empty boxes. Nobody is there to make them a home. Bishop used to feel like home. But now it feels like one of those boxes."

Stan looked over her head to Charlie. The man's lower lip eased out as he squinted toward the mountain. The slow nod came with heart and thought. "I've been feeling it, but I hadn't figured it out yet. Thorny is better at those things."

The Special Agent looked back at the steam shovel now

advancing another ten feet. His exhale was drawn out. "Here is hoping all of this work was not needed."

Charlie's cheeks scrunched up under his eyes. "I think you have reason to hope, but I also think it's a pipe dream to think either war will be over before this harvest. Everything I read about the war in the Pacific has been nothing but a slog through slop. Germany is a small country but seems to find more and more reserves." His head ground back and forth. Thorny could hear the frog in his throat as he rumbled to clear it.

The three stood in the chilly sunlight. The black smoke from the shovel was the blot on a cloudless sky and the echo to their thoughts.

Stanly's voice was soft and low. "Did you find what you needed in Los Angeles?"

"My boss misses me. I can have my old job back in a heart-beat. The boardinghouse now has old men allowed in, but is still half empty."

"And your investigation?"

"I need to find a case down in Independence." She looked up at Charlie. The smile was slow.

Stan fluttered one eye but also smiled. "I'll warn Burt and Ernest, so they don't end up in the river. It's cold this time of year."

Charlie heaved as his chest and back bounced with his quiet laugh. Thorny chuckled. "We can always light a fire for them."

28 OLD FIGHT SAME WAR

The day was overcast and dreary. Thorny couldn't smell any snow or rain in the air, but the sky hung low and threatening. It was as if the valley was saying spring wasn't around the corner.

The Chevrolet glided along the new patch of macadam. Surprisingly, there was enough spare old diesel oil to spray the road and then have the giant steamroller smooth out the chip stone and oil.

"Who was the guy?" Charlie didn't really care why they were driving down to Independence. He was just making small talk.

"Remember the crazy woman who lived up near the end of Dixon Lane? She had the goats running wild all the time."

He snapped his fingers. "She mixed the barn paint in with the whitewash. She brushed the house up as high as her arthritis wouldn't hurt her."

Thorny smirked at the forgotten memory. "Yes, the pink wainscoted house. Well, her husband was Jess Hessian. He was just as crazy as she was, but there were those who believed he was sane. Sane enough to vote him in as the county controller."

She leaned against the door as she looked out toward the last of the snow on the tops of the Sierra Nevada Mountains. "I don't know if he was controller back in 1927 or not, but your grandfather obviously remembered something."

"This is the type of work you did down in Los Angeles?"

"For the District Attorney?" She looked over at his nod. "In the beginning. I worked as a law clerk for a couple of different attorneys while I was in school. You spend your days in the law library or the county library going through old cases. Or you're sitting in court on cases being tried at the time, just in case their verdict might have a bearing on your case. It's boring slave labor, but it is the best way to learn the law. I was very lucky when I worked my final year of school. I worked for two attorneys in land law. The head researchist was named Meredith Wilks. She had worked for them for seventeen years. She could be a lawyer, but she loves digging through the library, finding case law and obscure laws dating back into the early eighteen hundreds. She is so important that they take her to court for every closing argument. When a judgment is coming back, she is there."

Charlie looked over with a smile. "She taught you how to do the research and to love the dusty old books?"

Thorny's eyes bulged. "Oh, my gosh, no. I still hate this. She taught me I never wanted to be stuck in her job for seventeen years. It made me study twice as hard for the bar exam. I told my boss at the District Attorney's office I would only clerk until I passed, and then I wouldn't spend a minute more in the library."

"Did it work?" Charlie drove around a farmer on his wagon with a team of horses. They both stole a look back and then watched the team and wagon in the mirrors.

"Nope. Even as a lawyer, you still need to go do research. The clerks do most of the work, but you need to finesse the fine stuff yourself. If you don't, you sound like every other lawyer."

"You said you need to do something soon. Are you running out of savings?"

"Running lower than I would prefer. I have enough to last probably another year, but I wouldn't be comfortable. I don't have any real bills, but I was looking at the roof of the house. I can see where Mr. Ferguson made some patches with flattened soup cans.

"When the war is over, and we can get tin roofing again, I know the house needs to be reroofed." She rubbed at her claw. "I think the missus would like to stop running out to the outhouse in the winters, as well. I don't know how much it will all cost, but I know I'll need to work to cover it."

The man eased the car to the edge of the wooden sidewalk. They looked across the street at the tan sandstone building. "Have you asked the mountain?"

Thorny snickered and then realized the man was serious. She reached to touch the pouch under her shirt. "Like go knock on the stone wall and start talking?"

He glowered at her as he opened his door. "We'll go up tomorrow night. The mountain is your family now. If you have a need or a question, you go ask the mountain." Her mouth started to open, and then with his look, it drew shut. She was at a loss.

He smiled. She was learning. "Besides, I'm sure the pool will feel good for both of us."

Her smile froze as she stepped out of the car. Two men were standing in the doorway of the pharmacy. From the cut of their suits, she didn't think they were Burt and Ernest.

"Good morning, Miss Wallace." The larger one in front adjusted his tie as he stepped out onto the sidewalk. "This is a pleasant surprise." His voice was nothing less than threatening.

Thorny gently closed the door. Her eyes never left the man or his hands. "Does that mean you plan to gun me down here on the street in front of witnesses?"

The man gazed across the street at the single gardener, half buried in the bushes he was trimming. Independence may be the county seat, but it never resembled the word *bustling*. The man's smile was flat and malicious. "Who, your Injun driver? Everyone knows they're nothing more than drunks and liars."

Charlie's head rose above the tall Chevrolet. The man's eyes took in the height and figured the size. He had never been close to the man with twin braids to his hips.

Thorny stepped into the man's face. "If you value having hair anywhere on your body, I strongly suggest you apologize to the man."

The rumble behind her barely resembled speech. "Miss Wallace, I'll take care of this." She felt the large hand cover her shoulder. As much as she didn't want to back down from any fight, she knew when to let Charlie take over.

The man was light on his feet as Thorny stepped back.

Charlie's right hand had reached up to slick back his tightly pulled hair. As the man's eyes followed the movement, his hand stopped from reaching under his suit coat by Charlie's left open fist striking his throat.

As he reached for his throat and choked, Charlie pushed him lightly. The man responded by leaning forward as the much larger man slapped his hands on both ears, and jerked the man's head down into his up-coming knee.

Thorny could hear the nose shatter.

Charlie reached into the man's coat as he held him up against his partner. He drew out the pistol and threw the man to one side. The pistol's barrel now floated in the other man's mouth. The man was a statue.

Charlie leaned in. "Now, I'm going to take your pistol so it's a fair fight. The last time she had to take on three guys, it didn't end pretty for the three. I think one is even walking now… with a cane." He fished into the man's armpit and withdrew the automatic. He eyed the large weapon. "Were you expecting Chinese assassins? She's big, but I think this little thirty-eight could do the job. That is *if* you could have got the drop on her."

He tossed his head back at Thorny, now leaning against the car. Turning back, he lowered his voice. "I think the smart play here is to pick up your friend and take him back to your boss in the city. Tell him there's a new woman in town, and she is keeping your balls in her makeup box. If we see you up here again, I won't step in. I'll let her do what she loves to do." He watched the last bit of blood drain from the man's face.

Charlie turned and stepped over to the car and Thorny. "Shall we go look at the boring files?"

Thorny looked around his shoulder at the smaller man struggling with the barely breathing body. "What about…?"

Charlie glanced back with a smirk. "Oh, he needs to go find a hospital for his friend."

He gently took her arm and guided her across the street.

As they crossed the lawn, he showed her the two pistols. "Which one do you want?"

She took the heavier forty-five caliber automatic. Weighing it in her hand, she thumbed the catch and slid the magazine out of the grip. It was full. Jamming the magazine into the pistol, she shoved it in her back pocket.

Looking over at the large man, she smiled at the pistol barely filling his palm.

"Just your size."

Charlie rolled around the table a few hours later. The few files had turned into a few boxes of files.

Thorny pulled the green glasses off the top of her head. She looked at her friend. "Hession wasn't crazy. His wife may have been, but he was making money right and left just from filing suits against farmers, ranchers, miners. Hell, this one starts with a landowner named Phelps, but I think there is another suit in these boxes where he files against not only Phelps but also the cities of Bishop and Big Pine."

"This doesn't make much sense to me." Charlie pointed to a short stack of files. "In one, he's filing for damages from something called transitory statute of assets. In another, he is suing for the mitigation of... of... well, something. I've got a degree in hydrography, but this stuff is something else. Do you understand this?"

She set down the file and washed her face with her hands. Drawing the skin around her eyes back, she blinked. "I had a professor in college. The man was brilliant, but I read a paper another student had written. I had to read most of it over and over to understand what he was saying. The kid had an amazing mind, but the professor gave the paper a low-grade. The kid was devastated, but the professor had printed in large red type across the top: Eschew Obfuscation. It means don't use language meant to confuse or hide the meaning." She smiled. "It was sarcasm but also got the point across."

Charlie pointed at the boxes and files. "There is nothing—"

"Clear and straightforward? No, there isn't. Later in law school, I had a professor who used to scream at the class,

'Obfuscate, obfuscate, but always call it research.'" She let it sink in for a moment. "In law, the language is to confuse to a point where a simple statement can be argued either way. It's why lawyers make fifteen- to twenty-dollars an hour. It doesn't make sense to you, so you hire a lawyer. Only this guy didn't need one. He probably went to law school and never told anyone." She leaned back, causing the chair to creak. "From what I've looked at, the man was suing for pieces of the whole pie. If there were mineral rights for a thousand acres, he didn't want the rights to ten acres, he wanted one percent of the whole."

"Why so little?"

"It's not little. Let's say you have mineral rights to the land under this building. But Joe Smith drills a well over in the middle of the pharmacy and hits oil. You spend the next five years drilling wells but only get water. But, originally, you could have bought one percent of the mineral rights for the whole town. It's only one percent."

He smiled. "But it's one percent of the oil."

"Now you understand."

"So what do you think happened to him?"

She stood and leaned over one of the boxes. Drawing out a fistful of thin files, she leafed through them. She laid one down and opened it, pointing to the date of the county clerk stamp. "I assume this is the last suit he filed. It was in October of 1929. But…" She opened another file. "His widow filed a handful of quitclaim deeds in the summer of 1930. All of them are for mineral rights, except the one on the homestead."

"Widow…?"

Thorny nodded. Somewhere in the county records is a death certificate. In those years, I won't be surprised if when we find it, we find the verdict to be suicide."

Charlie closed one eye. "Who did she sign the quitclaim over to?"

Thorny smiled. "Why, Charlie, I think this legal dust and paper is rubbing off on you." She grabbed the file and pointed to the receiving party of the deed. "It's called a legal trust. The board of trustees or owners are none other than, Mortimer J. Mann, Reginald Reseda, Cyril Royce Couch, and our old friend William Mulholland."

"Well, we know who Reseda and Mulholland are, but who are the other two?" He looked up. "Is there any way to find out how much they paid her?"

AN HOUR LATER, they stood in the county tax records office. They had their answer. The frumpy woman in a floral dress showing years of wear stood looking over Thorny's shoulder. She had kept sneaking peeks at the size of Charlie and his long braids. As she looked up records, she seemed to be working at keeping Thorny between her and the Indian.

"I wish my uncle Jedidiah had taught me how to whistle. That is a lot of money."

Thorny pointed at the date. "It's a lot of money even today, but after the stock market crashed, this would have set up several people for life."

The woman blinked as she thought about the money. "You could buy all of Independence and still have half left over. Who was this woman, and where is she now?"

Thorny put down the paper. "My guess is she moved to Los Angeles or San Diego to live out the rest of her life in luxury. As to who she was... she was the widow of a crooked man who stole land and water from many fine folks in this valley."

Charlie's rumble spoke to the darker side of the group in question. "I don't think her luxury lasted long."

Thorny turned to the woman. "I need copies of about twenty legal files, a couple of dozen deeds, and these tax files."

The woman blinked a few times and pushed on her large bun. "Do you need them to be conformed or just typed up?"

Thorny thought about the nature of what the woman was saying. If she only typed copies, nobody else would know. But if she typed up duplicates for conforming records, the evidence of Thorny finding all of this would be a matter of record.

"Refiling all of those records would be a large task." The two women stared at each other as they came to an understanding.

"Honey, I have filing in my bottom drawer that's been waiting since Taft was in office. This much work would have to go to the bottom of the pile."

Thorny smiled. "Eunice, you are a true gem. How long will it take for you to type all of this?"

"Can you give me a week? It's not busy... it never is, but we're closed for Good Friday."

"How about we come back down the following Friday. I'll bring you some fresh eggs, and I think we have a lamb ready for slaughter. How does a leg of lamb sound for Easter dinner?"

"My Harold and I would love it. We haven't had lamb in years."

"We'll see you next Friday then." She looked over at Charlie who nodded.

"I'll keep it all in the bottom drawer where it's safe from snooping noses." She leaned close to Thorny with her eyes rolled large. Out of the side of her mouth, she muttered, "I leave feminine necessaries on top of the files. Scares the hell out of men."

Thorny chuckled softly as she smiled. "I knew I'd like you, Eunice. The moment you gave the chief here a tough time by not flirting, I just knew we would be good friends."

29 HEATHER

"Either you need to wear a coat over your pistol or get one small enough to fit in your pocket."

Thorny frowned, confused, and then chuckled as she reached around and pulled the automatic from the back of her pants. She thumbed the button and dropped out the clip. Ejecting the one shell from the chamber, she eased the slide back into place and laid the clip and pistol in the drawer. "We found it down in Independence."

"In a store?"

She turned to look at the man. His face was scared and blotchy from the mustard gas during his time in the trenches of France. His service was only one reason Pop had taken them on as tenants and caretakers. "Somewhat. The men were standing in the doorway of the pharmacy. I guess they thought they could put a scare into me, but they didn't count on Charlie."

Mr. Ferguson smiled. "I liked the boy. I like the man even more... the more grown up he gets."

Thorny shied as she continued putting the folders and files in other drawers.

It didn't escape the older man's attention when she took the broken tack out of the large tack box, lifted the false bottom and withdrew a metal strongbox. Sliding a matching set of large envelopes into the box, she placed the box back into the secret compartment. She fitted the thick board of asbestos back over the box—sealing the fireproof chamber. Lowering the false bottom back into place, she dumped the damaged tack back into the box. She lowered the lid closed from the corners. The large wooden handle was liberally smeared with rancid elk grease and nettle spores.

Straightening as she turned, Thorny addressed the man's one raised eyebrow. "If I ever turn up dead, all the research is in there." His chin shoved toward the desk drawer. She shrugged. "Same files, but those might get stolen some night."

The man who moved into the house with his wife the year Thorny went away to college smiled. "I'll make sure we sleep soundly at night."

"Just don't snore. It makes the cows nervous."

His snort was as soft as his crooked smile. "Come on in. Maude made a roast out of the broken lamb."

Thorny dusted at her pants. "Shame about the little guy. He was one of the cuter bummer lambs."

As they walked across the wagon yard, he looked out at the pink blush starting on the last snow on White Mountain. "Bet he's one of the tastier of this year." He smiled over at Thorny. "She rubbed him down with mint and cilantro and used the last of the white wine."

"Wine..." She hadn't thought about how the rationing could affect in strange ways. "I wonder how it would taste cooked in moonshine?"

"Better than kerosene, but not by much." He opened the back

door and swept his hand toward the wonderful smells of dinner."

The three talked quietly as they ate. Thorny recognized the root vegetable chowder marking the end of the root cellar's vegetables from the previous summer. The chowder was the way to hide the cutaway rot, bruises, and hard sprouting. There were small slices of celery in the thick rue, but she politely didn't ask. She was sure there had been some serious horse-trading for something fresh. It could have only come from down in the Imperial Valley. As cute as the small lamb may have been, he proved to be even tastier. The meat all but fell from the bone. Their plates were more filled with chunks pulled than slices taken.

"There are three new pairs in the separator pasture."

Thorny pulled a small piece from the hack of bread torn from the round loaf. "I saw those as I drove in." Her one eyebrow nudged up as she looked sideways at the man. "And the brand?"

"It was her daddy's brand. The yeller horse was there too. The triangle is over a lazy halfmoon, so it's on its back. I commented it looked like a little sailboat. I don't think she liked the comment."

"What did she say?"

He dabbed some bread at the last smear of mint jelly. "Nothing. It were her eyes... They got like slits, and she got huffy. She told me to take the cows or not. When I held the hundred out, she nearly tore it from my hand and then stomped back into the house. She never offered to help me get them in the truck or nothin'."

Mrs. Ferguson, normally quiet, coughed quietly. Thorny rolled her eyes to the woman with a smile. The woman's quiet usually allowed her to observe many things and overhear conversations in town. For all the attention she drew, she may as well be the wallpaper.

"Excuse me for saying, but she always was a queer one. She and her mother—the judge's sister-in-law. Neither one ever really fit in. They kept to themselves pretty much, but I overheard some of their religious views. I would be hard-pressed to find them sentiments in any of the back chapters of the bible. I've read the book cover to cover many times, and I'm not sure I'd even find their beliefs in the early chapters either. There are bits and pieces, but nothing complete or fit for this modern world and people."

Thorny scrunched one side of her face as she thought. "I got the impression she wouldn't be sending her girls to school…"

"Doesn't surprise me. If they go to school, they might learn something she don't approve of."

"But she attended public school. She met Phillip at the high school."

The woman stood, taking up the plates. "She may have been there to learn how to read and write, but as for anything else, my guess is she wasn't a good student." She put the plates on the sideboard. Turning she smiled. "I made a savory pinion pie…"

Thorny's smile matched the cook's husband. Even with the end of winter and the stored food, there were some things worth waiting for.

THE SPRING SUN was warm on the shoulders of Thorny's barn coat. The tan had all but faded away to dusty white. The fraying was nothing more than a softening of the work cloth. She held up another half an apple. The piece of worm still wiggled near the exposed core. Heather didn't hesitate.

"My first reaction is we have him dead to rights." Pete turned back a few pages.

Thorny smirked. "Stan?"

The Special Agent barely twitched. Thorny almost thought he had drifted off to sleep on the short spring grass, but she had seen a foot twitch a few minutes before.

"My wife probably told you something about the difference between knowledge and actionable evidence."

Thorny held out the last piece of apple and then stroked Heather's neck. The mule moseyed off to find more food as Thorny leaned back on the log. "We might know it's him, but proving it's him is the separation. The use of fingerprints was rudimentary in the territories back then. To prove anything beyond a shadow of a doubt would require an eyewitness or physical proof."

The disjointed voice filtered back. "Or a confession."

Pete put down the file on his smaller log. He watched the mule as she cropped the fresh grass near the head of the FBI. "Heather..." His question trailed off.

Thorny's head turned. "What about her?"

"She's about as tame as any horse at a ranch... but you leave her here."

Thorny uncrossed her legs and held them in the air. Their weight gently rotated her body erect. "She gets plenty of food. I bring her treats. I rarely ride the horses at the ranch. I don't need her to carry anything I can't put in the Ford. She keeps my office neat and tidy, just the way I like it, and I have no need for her anywhere else."

Stan rolled over and braced himself with is one arm and

reached out to pet the close ear. He could hear some thinking grinding away in the deputy.

Pete pushed around to look at Thorny. "Exactly. You know where she is, and she is good where she is. You don't have to feed her or tend to her needs, and as long as she is where you left her, you don't worry about her."

Stan squeezed one eye down as he sat up with his legs bridged. Leaning forward, he laid his arms on each other, knee to knee. His chin softly landed on his wrist. "Are you talking about Heather or Reseda?"

"Bingo." The deputy's finger made a pistol at the other man. "As long as they know where he is, they will leave him alone. He grazes around Bishop and lets them know if there is anything wrong." His eyebrows raised in question. "So, what happens if he disappears for a few days?"

Thorny snorted. "So who's going to kidnap him?" She pointed at the two men. "The deputy sheriff or the federal agent who investigates kidnappings?"

Stan started laughing first. "Charlie was right. You are a party pooper."

"What?"

Pete, still serious, was bobbing his head. "You're the one who brought up work. Besides, we are all servants of the court."

"Okay, so we don't kidnap him. But how do we get him out of the way for a while?"

"You don't. I do."

They all turned at the sound of the deep voice. The head was all they first saw. The next was the Indian poling his canoe while standing up.

Charlie bent and grabbed a rope then stepped onto the bank. Pulling, he dragged the large canoe onto the grass.

Thorny smiled. "Good to see the old river runner is patched and working like new."

"Don't get any ideas. The hole you poked in the skin was not easy to patch. I had to get two elk to rebuild the whole front half." He sat on the end of her log as he scratched the hindquarter of the mule.

Thorny snorted softly. "The resemblance is uncanny. What did you have in mind for Reseda?"

He turned with a large toothy smile. "Squaw tea and milk-weed beetle."

Her eyes closed in memory as her eyebrows stretched high and her face grimaced. "Give him too much, and he won't leave the outhouse for a week."

"I thought you were scheming even longer."

The four were quiet, thinking about their positions and what needed to be done. Peter was the first to shift to the next page. "Did Mr. Ferguson find out anything about the brand?"

"Not from her, per se, but the hired hand up the road had some insight." She pushed her foot against Charlie's hip. "A negro who mucks out the barn and digs ditches around the ranch rarely gets any notice. If the man on the horse is a wealthy swell from down in the city, the ranch hand might as well be an invisible ghost. He's like a tiny tree frog. Almost not there until the dark of night, and then they all talk to each other."

Charlie frowned and turned. "Concho or Arturo?"

"Concho."

His face screwed up as he leaned back away from Thorny. "Concho isn't a negro, he's Mexican."

She smiled. "Just like the niggra…"

Stan crossed his legs and leaned in with his own frown. "Who are we talking about? Who is a negro but not a negro?"

Pete chuckled. "The niggra is the barber. For all purposes, he would be Thorny's uncle. But he is not a negro, he is a dark-skinned Mexican."

Charlie rumbled his throat. "To be more exact, he is the grandson of the Apache named Geronimo. They come from the northeast badlands of the Sonora region of Mexico. Negros, pronounced like egg rows, is Spanish or Mexican for dark or black. But he is not a negro."

Thorny leaned back on her elbow. "You might throw in a bit of Navaho there too."

Stan pulled some green grass to feed to Heather. "So, who are these other fellas?"

Thorny held out her arms—stopping the other two men. "Wait." She swung her right leg up and over Charlie's head and sat up. Leaning forward with her elbows on her thighs, she focused on Stan. "You've been up here what, nine months?"

"Eleven... but—"

Her hand snapped up. "How often do you buy fuel?"

"Now that I'm staying out at the Dude Ranch... about every two weeks."

"Where?"

"The Richfield station at Barlow and Line Street. It's on my way to and from town." He frowned his questioning.

"Who pumps your gas and washes your window?"

"Occasionally, there's a young girl, but most of the time, it's the old man with the cane."

"What about the girl's mother?"

He thought a moment. "I don't think I've ever seen her."

"What does the girl look like?"

He closed his eyes. "About ten or twelve, small, long curly blond hair. It looks like a mop that dried wrong. She wears a man shirt and old bib overalls mostly." His eyes opened, and he blinked at Thorny.

"What's her name?"

"Where are you going with this?" The agitation crept into his voice.

Thorny ignored it. "What? Is? Her? Name?"

His voice took on a clear edge. "I. Don't. Know."

Thorny leaned back against the single root on the log. "Some detective you are. And now I'm not sure you're the man your wife thinks you are."

Standing, his hands were half-clenched. "What is that supposed to mean?"

Charlie rumbled as he cleared his throat. "It means you don't pay attention. Edelman passed away over their Christmas dinner. His daughter Judith and her twin girls, Philomena and Wanda, run the place. If you had the common courtesy to find out names, you would know the three could pass for triplets. The differences are Judith doesn't smile anymore, and Wanda won't check your oil."

Thorny stood and stretched. "Check the tip of your passenger wiper. If there's a tiny piece of paper there, Pi washed your windows last. If the side windows are kind of smeared, it was Judith."

Still steamy but calming, Stan kicked at a clod of dirt. Thorny recognize the exploding ball as a former field mouse— tiny bones and skin were now dust. "What does this have to do with the fellas you were talking about?"

Pete stripped a leaf from the stem of grass he was fiddling with. "Many people, when they work in jobs separating them from labor, will lose touch with the people doing work for them. I'm sure if you were in a large office, there would be new agents. It's not your job to train them, so you only know their face." He stuck the stem in the side of his mouth. It bobbed as he spoke. "So you take a swell from the city, and he expects his horse ready and someone holding the reins, but he will never take the time to know who they are. The groom in a stable, or a ranch hand pushing water around, or the guy pumping gas— they're all just ghosts or invisible. They're there, and they see things, and hear things, but are never noticed."

Stan waved his finger back and forth. "And these guys…"

Thorny's head bobbed up. "Concho and Arturo. Yes, they are invisible. Actually…" She glanced at Charlie. "They are beyond invisible. Because they are Mexican, they aren't fit to shine the fancy boots of the man from down south. If we were a caste society, they would be the untouchables."

Stan's eyes looked up and down at the air and then focused. "As in India."

Thorny's face pulled back on one side. "Exactly."

Charlie hunched over and ground his head around to look at Thorny. "Concho?"

"The man parked his Duesenberg in the barn. He left word not to disturb it, but he wanted it washed."

Pete snorted. "Even this city boy can see the problem there."

Thorny smiled. "Well, I'm not sure if Debbie will ever be able to scour the foul barn out of the sheets they spread over the car, but Concho did wash it… and swept out the trunk and cab."

Stan was getting the gist of the humor mixed with the serious talk. "Did he find anything of interest?"

"The man's suitcase, which, when he moved it, it fell open."

Charlie snorted softly as he gave Thorny the eye. "Clumsy of that there Concho."

Thorny rolled her eyes back toward the federal agent. "His name is Reginald Abbotsford. His passport said he lives in Beverly Hills. Along with the clothes, there were two long barreled revolvers, a 30-30 with an open tube scope, and a large rifle packed in a case in pieces with a scope."

Pete nodded. "30-30 isn't much good over a quarter mile. It's more of a brush hunting rifle. The slug is slow, so twigs and brush don't affect it much. It's the rifle of choice for deer hunting."

Charlie sat up and took a deep breath. "Around here the rifle of choice is a .22 long rifle."

"A twenty-two sounds more like a squirrel gun..."

Stan smiled to one side. "Quite."

Thorny nodded at Pete's quizzical look. "Meat on the table, around here, gets taken any time of the year. You might call it poaching, but folk around here call it surviving. The .22 is a soft noise and doesn't carry far."

"So if it's not for deer hunting, why would you be carrying a 30-30 around in your fancy car?"

The other three replied at the same time. "People."

LATER, Thorny stopped Stan as he opened his car door. "Can I ask a favor?"

"You need a ride into town?"

"No, but thanks for asking. Charlie and I are going up to the mine. There is something I want to look at."

He half closed the door. "Then what can I do for you, Thorny?"

"This Reginald Abbotsford ... There was a corporation or collective of men. Reseda and Mulholland were two, but there was also an Abbotsford." Her finger held her glasses down her nose as she looked over the top.

"I'll see what I can find out."

"Thank you, I'd appreciate that."

"It's no problem. I've got to run down to Los Angeles next week, but I could go early and nose around."

"Does any of it include nosing around Ruth?"

"Next Wednesday is her birthday. I thought I'd take her down to the Pantry. Someone mentioned the violinist was back. She always loved waiting in line and dancing to the music there on the sidewalk."

"Sounds like a romantic time."

"These days, we don't get enough romance time. I want her to know she's still my special girl."

Thorny rested her claw on his shoulder. "I'm sure she always knows it, but it's good to let her know now and again. When do you think you'll go down?"

"My new ration cards aren't good until Monday..."

She thought a moment. "Stop out to the ranch tomorrow night. We got topped off yesterday, and we could only take half of our load. I'll fill you up, and I have something you can give Ruth for her birthday."

He softened. "Thanks, Thorny. You're a swell friend. A tank full will get me down to Mojave, and I've got enough cards left to get me to the federal building."

She noticed Charlie standing with the truck's door open. "I'll see you tomorrow night."

30 DEEP MINE

Thorny read the passage again and then wrote on the piece of paper. She figured if something happened, at least Stan knew where they were. The directions on the paper were more direct than the cryptic note Ulysses had left for her.

Putting down the pencil, she and Charlie checked the new lights she had picked up in Los Angeles. The battery pack took six cells, and the store owner said the light would last for a full week's shift of eighty hours. The lights had an elastic band to go around a helmet or on their heads. She didn't want to think about a miner working backbreaking labor eighty hours a week.

The mine soon became quiet and cool. The summer desert heat would never penetrate more than a handful of yards. From experience, Thorny knew the barn coat on her arm would become necessary. They stopped as Charlie struggled with his coat in the confines of the mine.

Thorny slipped the barn coat on. "Just don't hit a timber or header and bring this old mine down on top of us."

Charlie finally knelt for more arm room. The header beams

were set about the level of his head. Warmer, they continued into the mine. Charlie stooped instead of risking a large bruise on his forehead, or worse yet, shattering his light.

Most of the upright timbers were gray from time and air. The headers were stained dark by what little moisture the White Mountains could squeeze out. The rubber boots they wore were never for the upper layer. The ankle-deep water would be in the drifts two layers lower.

A short wall ran along the one side of the drift. The narrow bench of rock was for the miners to sit while they ate from their lunch pails and to catch their breath. The oxygen in the top level, also known as the horizontal drift of the mine, would have the most oxygen. The older the mine, the more drifts were dug from the outside. The problem was the oxygen also made fires more problematic. The rotting timbers and compression of the unmoving air created sulfur dioxide which can be deadly to breathe, but in lower concentrations, it can cause explosions or fires.

Charlie looked back at the solid black they had come through. "How far in do you think this is?"

"From the map, this first shaft is only a quarter mile in. There is another shaft about two hundred yards further in, but it goes to a gobbed drift. There was a fire down there at one time, so they built the wall and marked it with a red and white marker."

"Gobbed?"

"It means walled off. The marker is just an X, but the red and white means the only way to know if it's still burning is to open it up."

His light crawled around until it was shining on her knee. "How could it still be burning?"

"Burn, as in flame, is the wrong image. There are minerals in the mountain that burn at temperatures above a thousand degrees. The heat causes them to break down like a hardwood log in a stove with the damper turned down. There are coal deposits back east, ignited in mines before the Civil War. The snow falls but never sticks on the ground above the burn. Elsewhere on the mountain, it can stack feet deep. The ground is too hot, so they know it's still burning."

Charlie pointed at the top of the ladder sticking out of the shaft. "How far down does this go?"

"The next drift floor is about eighty feet."

"It can't be all one ladder…"

Thorny stood. "No. The ladders will be about twenty or so. There are decks… Well, you'll see."

He eyed the old ladder. "Do you think the ladders will hold me?"

She looked at the tall, muscular man. "Ulysses was about two-ten…"

"I'm two-forty."

She swung at his upper arm. "You lie like your Husky wife. But they built these ladders to handle more than one man at a time. If there is a problem, we can always haul you up in an ore shaft."

As they started down the ladders, the wood creaked. Thorny looked up as Charlie looked down. He shifted his weight on the rung and the wood moaned again.

"It was a long winter. Without the chief, I had to eat for both of us."

Thorny took in a sharp breath at the memory of the old man. "Just keep your feet spread near the rails. Let the joints carry the weight."

They continued in silence until they got to the next shaft. The drift floor lay scattered with rocks and piles of ceiling leak. Thorny chalked it up to the mine not being used for decades.

Charlie grabbed the one rail and started to swing his foot around onto the ladder. "I'll go first this time."

The marks on the wall were small, but for a mine, it was out of place. "Stop."

He looked over his shoulder at her. "No, really, I can go first—"

She grabbed his jacket. Quietly, she pulled. "Step back."

"What's wrong?" He too was looking around, but he pulled his foot back and stepped away from the shaft.

Thorny thought for a moment. "Let's take a seat."

They sat on the air ridge as they looked across the drift at the shaft. Thorny kept looking at the debris scattered about on the floor. Something was out of place, and she knew she was missing what it was. Finally, she reached down between her feet and picked up a rock half the size of a small hen egg. She bounced it in her palm—thinking.

Just as Charlie started to ask, she pitched it softly over to the shaft. It barely cleared the ladder, which was on their side of the shaft. They listened. If it landed, they didn't hear it. But it never landed on wood. If there had been a series of ladders, it would have rattled its way to the bottom.

She looked at Charlie and then picked up a rock the size of her fist. Several seconds and they heard a dull, soft thud of the stone landing on sand or soft dirt.

They stood at the edge of the shaft, holding their lights facing down. There was no platform dimly showing back—only a pole holding the ladder up.

"How did you know?"

She pointed at the marks on the wall near the edge of the shaft. "Ulysses wasn't just a desert rat. He was also a well-traveled hobo. Those three diagonal lines mean this is a bad place. I'm not sure, but the large X with the little circles on each side mean bad also. Think of it as the skull and crossbones of a pirate. The wiggly line over it, you should know."

"It's a snake."

"What kind of snake?"

"Deadly."

She started back the way they came and then stopped. "Smell that?"

"Smells like the mine."

She turned and led back to the shaft. "Now what do you smell?"

"Sulfur. How did I miss that?"

"You didn't. It's very faint, but I should have caught it. In this mine, it is the one thing Ulysses drilled into me. Always smell for sulfur. Throw a torch down there, and the whole drift and shaft will turn into a firebox until the timbers collapse. Come on. We need to go read something again."

CHARLIE STRETCHED in the late afternoon sun. The blue enameled cup was only half full. He sipped again.

"Lizard, you can marry me any time now."

Thorny pulled the letter out of her way as she spat her coffee. He hadn't called her Lizard since the seventh grade—right before she kicked him between the legs.

"Why, Frog, I didn't know you cared."

He looked at his coffee and took another sip. "I've got a good coffee percolator, but this coffee you fried up in an iron skillet puts my coffee to shame." He smiled at her with honest admiration.

She thought about how rare the man was willing to offer a good word. His life was not easy, and he survived through his guts, determination, and exhausting work. Few could keep up. Fewer still could best him.

"Did you see any dog hairs in my skillet?"

"No."

She leaned back against the building. Closing her eyes behind her glasses, she angled her face toward the sun. "Well, there you go."

THE SUN WASN'T EVEN BEGINNING to rise when Charlie rolled over and reached for more blanket. He wasn't cold, but his body responded to the awakening. His hand reached out looking for the blankets where they were usually bundled around his dog.

There was no dog, and there were no blankets. He sat up. He could feel the heat from the stove. Still at the mine. Exhausted, they had slept on the hard wooden cots—any soft padding had become mouse food long ago.

"There's coffee." The soft voice came out of the dark where the other cot was against the far wall.

He washed his hands over his face. "Mmfp." He padded his way to the door. Middle of the night or early morning, he needed to make room for more coffee.

Charlie looked at the letter. He pushed his chin at it.

"I had it all wrong. I thought he wrote a straightforward description of where he was. But the second shaft is impossible, and even if he had been on the second level, he never could have pulled himself up the ladders."

Charlie pulled his braid out of his plate and flipped it to his back. Lifting his mug, his eyes rose to meet hers. "So, where was he?"

She pushed back in her chair as she brought her mug to her smirk. "He wasn't in the old mine." She sipped as she let the information sink in. "He was in the new mine."

***

TEN MINUTES LATER, they confirmed the right location. If nothing else, they only had to follow the drag marks on the dirt floor of the drift. "When the large mine played out, you have two choices. You either dig deeper, which is very expensive, or you walk away. When you have thirty or forty miners to feed and pay…"

"So who started this mine?"

"Someone who was working mean and lean. Probably a foursome." She pointed out the timbers and back stacks to hold the rock back. "They scrimped on the stacks by leaving four to six inches between the boards. They weren't expecting to be here long. My guess would be they expected to be here four to eight years and move on. I'd even guess they never filed the claim because the old claim was still running."

The drag marks swerved to the right into a branch in the tunnels. The drift had enough slope to be more of a ramp. "They were following a vein."

"So the main tunnel is straight until they get distracted?"

Thorny glanced back. "Like you in the seventh grade."

"Oh, I was focused… until someone kicked me."

"Don't hit girls."

The drift widened. The start of a shaft on the one side never went far.

Thorny looked down into the shaft to the rubble-strewn floor, eight or ten feet below. The short ladder was battered but still serviceable. The drag marks to the one side certified to this being where Ulysses fell. Glinting on the floor was a rock hammer—Ulysses's. The wall where the timbers and header should have been was broken out. The lumber had never been installed.

The vein started about two feet from the edge of the shaft. Thorny's guess was, if they had known the vein was there, the original miners would not have started the shaft. The wall had caved at one time, exposing what Ulysses had reached for. Thorny pointed at the vein. It started as thin as a thread but, shortly, was as thick as Charlie's arm.

Charlie let out a low whistle. "But what do you think was in reach for him to try getting it?"

"I'm going to find out. Steady the ladder."

Using the rock hammer, she turned the top chunks of debris. In the light, she began to see the difference between the two strata of rock the inclusion ran between. She cleared away the lighter color. This had fallen after Ulysses had. Soon, she found a few other rocks. The inclusion ran along the surface. Hammering away the rock, she soon had her pockets full of the pure mineral.

In the sunlight, she handed Charlie a slab of the inclusion. The piece was the size and thickness of a serving of liver. The silver was dull gray in its natural state, but Charlie could see why the other man had overreached his balance. He hefted the ore. "About two or three pounds."

"More. I think I have about ten pounds in my pockets."

Charlie looked over. "I guess you don't need to find a job."

She looked across at the sun setting behind Mt. Tom. "I still have a job. I just need to figure out how to finish it."

———

As the truck reached the river road, Charlie stopped. They had both been silent as they packed up and left the mine. He knew something was on Thorny's mind but wondered if it was the same as his.

He studied the night out across the valley to the few twinkling lights not shaded by blackout curtains. "When we were in the mine…?"

"Which one?"

He paused. The tip of his tongue wetted only the center of his upper lip. "When we were in the mountain…"

"Was it the same as when I stuck my arm in the other mountain?"

"Yeah…"

"Did you ever get your spirit from the mountain?"

"In a way. I was a young boy. Grandpa took me hunting. I fell down a short waterfall, and it knocked me out. Grandpa took me to the pool. Over the three days, I had dreams, and my spirit came to me. When I woke, my hands were clenched. It was only sand, but it was the sand coming with the water. It was not a spirit fetish, it was just part of what my spirit gives." He looked out through the dusk toward the river. "I don't feel the mountain the same as you and Grandpa. I never had the golden hand.

But when I am in the Sierras, I feel the blood of the mountain, flowing in and sometimes out. There is very little blood left in the Whites."

"You feel the water?" Thorny turned on the seat. "I feel the rock, but the two mountains are not the same. The Sierras are young and still growing. The Whites... they aren't dead, but they are old. They know they are dying, so they are willing to give up the silver to Ulysses... and now me."

Charlie rolled his shoulders and cracked his neck. He was uncomfortable with talking about the things his grandfather understood and lived in but were only forced on his grandson. "So does this mean you're going to be a miner?"

Thorny bit lightly at her half smiling lower lip. "I have the feeling I don't have to. I started feeling it the day the mountain gave us the water."

Charlie only hummed as he let out the clutch and nosed the truck right toward Bishop. He wasn't sure he was comfortable with his best friend swimming in his spirit pond.

As they approached the bridge over the Owens River, Charlie stopped the truck on the bridge. He looked at the darker path in the dark of the night. Almost to himself, his words were more of introspection. "Everyone swims and fishes in this river. I've never even eaten a fish caught in it. I have been in every other water within a hundred or more miles, I even swam in Mono Lake, but I've never been in this water."

They sat silent for a while. Thorny digested what he had just told her and what he had said earlier. "Are you asking me to marry you, Frog?"

He turned his head. She could only see the dark silhouette, but she could feel his eyes on her. They had stepped out on cracking ice, and it wasn't safe or comfortable.

"Because, if you are, you better talk to your wife first."

He snickered. "She'd only lie. I think she's sweet on you."

The single red light of the truck got smaller in the dark. A sliver of silver moon peeked up over the White Mountains—turning the old snowcap to a satin bridal dress.

31 COME BACK

The man squinted around the jeweler's loupe. He turned the chunks over one by one as he hummed. "These all came from the same mine."

Thorny slouched further down in the comfortable club chair. "They all came from the same vein. Not even three feet separated them from sample to sample."

The Bakelite loupe fell from his eye socket into his right hand. He softly placed it beside the pile of silver. He fed his fingers through his thinning snow of hair as his eyes became larger while focused on the ore.

"Ulysses used to occasionally bring me vein ore like this. I always wondered why he alone brought me the vein when every other miner hauls graded ore to the stamp mill. There is a protracted process to get pure silver from the earth."

He paused and leaned forward. Taking up the large flat he weighed it in his hand.

"Spot price on 99.9 fine silver last month was thirty-eight cents a troy ounce. My guess is this is worth close to at least thirty-five. At just over fourteen troy ounces a pound, we are looking at five dollars a pound. This piece alone is thirty-two dollars."

He looked at the girl in bibbed overalls who he had watched grow into a woman.

"And all of it, Wilber?"

The wooden chair squealed as he leaned back. "With this pure, I think I can smelt it right here. I think I can go about sixty-five or seventy. How soon do you need the money?"

She shook her head as she stood. "Not for a while." She scratched at her hair and suddenly felt guilty for not taking the time to bathe before coming to town. "Look, I know you don't have much of a market here in Bishop, but what about down in the city?"

"There are always people who have money to spend. What are you asking?"

"Down in the city... they're going to want the silver in ingots, right?" He nodded. "Can you make ingots they will buy?"

He shrugged a nod. "Of course. I'm a certified assay, and so I can cast certified ingots."

"Then I'll make you a deal. I'll bring you the clean ore, you do the rest, and we'll split it straight down the middle."

His deep breath was noisy. He thought a moment. "I had a different arrangement with Ulysses."

"What was the split?"

"Sixty-forty, his favor."

She snorted softly and smiled. "He had a girl he wanted to send to college. I don't have such a burden. I'm more comfortable with a fifty-fifty split. This way we both are paid fairly for our labor and knowledge."

He stood and put out his hand. "You drive a hard bargain,

but I guess I can live with it." As they shook hands, he continued. "What about the gold?"

"What about it?"

"It's a hundred-fold the price."

"Thirty-dollars...?"

"Thirty-five last Monday. Your share on a pile this big will be over three thousand dollars."

"Did Ulysses ever bring you this much at one time?"

The man hung his head and looked at her sideways with a smirk. "Of gold... no. Of silver, there were more than a few large bags. I didn't see him for a few months one time. He walked his old mule right into the jewelry store. We unloaded her right there." He pointed next to where Thorny stood.

"How much?"

"The most he said he would ever put on a mule. It was just under ninety-four pounds. He brought the other eighty-seven pounds in the next week. The week after was your high school graduation, and he brought me seven pounds of pure nuggets. It all retorted down to pure."

Thorny stood stunned. "Even if the value was..."

He shook his head. "It all went into the account for you, another, and the schools to draw on. He didn't want a dollar of it. He said you would need all the help we could give. We expected important things from you."

She quietly looked down at her bare feet.

The jeweler stepped around his desk. His hand settled warmly on her shoulder.

"Don't ever doubt your value and the worth of what you do." She looked up in askance. "Your returning home to stay is more important to him and this town than you think. I know he thought you would stay with the big office down in the city. But

I didn't think so. I watched you grow up. I knew your grandfather, Ulysses, Harold, and Monte." He pointed at her bare feet. "I told him, one day, the city shoes would pinch, and you would remember where your feet felt at home."

She smiled shyly. "I used to go over to a tiny park at lunchtime. I didn't eat, I took off my shoes and walked on the grass. It was the only way I could clear my mind." She stood straight and drew in a long breath. "I had a case. The man had been beating his wife for years. Finally, he got into a fight at a bar which resulted in him killing a man in front of several people. When the conviction was delivered, and he was going away for the rest of his life, his wife hugged me." She looked over at the elderly jeweler. "We as a society had failed the well-being of the woman. It took the death of a young man to right the balance. I had slipped my shoes off for the reading and sentencing. They were still there when I walked into my boss's office and resigned. The shoes, the job, the city, all pinched my feet."

Wilber squinted back at his desk and the pile of silver. "Well, I don't think you need to have pinched feet anymore. I'll let you know when I have it sold. Do you have an account set up here yet?"

"Kind of, but just hold it in trust for now. We'll work it out soon." She pulled at her hair. "For now, I need a haircut."

"Say hello to Monte for me. Remind him Wednesday night is at his house this week."

She chuckled. "Sounds like Gin with a little Bourbon."

"Hah." He snapped. "It's more like Scotch with a little Gin on the side." He leaned in. "We may need a fourth."

She looked over their shoulder at the desk. "What are the stakes?"

"Steep. It's a three-eagle buy-in and penny a point."

"You do know Monte cheats at cards."

"We all do. It's why we're friends. Join us Wednesday, we'll teach you how to cheat."

"You forget who raised me."

His smile grew. "Then I look forward to losing this Wednesday."

THE HEAT WAS TEMPERED by a scattering of clouds, but the shady side of Main Street felt warm and comforting. Thorny stopped at the bookstore window. The books with little signs proclaiming them as the newest were the same books she had seen before she became a lawyer. Time moved slower in Bishop. She counted the dead flies in the window display and thought about how many young men the war had drained out of the town.

As she turned into the door of the barbershop, she looked back down Main Street for a few seconds. There weren't even four cars moving on the street. Fewer than double the number parked in the several blocks she could see. Bishop was not dying or dead, but it definitely was holding its breath.

Monte looked over his paper. The thumbed to death corner told Thorny he had almost read the paper so many times, it needed to be used as fire starter.

She pulled at her hair. Her hand contained a few stray pieces of straw. Monte laughed. "Do I get to shampoo it first?"

As she eased back in the reclined chair, Monte dropped a small envelope on her lap. "It was slid under the door this morning when I opened. I guess everyone knows how you get your mail."

The envelope simply read *Thorny*. It was not a number ten business envelope, nor was it one she would construe as personal. It was small, but carried more of a look of anonymity than intimacy.

"Are you going to open it?"

She looked up at the man. His impatience was almost humorous. "Are you going to wash my hair?"

He growled and rumbled as he turned on the water. "Let me go get the lye soap."

Thorny smiled as she smelled the juniper oil in his personal shampoo. The lye soap joke had probably been running since Cuba. She folded her hands around the letter. The letter could wait. No matter what it was could wait until after this tiny slice of heaven.

HE HELD up the hand mirror slightly behind the letter opener. Smiling, Thorny took the slender knife and slit open the envelope.

She unfolded the telegram. Monte read over her shoulder the five words and letters.

'COME. HAVE S DRIVE. R'

Thorny tossed the telegram and envelope onto the chair as she stood. She grabbed the rarely used phone and dialed.

"Danny, please. Tell him it's Thorny, and it's more important than his lunch. Thank you."

Monte glowered at her. "Saying thank you doesn't make up for being rude and not asking politely."

She glared back at him. "Next time, I'll use a large pistol and say please."

She heard the tiny 'eep' first. "Excuse me?"

Thorny rolled her eyes. "Sorry, I was having two conversations. Can you find Danny, please?"

"He's right here."

Thorny could hear the mouthpiece rub against an unshaved cheek. It wasn't like Danny. "What have you been up to?" His voice was more demanding than inquisitive.

"None of your business, but I need to find Stan Manly right away, and we need a car that will make it to Los Angeles before sundown."

"Stan is right here. We were just having lunch. You can use my Desoto. It has a long-range gas tank. You'll need to stop in Mojave. Where are you?"

"I'm at Monte's."

"I'll have the kitchen pack a basket when they fuel the car. Stan needs a fresh shirt."

"What's wrong with the one he has on now?"

"There's blood on it."

"Do I need to drive?"

She could hear Danny looking elsewhere. "Probably would be for the better. I still want to know what you've been up to when you get back."

"You can buy me dinner."

"Is that a date?"

"Keep dreaming, big guy. Hurry with Stan and the car."

Twenty minutes later, the car pulled to the curb facing the wrong way. Danny stepped out of the driver's door. As Thorny came out, she could see Stan lying in the backseat.

"He caught a bullet from a long-range rifle. It's a through-

and-through, so I cleaned it and sewed him up. It's just under his right armpit. He slipped and was falling to one side, or it would have been through the heart. He got lucky. Better if you drive. I gave him a couple of these."

The bottle was small, dark, and without a label. She held it up to the light.

Danny covered her hand with his. "It's morphine. No more than two every four hours. He needs a hospital. Make sure the feds shackle him to the bed."

Her one eyebrow cocked above her dark glasses. "I'm taking him to see his wife."

"That should work. On the macadam, you should be good for fifty or sixty. Once you hit pavement, she'll run at eighty all day long."

She slid into the car. "Thanks, Danny. I'll try not to scratch the paint." She closed the door and put the car in gear. She looked back at the sleeping man. Turning back to Danny, she thought a moment. "Where was he?"

"We were up at the drill site. Someone had been trying to dig up the pipe."

Her lips curled in tight against her teeth. She adjusted the rearview mirror. "Thanks."

The car pulled away.

Danny turned as he plucked at his hair. Monte had a half smile on his face.

Danny slumped. "Yeah, and I need a shave too."

32 HEADING SOUTH

Two hours later, the hard-packed oiled macadam finally turned to the narrow ribbon of asphalt Los Angeles had forced the state of California to lay across some of the worst deserts within the state. The smoothness wasn't much difference, but as Thorny pushed the powerful engine, she could tell the grip was better.

As she pushed the car past seventy-five, the extra wind through the wind-wing helped keep the car cooler. She glanced back at the man, either sleeping or passed out, in the backseat. She had stopped in Olancha. The old pony expressway station had all but tumbled down, but the large cottonwood trees, planted by the original station master, provided deep shade. Thorny was able to get Stan to take another morphine as well as more water. She knew the pain was bad, but dehydration would turn you into a puffball of dried skin and crushed bones.

She stopped at the Manzanar internment camp on the off chance of getting a medic to check his bandages. One of the wraps was showing the dark blot of a leak. The doctor thought it was natural for the wound to leak but changed the wrap anyway. Stan's FBI identification had waylaid any questions. But word got out, and two of his friends came by to say hello. Sullivan and Hughes both agreed on where to take him in Los Angeles, and the one said he would call ahead. Thorny knew where Angeles Hospital was.

She ate half a sandwich, but Stan choked on the second small bite. She let him lay back down and just sleep. There would be time enough for food later.

The desert wound down the valley. Around Long Lake, the highway turned to a snake of dips, turns, and humps. Cresting the last rise, Thorny spotted a dot of a car just entering the snake pit. She guessed about five miles behind her. As the valley opened out onto the desert floor, she could see the smudge of the ore refinery at Mojave, fifty-eight miles away.

She eased her foot down.

The long sweeping left turn was a branch in the highway. Take the branch to the right, and the asphalt stopped. The macadam ran the sixty miles up to the dam at Kernville. Continue driving on the asphalt highway, and in forty more miles, the small town of Mojave rose squalid from the dust and grime of the fourth deadliest desert in the United States. The twenty-mule team of the Borax company had crossed the valley floor of Death Valley, but the Mojave Desert had been their death.

Thorny glanced back at the unmoving Stan. She hoped the sound was his snoring, not just the large engine vibrating through the floorboards.

In the rearview mirror, the dot had become the shape of a dark car. Even with Thorny holding the heavy car at a steady eighty, the dark car had closed the nine-mile gap in less than forty-five miles. She glanced back at Stan. The man had no touch with the world. She was on her own.

Her right hand reached for the seat beside her. She raised the pistol and thumbed the clip release. She jammed the nose of the gun into her lap and grabbed the clip. Through the slots in the side, she could see she had only four or five bullets left. She jammed the clip back into the handle of the pistol until she could hear the metallic click.

Looking in the side mirror was enough to solidify her plan. The car was close enough to tell it was a Chevrolet Master Deluxe or Supreme. If it hadn't been for her work in Los Angeles, it could have been a black car. The Deluxe and Supreme were the cars of choice for those who made their living with a gun. Black or black were the two standard choices.

She eased her foot off the gas and let the car coast down to a stop at the edge of the road. As the other car pulled up behind, she watched the two doors start to open. She jumped the car ahead, but only a few feet as the front turned toward the centerline. She threw the transmission in neutral and pulled on the parking brake. Her door was already opening.

Her feet hit the asphalt as the forty-five automatic came up from her side. She didn't wait for the driver to finish coming around his door. She knew the passenger was already creeping along the front of the car. She aimed high and low with two shots through the radiator. The nose of the car erupted in steam as the hot water hit the hotter metal of the hard-pushed engine. There was a high-pitched metallic bang. Thorny hoped it meant the engine had just cracked.

She held the pistol level on the chest of the driver. "Passenger. Come up slow with your gun held by the barrel or your friend gets the next two holes."

The driver's voice stumbled. "Miss Wallace…"

"Mister, you need to grab a whole bunch of silence before your friend gets you killed."

The driver's hands rose. "Hank… do what she says."

Thorny watched as the hand rose with a revolver. The rest of the man followed.

"Don't take a big wind up, but throw it out into the desert. I want you to find it, but not for a while." She nodded the automatic at the driver. "You too."

She watched as the man slowly drew the pistol out of the shoulder holster. His grip was with only his thumb and middle finger. She wiggled her pistol at the desert on the other side of the road. "Come on, you can spend the next few hours cleaning it after I'm gone."

The passenger shoved his chin up to one side. "You are Elizabeth Wallace, are you not?"

She glanced over at him. "Hank, if you don't grab a whole bushel of shut up, you're going to get your friend killed. Now, Hank, I want you to come around and stand by your friend."

The shorter man came around the front of the car. As they lined up, she waved the gun for the driver to close the door.

"Now, I want you to know… I was raised with a gun in my hand. I can still take the head off a dove in flight across a ten-acre field. So I want you two to lay down on the road. If I see either of you move in the next ten minutes, I will be forced to trade my sidearm for my carbine with a scope. At one mile, that bird is still dead. Do you understand me?"

They both nodded and then rested their foreheads on the

hot asphalt. She was sure they would have a few blisters to remind them of who they had tried to deal with. She didn't smile until the last rise, and she saw their forms still as shadows next to their now dead car.

"Who were they?" The voice was groggy and weak.

She glanced back. The man had drawn himself up halfway as he leaned against the door. His usual tan was all but gone. She pushed harder on the gas pedal.

"I didn't ask. They knew my name. I didn't think we had time for any niceties like tea and exchanging love letters. How are you doing?"

"I need another pill. But I also need to go to the bathroom."

"Number one or two?"

She eased to the side of the road. Glancing at the mirror, she set the brake. In the desert, you don't turn your motor off. It might not start again.

She pulled him out, and they stood by the side of the car. His complaint was barely above a whisper and held no energy. "I can lean against the car. You don't have to hold me."

"What? And have you urinate all over your pants and then get back in the car on the fine upholstery? Danny would skin both of us alive to make new upholstery."

"I can do this."

She sighed and grabbed hold of his arm tighter. "Just get on with it. A man pissing or defecating or heaving his drunken guts. I've seen it all, and I've seen worse," she lied, but she looked out across the desert. She thought about how worldly in few things she truly was.

As the sound of water hitting the hard sand stopped, she could feel him sag. Not caring if he was buttoned up or not, she manhandled him back into the car. Grabbing the bottle, she fished out a pill and opened the canteen. She helped him drink as she thought about the race to Angeles Hospital. Even at high speed, it was still another three hours away.

If nothing else happened...

33 BRIEF

The woman stood in front of her. Thorny knew she should know who she was. The leather and wool jacket over the khaki slacks and low heels didn't fit the image of anyone she knew.

She looked up at the face of the brunette, the hair pulled back tight in a no-nonsense bun. The whole look was military, and yet not.

The woman quietly sat on the couch next to Thorny. She took in the bandage on Thorny's forehead and the arm in a sling. The hazel eyes stared glazed but lifeless. Her face was as if she hadn't slept for days. Ruth was certain it was not the case, but more because of Thorny hitting her head.

"You were in a car crash."

Thorny looked at the woman. Somehow, she felt she could trust her, but recent habits dictated otherwise. She nodded.

"Do you remember the crash?"

Thorny tried, but the cars and cliff or was it the ocean… The swimming motion of everything tumbling made her…

"Excuse me." She lurched to her feet and made it as far as

splaying out across the hospital linoleum. Her stomach heaved and the vomit leaked from her mouth. There was little left from the last six hours.

"Nurse. We need help here." And there was a soft hand on her shoulder... and then there was blackness.

THE WHITE OF the walls and ceiling meant nothing to Thorny. The rails on the bed and the green of the hallway told her everything. She thought about what hospital and what it could mean. Finally, she closed her eyes. Just the thinking of possibilities was making her tired, and she wasn't focusing. She rolled over onto her right side toward the window.

"It's good to see you're finally waking up. You gave us quite the scare."

Thorny squinted. A woman with dark hair sat in the lounge chair. The bright light of the window flared Thorny's vision, and she couldn't make out much else. She tried to talk, but her mouth was dry and only croaked. The woman stood and poured water from the pitcher. She held the glass so Thorny could drink.

"Do you remember anything?"

Thorny rolled over on her back. "There was a wreck."

"Do you remember anything about it?"

"No..." She squinted her face as she rolled her head. Something was there... "Maybe..." It washed away in a hiss of static in her mind. "No."

The woman's hand rested on her arm. "The wreck was six days ago. You saved my husband's life."

Thorny took a breath through her nose. "Stan..." There was something else, but it was just out of reach. She coughed softly.

"Yes, Stan Manly. He was shot. You told the Highway Patrol he had fallen on rebar at a construction site, and you were taking him to Angeles Memorial. They brought him and you here by ambulance instead of to the clinic in Lancaster. They found your identification card for the District Attorney's office."

Thorny struggled and frowned. She looked out of her slit for a right eye. "You're Ruth."

The woman smiled. She patted Thorny's arm. "Bingo. Now get some sleep. Stan is down the hall, and we'll try again tomorrow."

THE MAN SAT in the sunshine. The light through the window turned his head of white hair to an aura. The three-piece suit was silk and wool, perfectly hand sewn. He raised his right foot and twisted the shoe, making a mental note to stop for a shine. The stockings were almost shear.

Thorny rolled over in her sleep. The man looked up and ran the side of his index finger along his pencil-thin mustache. Hiding in the thin line, there were still a few blond hairs that would match his son's hair.

The man cleared his throat, and Thorny's exposed eye came half open. She thought for a few minutes. The man had always dressed exactly right. It was only for special occasions she had ever seen him in a suit. The last time was at graduation. He had purposely congratulated and shaken Charlie's, hers, and his son's hands. At the time, she had thought it was strangely formal for Bishop, but now she realized how formal the man was.

She groaned. "Mr. Rambino."

He stood, checking the center button on his suit. "Hello, Miss Wallace. I would ask you how you are, but the doctors have already done me the courtesy. However, how are you feeling?"

She tried to pull her arm under her to rise. He could see the strain. He held his hand out.

"Please, just you being awake is enough. There is no ceremony here.

Her smile was soft but weak. "Except you are all dressed up."

He chuckled. "I'll make a note to wear my dungarees next time to make you more comfortable." He caught himself and smiled. "Or was it bibbed overalls you preferred?"

Her eyes rolled as the smile filled her face. "I truly miss those days."

"Danial tells me you still walk miles and miles—still barefoot." He chuckled. "I think he's fond of that side of you. You were always a good friend to my son when he had no others."

"It was a tough time to grow up, but even more so to be the son of the richest man in the county. The business didn't make it any easier."

The man winced at the scrutiny. "Sometimes, when we make our choices, we don't think of long-term or of how it will affect a family."

She reached her hand out and covered his on the rail. "Your son proved to be bigger than the trials. He turned out to be a fine man, and one I value highly as a friend. Rest assured you can be proud."

His voice softened with warm. "Thank you. It means a lot—coming from you especially. He tells me you have done proudly, as well. Your grandfather should be very proud of you."

She squeezed his hand gently. He may occasionally talk with his son, but not about the valley that he'd left. "Eustis passed away about four years ago, but I'm sure he is watching over me somehow."

"I'm sorry. I didn't know. Do you have other family?"

"Other than your son, Charlie, and Monte…not really."

The man smiled and arched his back as he chuckled. "Charlie… I was trying to remember his name. I understand he is now the chief of the reservation. How is he doing?"

"I think the passing of his grandfather hit him a little harder than he lets on, but he's doing okay. He's the hydrographer for the county, and he delivers fuel to make ends meet. But in the end, I think he's happy. I think he would have done a better job at driving the car."

The man pinched his lips between his thumb and knuckle of his finger. "Hmm, how much do you remember?"

She studied his face. His eyes were clear. There was no duplicity or hidden motive in his question. "There was a second car. They caused the crash trying to drive us off the road."

His eyes narrowed. "Your passenger was the FBI friend. Danial told me about the sniper. But the crash wasn't the end of it…"

Thorny wasn't sure she was confirming what the man knew or filling in blanks. "One of them survived and tried to kill us. I shot him with my last bullet, and then I think I passed out."

The gray mustache rolled into the lower lip as the man quietly nodded. "Your FBI man put three more into the other man." He put his hand on hers. "I've been assured the report will reflect a blown tire at high speed to be the cause of the single-car accident. Anything else—we're looking into… quietly."

"It was Danny's car…"

The man's smile pursed and drew back to one side. "Yes, well, the previous history of the car was wiped clean by the resulting fire. I'm sure we can see our way clear to find him a newer car."

"History?"

The man tossed his head with a shrug of his eyebrows. "There was an extra forty-gallon copper tank secreted in the underframe. We have no need for those cars anymore. However, Danial mentioned you might need a car yourself. What kind did you have in mind?"

She leaned back into the pillow with a smile. "Why, Mr. Rambino, are you suggesting a bribe to an officer of the court?"

He smiled and chuckled. His eyes twinkled like his son's. "Maybe we could just call it a belated graduation gift. After all, we can't have a lawyer walking barefoot everywhere."

Her eyes slid shut as she rolled her head back and forth. "Just take care of Danny. I'm fine for now, and barefoot suits my job."

His face cleared and he became serious. "Just so you can rest better, what the FBI doesn't cover with all this, the Rambino Corporation has asked for all bills to be sent to them. We want you to get well and finish the work you're doing."

"You don't… I mean…"

"Shh…" He leaned in. His hand rested on hers. "Danial insisted. I was given no choice. Rest and when they let you out, give me a call. I would love to take you to the Brown Derby or Mousso and Frank's for dinner."

Her eyes searched for an answer before looking up. "It would be my first date. I think I'd like that."

"Well, for such an auspicious occasion, maybe I'll have to

change it to the Hotel Bel Aire and their amazing Lobster Thermidor."

She smirked. "Do they allow bibbed overalls?"

He twinkled at their shared joke. "Maybe if they were out of black satin, you might just get away with it." He patted her hand as he turned. "Rest, my dear. You have an important date to be well for."

She smiled as she rolled over. She was asleep before the pillow was fully adjusted.

THEY SAT IN THE ATRIUM. The stars weren't obvious through the glass overhead, but the night was clear. The small light from the hall showed a pool of illumination on the documents. Ruth pushed and turned papers as she explained the research she and others had done.

Thorny held her hand on one paper and pointed at another. "So the Abbotsford here is not the Abbotsford who is Debra Hudgins's uncle through her mother."

"No, her uncle is Reginald. Reggie and Debbie's mother are the children of Edger Abbotsford. Edger was Mulholland's friend who ran a shady string of small banks. When land was cheap, they bought up a lot of it in Los Angeles, and then through shell companies, sold the land during the land rush they all created with the help of Hollywood."

"How did the movie companies…?"

Ruth spread her hands across all the papers. "Okay, first, stop thinking about the city or the industry. Shortly before the turn of the century, there was a snake named Theodore Holly-wood. He came out and bought land on the lower slope of the hill overlooking Los Angeles. He rented much of the flatter land to some people with the idea called movies. The stages were little more than a row of small tent sets built on a long platform. Several short movies, about a minute or two long, and filmed side by side. Usually, there wasn't even a writer. The director would think up a skit, the actors would ham it up, and that was that. But, soon, they found cheaper land to buy, and the moviemaking moved over the mountain to Toluca Lake and Burbank. Soon, there were large studios with stages and lights they could control. Filming didn't have to be only on sunny days."

Ruth pointed to one of the documents, and then she continued. "The area was already known by the landlord's name. With the last funds he hadn't squandered, he turned to developing the land. He hired some carpenters to put up a huge sign he hoped people could see from the trains bringing new suckers to buy his land. He couldn't afford a solid sign, so he contracted for seventeen letters standing forty-four-feet tall. One thing led to another, and he couldn't pay for the lumber. He drifted into obscurity, but not before his idea caught the attention of none other than Harry Chandler, the publisher of the Los Angeles Times. The paper was doing an article on Hollywood's contribution to Los Angeles becoming famous for its movies and glamor. By 1923, he had built the sign and was hip deep in Hollywoodland."

"So where did Edger Abbotsford come in?"

"His banks were the only place you could get a loan for some of the new houses being slapped together to house the new Hollywood, but these weren't the houses you think of in Hollywood and Los Feliz. His loans were made on the shacks the workers bought. They had almost nothing to put down, so he charged huge interest on the loan. When the weather turned cold and ugly, the construction they depended on to make the payments stopped. Mann banks had a small army of thugs to throw you and your family out on the street, clean up the shack, and resell it."

Thorny smiled. "I wonder if that is where the movies got the idea?"

"Undoubtedly. However, it didn't take long before the government caught wind of the strong-arm tactics and put a stop to it—not before Edger had hitched his wagon to Mulholland's team, though."

Thorny sat back into the deeper dark. "But his son Reginald is still in the business."

"We have a clear indication, but no documentable proof that he is the strong arm of the business. Or, at least, he is a major part of the nastier end of it all."

Thorny closed her eyes as she softly scratched at her hair. "And it's Debbie's mother who was an Abbotsford, not her father."

"Correct. Debbie's father was Harold Hudgins older brother, Donald. In his youth, he was a firebrand traveling evangelist—a real con artist. He left a trail of fleeced widows and many wives. Some he left before the nuptials were dry in the sheets—one step ahead of the law. His ministering to the flocks before the fleecing were legendary. His stuff put Aimee Semple McPherson in the back row with the paupers. We're talking the full-blown tent show with witnesses, snake handlers, a woman who talked in tongues, healing cripples, and raising one man from the dead with his Holy Scripture elixir."

Thorny laughed. "From the dead?"

Ruth shuffled through a small pile of papers. "Hold on, I

have it… right here." She ran her finger down the page. "One Dardanelle Dietrich. He seemed to have a nasty habit of dying at the peak of a tent meeting. Every new town was another new death."

Thorny moaned. "Lucky for him, the tent had a full supply of restorative elixir."

Ruth pointed at the one line. "Blessed by the Pope and nine of the only living saints."

"So, he gets to the Owens Valley and settles down?"

"It's more like he ran from the law across ten states and went into hiding."

Thorny squinted one eye. "By using his real name?"

Ruth laughed with her rejoinder. "Nine living saints?"

"Point taken." She looked sideways at Ruth. "We've covered Debbie's parents… what about uncle Reggie?"

Ruth shuffled through the stack of files and found the slim folder she was looking for. Opening it, she found the notation she was looking for. She pointed it out to Thorny.

Thorny's eyes opened wide as she looked up. "Holy tornadoes. His longest kill was over a mile away. How do you even see a person a mile away?"

"The snipers use different telescopes mounted on a rifle these days. My uncle used to talk about some snipers back in the mid-eighteen-hundreds. They called them Regulators. Their only telescope was a long tube. They could adjust the tube to account for distance and windage. He said he had heard of a Regulator who took the head off an Indian scout from almost two miles. The man was using a muzzle-loaded Sharp's seventy-caliber with a four-foot barrel."

"Do they know what went through Stan?"

Ruth's mouth pulled flat and hard. "There is a rifle the

government is looking at. It's a fifty caliber with an extra-long barrel. Because of the length—the whole rifle breaks down into its parts and fits in a small case. It's an experimental model, but there are rumors it was tried out in Africa by a big game hunter."

Thorny's face sagged into anger. Raising animals for food was one thing, but hunting for just the sport was a different area. "Do we know the hunter's name?"

The brunette nodded with a confirming glare. "Abbotsford."

Thorny chewed on the words she wanted to say.

Ruth started straightening the files and then peeked at her watch. It was getting late.

Thorny turned her wheelchair. "Here, I'll do that. I'll take them back to my room. I want to read a few of the details again about the landholding. You go see Stan until they throw you out, and then stop by to pick them up."

Ruth stood with a soft squeeze on Thorny's shoulder. "Thanks, you're a champ. The nurses don't throw me out. It's Stanley. When he falls asleep, his mouth falls open, and his snoring sounds more like a death rattle."

"What do you do at home?"

Ruth leaned over with her one eye cocked in conspiratorial fun. "He has a choice. Sleep on his side or sleep on the couch."

Thorny snickered at her friend. "The couch must be well broken in."

"After the war, we're getting a new couch. Even the dog sleeps in with me now."

"My close friend in Bishop... his wife sleeps with him. She's a Malamute husky."

"A large dog?"

Thorny chuckled as she held her hand out to the height of a small pony. "She's big enough to push anybody out of bed."

Ruth shook her head. "I think we'll stick with our little schnauzer."

Thorny smiled at the thought of the FBI agent and a small dog. "Go tuck Stan in. I'll see you in a bit."

34 ALLIANCES

T horny stood looking in the small closet. The clothes she expected were not there. A black cloth garment bag hung thickly from the rod. A shoe box sat on the floor. Thorny had never seen a shoe box like it before. Even shoes from J.W. Robinson came in pasteboard with labels printed or affixed. This box was covered with black satin. The ribbon was a soft crepe silk.

She stooped and picked up the box. Carrying it to the bed, she untied the bow and opened it to find a pair of sensible low heels. The leather was fine, but not patent. The polish glowed instead of shined. She could have worn these to work at the District Attorney's office.

The fit was perfect, and they were as soft as a five-year-old pair. She walked around. She stood, holding the hospital gown back.

Her mind went back to her first day at court. Her shoes had been sensible lace-up shoes. She had walked many miles across UCLA both as an underclassman and as a law student. She could apply polish and read, and then lean over and read as she buffed the shoes to a shine. It was her senior year when she saw another woman wearing the shoes. The woman was in her seventies and visiting her granddaughter.

"A blue would have been a nicer match to the gown."

Thorny looked up. The nurse stood with her folded clothes and boots.

The nurse smiled. "Those were delivered while you were down at physical therapy. I took the liberty to have these cleaned. Sometimes blood can be hard to get out."

Stan wheeled up in a chair behind the nurse. "I heard your plea bargain for an early release came through."

The nurse flinched but moved around Thorny to put the clothes down on the bed.

"What are you talking about? Nobody has released me."

The nurse turned. "Not so much of a release as being let out for a short trial. Obviously, you have a date." The woman turned red and started past.

Thorny grabbed her arm. "Excuse me?"

The young woman's eyes looked down and slid toward Stan. Her chin buried in her shoulder and her voice hushed. "Evidently, you are being let out at four to attend a function or something." The big sister in her took over. She plucked at Thorny's hair. "We have just enough time to get you showered and your hair done. I think I can find some makeup arou—"

"I don't wear makeup."

The woman leaned in with a soft wink. "Better yet. Neither does Kate Hepburn."

Thorny turned on Stan. "You knew about this?"

The man shrugged. "I've heard rumors."

"And the function is…?"

He looked down the hall and wheeled into the room. "Do you want me to ruin all the surprise or just some of it?"

She leveled her right eye at him. "Someone should put a bullet through you."

His quick smirk was buoyed by a soft snort. "It's been tried. You are being picked up by Danny's father, but dinner will also be with your old boss, among others."

"Oh, great. The District Attorney and a mobster. Where are we going?"

"I heard you already knew."

"If I knew, I don't think I'd be asking—" She turned to find the nurse drawing the clothes out of the hanging garment bag.

At the sight of the white silk blouse, the nurse let out a small mew. But the black bridal satin bibbed overalls took her breath away. Thorny was just as impressed. Even Stan took a small sharp breath in.

The nurse turned with the short velvet jacket in one hand and the overalls in the other. "Where do you wear something like this?"

Thorny smiled and responded with a breathy movie star voice. "Why, the Hotel Bel Aire for Lobster, my dear. I'm sure it will be all the rage."

Thorny drew back the privacy curtain and stood to look in the mirror. The woman looking back only distantly resembled the famous aviatrix. The hair and face were the same, but the whole appearance changed everything.

"Wow."

Thorny turned to see Stan sitting in the doorway. Down the hall, the familiar voice of the young nurse sounded out of breath. "Wait, I want to see." She slid to a stop at the wheelchair as her head turned. Her mouth was a round exclamation. A tiny 'oh my' escaped.

Thorny felt uncomfortable. She had never been the center of scrutiny, except in court. "It's okay?"

"Oh, honey, it looks like a million bucks."

Stan slowly rolled in. "At least a couple of thousand." He handed her an unmarked envelope.

Thorny frowned. "What's this?" Her finger slid open the flap, and she drew out a check.

Stan's face was stone. "It's the first payment for the water. Next month, they will begin to harvest. By Thanksgiving, they'll know if it all works. You can get used to those clothes."

There was a soft knock at the door.

They turned to find Mr. Rambino standing next to Mr. Rambino. Both were in tuxedos.

"Danny. Mr. Rambino. Please come in."

Danny took the lead. "Hello, Stan. Good to see you're up and about."

"I wouldn't miss this for the world." His hand leveled up and down in Thorny's direction.

Danny's lips rolled as his eyes twinkled. "Like a freshly born colt. You look marvelous, Thorny." He slipped around behind her and opened a slim box. As he gently pulled the pearls around her throat, his father cleared his.

"Those were my Katherine's favorite string. I haven't given up hope on Danial needing them for a wife... but I think we have found the right home for them."

Thorny's fingers found the cool line of delicate orbs. She sensed by the intense stare the memories of his wife were all the man could see. Danny's hands on her shoulders gave a soft lingering squeeze.

She swallowed. "I'd be honored."

THE EVENING HAD STARTED with a leisurely stroll through the extensive gardens. Thorny thought about the morning paper and how, if she hadn't seen the news, she could imagine the war wasn't real. At a certain point in the social structure, not even war had a visible effect.

The lobster was as good as promised. Danny laughed at how they had to explain what a lobster tasted like. Thorny hadn't even tasted a shrimp. Danny remembered a few times of them riding horses out to a spring in the desert named Fish Slough. They had chased and caught a dozen of the crawdads and then roasted them over a small fire.

As the older men about the table laughed at the younger one's childhood memories, the District Attorney waved the waiter over and quietly asked for shrimp cocktails. Thorny's response to her first bite was to backhand Danny's arm.

He grabbed his arm and looked in horror at being so accosted.

"You never told me those crawdads were supposed to taste this good."

Stan's boss, Special Agent in Charge, Terrance J. Taylor, assured her no matter how you prepared crayfish or crawdads, they could never taste as good as shrimp. The man continued with stories of his growing up in the mud where the bayou met Lake Ponchartrain, just north of New Orleans. He held his right hand aloft as he swore there were over one hundred and seventy-eight ways to cook bayou shrimp and crabs which did not involve direct fire at a desert oasis.

The waiter cleared away the desert, carefully scraped any crumbs from the brilliant white tablecloth, and laid out preparations for after-dinner drinks. Thorny sat back with her eyes sparkling from the low candles on the table.

Her voice was low. "When I was eleven, one of the goats threw a kid. The goat was mostly brown with white speckles. Where most goats had a black nose, hers was pink. Even from the first few days, she had a way of bouncing around in the yard. She didn't walk, she bounced around like she had four pogo sticks for legs. We laughed just to watch her. I don't know why, but I insisted on naming her Pixie. The one and foremost rule of farms and ranches is to never name an animal."

Danny reached over and rested his hand on her claw. The men were quiet as the drinks were served, each with their own understanding and feelings.

Mr. Rambino softly cleared his throat and lifted his small fluted glass. "What shall we drink to?"

Danny squeezed Thorny's claw. "I think the only woman here should do the honors."

Thorny rolled her head to her friend and mouthed the words 'thank you.' Raising her glass, she continued. "Gentlemen, here is to the fatted goat... who got away because she was pregnant with twins."

The men started and then chuckled with a 'hear, hear' and sipped their drinks.

"So you didn't eat her?"

Thorny shook her head. "Not yet. She's too old to kid, but she calms the horses when they are foaling. She is every bit a part of our ranch as the tractor. In fact, I would bet she's curled up in my bed right now... wondering when I'll be home."

The senior Rambino was delicately aghast. "You sleep with a goat?"

"Well, she snores less than most horses, and some men—I've been told." She glanced at Danny. Only his neck above the collar was red.

The senior FBI agent leaned back with his fingers steepled. "I don't think the story of your memory was about revealing your bedroom arrangements."

Thorny leaned her mouth into her propped hand. Her eyes studied the man. Mentally, none were left behind at this table. Mr. Rambino had survived decades of scrutiny by law enforcement at all levels as he built an empire. His son continued to create his own, as he danced between reputation, history, the senior's shadow, and his own vision of a more legal empire. The agent, she studied, didn't rise from the swamps of a southern state to the highest rank in law enforcement by being a fool.

"No, this isn't about Pixie." She sipped at her water and taking her time dabbing at her mouth. This was her time. This was her opening argument, and her court was in session.

"We fed Pixie and all the other animals on the ranch. You feed them to be healthy and grow. You also feed them to get as much muscle and fat on them before you slaughter them. Hence, the term the fatted calf."

"And you feel we brought you here tonight to fatten you up?"

Her eyes slid over to Mr. Rambino. "The thought crossed my mind. But then, the players were all wrong for the butchering. Not that I would ever think such gruesome acts ever went on with your people, but what I can't figure out is you and Mr. Taylor."

The agent leaned forward as he leveled out his hand to the other's arm. "Let me stop you right there for just a moment, please." Indicating the table, he circled it with his palm up. "I think I can speak for all of us tonight when I say we enjoyed an extremely pleasant dinner. In the south, we call this breaking bread. Once you have broken bread with another, you are friends. So, please, you have allowed us to refer to you by your nickname, at least would you do us the honor by using our given names."

He looked toward the older Rambino, who nodded.

"Thorny, I have known you since you sent Danial home with a bloody nose. Not once did you ever insist on being called Miss Wallace, but I don't think this is about names."

Thorny leaned forward. "No, no it's not... Is it Mike or Michael?"

The man smiled. "Mike works for me, Thorny, but you're way past Terrance so go straight for Tony or Tornado. He boxed in the Army and was a two-time Golden Gloves. I lost some money the first time, but made a lot more the second time."

"So, you two go back a long time?"

Tony chuckled. "Long enough for our friendship to not get in the way of our work, or vice versa. In fact, we go back so far, Mikey doesn't remember the third Golden Gloves championship—but my boxing isn't your question."

"No, but it answered much of it, Tony." She turned to the one person who had been quiet through the whole meal. "Paul, you haven't said more than ten words all-night."

Her old boss held his hands up, palms out. "My job tonight was to make sure there wasn't a mugging." He pointed at the two smiling men. "This is their show. I'm only along to enjoy the ride... so to speak."

She only marginally accepted his words, and her eyes stayed

on him as her head ground toward the other. "So where is this little sleigh ride going, Mike?"

"Danny here, and Stan have been reporting on certain… um… arrangements in Bishop which are about to come to an end. With what we know, and what we suspect, there are about to be a few jobs available. Danny said you were talking about needing a job… and well… we thought we would like your take on the positions, Thorny."

"So this has been a job interview?" She flapped the velvet jacket over the silk blouse and satin overalls. "Because, from where I'm sitting, it feels more like a bribe or a payoff."

Tony held up his index finger, but Paul answered. "That's what Tony and I are here for. To keep it all on the up and up."

"So what is it you are asking?"

Tony adjusted in his seat. "When it comes to the valley, our interests align. We have watched the corrupt control for far too long. What we would like to know is your gut. How far do you think this will all go?"

Thorny noted the heads bobbing in unison. What was being presented was what was there. She thought and then recapped the last few months. "We know about Reseda and Abbotsford. Beyond them is only conjecture. I'm not sure once we lock up Reseda, the mayor doesn't decide he needs to go be with his family back east. Beyond there, I'm not sure."

Danny lay the back of his hand on her arm. "What about Abbotsford's niece?"

Her head ground back and forth. "Tough one there. There is an argument for acquiescing, but complicity is another state of conditions."

"What about the land records?"

She looked at the head of the FBI, and her lips rolled into a grimace. "Nothing showed up that we could call hard evidence without a confession. My gut is Debbie is just what she appears —a mother and a niece. Nothing more."

LATER, both wheelchairs sat under the glass roof. The black of night was tempered only by the sliver of a new moon.

"Must have felt strange." Stan's head rolled back and then in circles. The bones cracking sounded like sand on a tin roof. "Strange enough, just having Danny's father and my boss in the same room... but actually talking...? Not only talking but old friends. Then there was my boss, who has a reputation for dominating conversations. I almost wanted to go over and check for a pulse during dinner."

"Ah, yes, dinner. How was the lobster?"

"I think I need more. I can tell you, the crawdads out at Fish Slough aren't even in the same universe as this. I wanted the recipe just for the sauce."

He chuckled. "I'll nose around to see if it's a national secret. Maybe if I take Ruth out there, she can get them to talk."

"I want to go along just to hold them down or something."

"The lobster or the chef for the recipe?"

Thorny laughed. "Yes."

A mule's lips are sensitive. They can tell if a person feeding them apples is cheating by taking a bite out of the back side. The tastier side without the worm. Heather took the apple and then pushed her shoulder against the man.

Pete laughed at the mule from the grass. While Stan and Thorny were in Los Angeles, he had taken to gleaning all the fruits or vegetables he could find. His afternoons were in quiet contemplation as he bribed the jenny for company.

Laying back, he shaded his eyes with his hat. "I know. I miss her too."

"She's cuter than you too."

Pete sat up and looked toward the river. The deep voice could only come from one man.

"River's too cold. It makes my feet ache. Southern California Edison is dumping water before the winter. The extra water comes from up high and is near freezing. But the trout like it. It cools the river during the hottest months."

Peter turned around. The big Indian was sitting on the log.

"A few minutes ago. Just before she knocked you on your

ass." Charlie answered the man's question before he could ask it. He was getting good at his grandfather's old game. He tossed a couple of large carrots in front of Heather. She took a step and nibbled at the greens. The orange tubers sucked into her nibbling lips. "Thorny will be home on tomorrow's bus. Stan has to stay put for a few more weeks before his wife will let him come back up for more ventilation."

The deputy reclined in the sun. His composure said relaxed, but Charlie could tell by the movement on the eyelids, it was more of looking at the blackboard of items undone. Both worried about the shooting. A pistol or a deer rifle were common tools used in the valley, but what had punctured a hole in Stan was anything but common. Someone was getting extremely serious about the water. Serious enough to try killing a federal agent.

"Did she say anything about the shooting?"

"Pretty much what we already knew, except some additional information confirming the long-range theory. Mr. Clark Gable is definitely our man."

Pete rolled over and pushed his hat back.

Charlie bumped his chin out. "Do you know what a sniper is?"

"The bird is a snipe, but a sniper is a person trained to make long distant shoots with a rifle."

"Confirmed at over a mile, and suspected to have made shots close to two miles."

Pete thought about where Stan was shot. "If you continue up the road toward the Bishop Creek dams and lakes, there's a hump just past the switchback. When the water was still blowing, I hiked up there with binoculars. It would be a straight shot, but it's at least two miles."

Charlie raised his hand to look west into the afternoon. There was plenty of time. He looked down at the other man. "Lovely day for a hike."

Pete dusted off his pants. "Where'd you park?"

"Truck is still up at the mine. We'll take yours."

The sun was on their backs and left shoulders. The hill was an effortless walk up from the flat expanse they were sure had been the shooters parking spot. They had stopped for an extra pair of binoculars. Both braced their elbows on their thighs as they sat on the sand.

"It's downhill," Charlie noted. "I've missed some kill shots shooting downhill."

"Danny said they had just turned to look across at Chalk Bluffs to the northeast..."

Charlie lowered his binoculars and scanned the sandy saddle of the low hills, almost two miles away. "If he was aiming for a headshot at this distance, he was either god good or overconfident. I think he was going for an upper body mass shot with the hope of tearing the holy hell out of everything important. The sudden turn and a lower hit might be from the colder air falling down Horton Creek canyon. Unless he had hiked around Buttermilk a lot, he couldn't know about the steady two or three miles-per-hour wind."

The man stood and looked around at the low sage.

"What do you see, Charlie?"

The large man mussed to himself as much as the deputy. "It's all wrong. This isn't where he was."

"What do you mean?"

"The brush. It would be in his way."

Pete stood and looked at what Charlie meant. The brush was only a foot high.

Charlie thought about what he would look for in a perch for deer or elk. He deftly moved along the ridgeline, looking down the gentle slope. He stopped and looked out at the saddle where Stan had been shot. "Here." He moved down the slope.

The small dished-out area was a drop of under two feet. Two small bushes lay pulled out of the soft sand and thrown aside. There was a small mound of sandy dirt. The scrape marks were still obvious. Until the winter rain and winds, nothing changes in the desert.

Charlie pointed along the line. "He laid a blanket down. He's left-handed. See how the depression is running downhill to the right."

"It looks like he placed the rifle twice..."

Charlie smiled. "The second line of depression is for his telescope. I do the same thing. You use a powerful telescope to make sure of what you are shooting. Check the target for any other hunters. Then, when it is all good... you take your shot."

Pete narrowed his eyes at the other man. "You were a sniper?"

Charlie snorted. "My great-uncle was a buffalo hunter."

"I thought the buffalo were almost gone."

"A buffalo hunter was a hunter for the Cavalry. Tepo's job was to put meat on the table, even if it meant prairie dogs or coyote. He taught me how to shoot from a great distance."

"How good are you?"

Charlie pointed at the saddle. "From here? I'd let you choose the front or back door of your car."

"What scope do you have on your rifle?"

"My model 1894 doesn't have a scope."

"You could make this shot using a 30-30 lever-action with the standard iron sights?"

The smile was slow growing, followed by a quick single shoulder shrug. "It's your car."

The deputy mulled over the man's displayed lack of bravado and proven skill with a gun. "When this is all over, I think I'd wager a ten-spot on that shot."

Thorny laughed as they lay in the hot water looking at the stars. "Ten? Either the county doesn't pay him enough, or he knows you can make the shot. Has he seen you shoot?"

"I had him over for dinner a few times."

"Dinner?"

"He'd never had rabbit or squirrel."

Thorny laughed. "Where did you find a squirrel big enough to eat?"

The waves of Charlie laughing came first. "There aren't any. I took four pigeons on the high school front lawn."

"With a rifle?"

"Slingshot. One of the neighbors complained, so I got four more for her."

"How were they?"

"Good as usual, but a little greasy. The coyote was better."

"Mr. Ferguson said the elk are back. He has had to double the top line of barbwire."

"I could hang two or three carcasses at Johnny's. Maybe another or two down at Merkle's."

"It would be a blessing through the winter. It could add meat to many needing pots."

"I'll put the racks up, and we could jerk a few more."

Thorny thought about the barn. "We could build some racks in the barn and hang some chunk jerky."

Charlie surged out of the hot water and sat on the edge. "How much killing are we talking about?"

Thorny joined him. Her white skin glowed soft in the moonlight. The scaring on her arm and side were darker. Charlie had seen it all before. "We haven't even got to the humans yet. We're still talking about putting meat on the table for the winter."

He cleared his throat with a swallowed growl. "Speaking of food for the winter... I gave a couple of people seeds."

"Out in Round Valley?"

He rumble-hummed an affirmative. "The carrots are sweet, and the radishes are so hot, I don't even want to try the peppers." He smiled at her in the dark. Only his teeth shown through the steamy air. "The potatoes have pushed up large mounds, and the cabbages are bigger than my head."

Thorny chewed at the side of her mouth. She looked up at the pond built before she was born. The mountain behind was more of a presence in the dark than an object she could see. She turned to her friend. "The government gave me a very large check for the water. Next month and each month after, there will be more."

"What are you saying, Thorny?"

The tip of her tongue dipped out to wet the center of her lips. "I won't need it. We need to find places for it to flow to."

He studied her face. Nothing had changed in the twenty years they had known each other. She had kicked him in the crotch, brought him soup when he was sick, hit him in the arm at odd times, and helped him study for exams. She snuggled on his couch with his dog and mucked out the horse stalls because she just stopped to say hello. Her claw had never got in her way or defined her. His being Paiute had never been a part of their being friends. There was no romance in their relationship, but no romance was as deep as their friendship, nor as supportive or defining. Thorny was Thorny, and Charlie was Charlie—everything else was just extra.

He slid back down into the heat. "We'll find a way." The silence of the night was defined by the symphony of the crickets and tree frogs. Silence in a desert, for some, is the definition of quiet. For others, it is the loud deafening noise of life itself. When it is truly silent, a human can hear their own heart beating. Charlie knew he didn't have to listen to hear Thorny's heart beating. It surrounded him—it had for as long as he could remember.

Thorny wound her arm in the air. There was no pain, but the stiffness bothered her. She bit her teeth as she imagined what the pain must be like for other people. The long table in the bank's conference room was divided into piles of folders and paperwork. She looked up at the soft knock on the ajar door.

The elderly banker stood with his fingers through the handles of the two steaming mugs. His right hand was free. "I thought you might like a cup of coffee." He extended his hand. "I didn't know how you took it."

Thorny took the mug from the one finger. "Black is fine. It's rare I'm ever near fresh milk straight from a cow. Anything more than an hour old tastes…"

"Old?"

They both smiled. She hadn't known if he had a cow or grew up with one. She now had her confirmation. "What kind do you have?"

"Nipper?" He smiled. "Good old black and white Holstein. Got her when one of the accounts passed away. The widower didn't know beans about cows and was just happy I would take her. You?"

"Dorothy's some kind of Jersey mix. Some days I think she has some Angus in her, others she is as gentle as a lamb." She sipped as she pointed at his right hand. "I noticed you always keep your right hand free…"

He turned and drew back his suit coat. Stuck in his back was a holster with a revolver. "Old habits. My father was a stagecoach driver for the Overland. He taught me always to leave my gun hand free."

Thorny thought about the habit. "Do you eat left-handed?"

"And everything but write." The man waved his finger at all the files. "Is this what was in the box that belonged to Ulysses?"

Thorny glanced back. "And a few more. They had originally been Judge Harold Hudgins's. These are old cases never solved or resolved."

The man opened a folder and peeked at the contents. Thorny could tell he wasn't looking, or even seeing, but just curious. "What are you going to do with them?"

Thorny pushed back in the chair as she cradled the warm mug. "I'm not sure. But I'm thinking I might take a stab at solving a few of them."

The man beamed as he looked at how she sat in the chair and talked. "Ah, the cocky confidence of youth. Your grandfather would be popping with pride right now."

Thorny shrugged her eyes at the piles. "Well, I'd just be happy if I can solve the mystery on my plate at the moment."

"The judge?"

She nodded. "With a few other twists."

A woman appeared in the doorway. She wore a blue gingham dress. A heart-shaped gold locket drew down the small silver chain. The locket and chain were not a match. Thorny guessed she had a loved one in one of the conflicts.

"Sir, miss, there is a Mrs. Ruth Mann on the phone. She wants to talk to Miss Wallace?"

The banker frowned for a moment. "Thank you, Ethel." Turning, he tossed his head. "You can take it in my office."

Thorny didn't sit. "Yes, Ruth. It's Thorny."

The strained voice sounded like it was coming down a chimney with a roaring fire going. "Thorny, Errol Flynn's headed your way."

Thorny cocked one eye. She guessed the phone could be sharing with someone listening. "Is he bringing Douglas Fairbanks or James Cagney?"

"Mrs. Murphy said she thought he was coming alone, but if anyone, I'd bet on Cagney."

"Thanks, Ruth. We'll clean the house and make a bed for him." She started to hang up but put the phone back to her head. "Oh, Ruth?"

"Yes?"

"How did you know where I was?"

"Monte gave me the phone number."

"Thank you. Say hello to your other half."

"Will do. You take care. Good-bye."

Thorny gently returned the handset into the cradle. Her mind was elsewhere.

"I don't for a moment believe that call had anything to do with movie actors."

Thorny turned. "Hmm? Oh, no. No, it didn't. And thank you." She distractedly pointed back at the phone.

He waved his hand in dismissal. "Anything I can do to help?"

Thorny's eyes clicked as if she had just noticed the man. "Yes, as a matter of fact, there is something you can do." She walked over to the man. "Let me take another look at your holster."

He drew his coat back, and then unsnapping the keeper, drew out the holster and gun as one and handed it to her.

She turned it over and over. Studying the unique design. "Where did you get this?"

"Where everyone gets leather work in this town. Victor made this for me a long time ago."

"Do you think he could make one for a model 1911?"

"A forty-five automatic? Sure. Those are becoming popular as the preferred sidearm for officers in the Army."

"But I want it to sit down low on my back."

The man smiled. "Go talk to Victor. Tell him you saw mine. His son Vic is turning out some clever work also." He looked down as he drew up his pant leg and held his shoe up. The saddled shoe was all black. The top came above the ankle and then some. The laces hooked instead of drawing through holes. "I have a problem with my ankles. With this, I can pull the laces snug for the support. The kid is creative."

AT THE MENTION of the banker and Thorny's presentation of the pistol, the man rummaged about on a large workbench cluttered with half-finished leather projects. The younger edition of the leather smith walked in from working on a few pack mules. He stood behind Thorny. She was aware of him studying her backside. She was about to turn and confront him when he spoke.

"Reach back with your shooting hand and stick it inside your pants."

She turned with a frown. "Excuse me?"

Vic waved his finger at her hand and the back of her pants. Finally, he rolled his eyes and turned so she could watch him. He reached back and into his jeans. His hand withdrew a revolver she hadn't seen or noticed.

"I'm assuming you don't normally wear a suit coat or jacket. So you'll need a deeper holster to hide the handle as well."

She cautiously turned and slid her right hand into her pants with the palm facing out. She felt his hand move her arm slightly.

"Is this more comfortable?"

"It's easier." Thorny turned. "What's your thinking?"

The other leather smith walked up with the pistol in what looked like a small frying pan sized pancake. He handed it to his son.

"It will take some practice getting used to the feel of the draw, but the barrel and slide of the model eleven are large. So we have to hide them where they'll fit." He moved the pistol in and out of the holster. Satisfied with the ease and fit, he started to turn Thorny around but stopped. His throat and lower face flushed.

Thorny blinked lazily and turned around. She unbuckled her belt and slit it out of the few loops. She felt the holster slide down into her pants. The man was right. The fit went where it could. She noticed him feeding the belt through her side loop. She pulled and with the last loop, completed the circle. She let him turn her from side to side.

"What do you think, Dad?"

The older man stepped behind her, and she could hear him humming. "Well, we could feather the edges out more, but it would weaken the stitching."

He walked past her and went back to the saddle he was stitching. "Wear it for a week and see if there is any chafing. Silk underthings would allow it to move better than the cotton. Just sayin'."

She looked at the younger man. "Do you wear silk underthings?"

His face was sunset red. "My dungarees are looser, and so it moves just fine."

Thorny held his eyes as she reached, grabbed the pistol, and drew. "You're right. It'll take some time to get used to the draw, but the snugness keeps it from moving around."

A FEW MINUTES LATER, she showed it to Monte. She just didn't tell him what she was showing him.

She stood with her body cranked around. Her right hand was on her left hip. "What do you think?"

Monte thought a moment. "Well, I think walking all over has been good for you. But your pants look a little baggy. Maybe if I take a couple of darts in—"

Thorny spun around. "I'm showing you my new holster, and you're talking fashion?"

Both were silent. The rebuke was uncharacteristic of her. Thorny stumbled. "I'm... I'm sorry. I didn't mean... Wait. You know how to sew?"

The vibration in his chest was her first hint. The second was him grabbing at the arm of the barber chair to steady himself. The laughter only became audible when he fell into the chair. "Do you remember those shirts you wore. Sometimes the sign of the flour company showed, but most of the time, your over-alls would hide that part."

She cautiously watched him as she gradually sunk onto the window bench. "I hated those. But it was all we had. A few kids made fun of them, but only until I hit or kicked them."

Monte smirked warmly. His fingers picked at his shirt. He looked up with his right eye and brow leading. "Who do you think sewed those for you? Your dead mother? Eustis?"

She sat watching the late sun warm the tiles of the floor. The patterns made as much sense as for how she felt. She had never thought about how she dressed as a child. Now, the shirts made more sense than wondering as a child which store sold shirts made from old sacks. Her voice was quiet. "I never thought about it." She looked up at the man she had always thought of as one of her uncles. Now she realized he was more a favored aunt. "I guess a thank-you is in order."

He dipped his head. "Times were tough. We did what we needed to do." He let the weight of the statement hang in the air. Monte, afraid of the moment becoming too much, waved his hand about. "Well, show me this holster."

Her smile crept sideways as she stood and paced her turn. She made two complete revolutions.

"Well? Where is it?"

She reached and drew the gun. His eyes opened larger than she had ever seen them before. She knew the holster was a success.

With the pistol restored to the holster, the tailor or seam-stress in Monte took over. He thought about how the extended flat pan of the holster spread flat across her backside. His hands moved about the cloth. "Besides the straight up pull you must contend with, there is the sweep of the spine. We can let these pleats out a tiny bit, but for the draw, try bending forward about an inch or so as you draw."

She bent and drew a few times. "Yes. It doesn't scrape along the back as much."

Monte demonstrated his next guidance. "As you draw, reduce your silhouette by turning slightly right and dropping to your right knee. You can brace your left elbow on the knee and cup your right hand. We used to do this with the old thirty-six because it was so damn wild. Bracing will increase your accuracy range." He stood as he watched her mimic his moves.

Movement caught his eye. A woman's mouth was a small circle of horror. Her gloved hands were on her cheeks. He smiled and waved. As the woman rushed past the open door, he called a good afternoon and reminded her of her husband's end of the month haircut.

Thorny bit on her claw to keep from laughing.

Monte watched the woman cross Line Street and continue down Main. She only glanced back twice. He ignored Thorny laughing on the floor. "So why the sudden rush to start carrying a hidden pistol?"

"Ruth Mann's telephone call."

He turned on his heel. His one eyebrow was slightly cocked. She had his attention.

"She called to warn me. Reginald Abbotsford is either on his way or in the area."

"He's the one you think shot Stan?"

"By all indications, he is the long-range shooter. There are records of him using the same rifle needed to make the long shot. I'm sure Ruth has reason to believe he's headed this way to stop my nosing around."

"Not to mention some water?"

Her mouth pulled taut as she looked toward the sun hanging above Humphry's basin. The curve of the mountain ridge pointed down toward Upper Buttermilk and her well. If the hemp worked, any meddling with the water and its use would constitute treason. She had a tough time believing even the cold-blooded killers of Mulholland's crew or Los Angeles Department of Water and Power would tolerate or walk such a dangerous path. But desperate times created desperate men who performed acts a prudent man would not.

She turned and looked at Monte. They both understood the shift in circumstances. One from experience, the other from a guess.

37 THE PASS

Danny shook his head. "I don't remember a Debbie Brockman."

Thorny snorted softly as she pulled at the tan, late-summer grass. Turning, she squinted behind her green glasses at her friend. Looking back at the Sierra Nevada mountains, across the valley, she bit her lip for a second. "Okay. Do you remember a Debra Hudgins? She had a large wine stain on her face. Looks like someone splashed—"

"Yes. What about her?" He frowned a moment. "Wasn't she sickly or something? I don't remember her being at school much."

Thorny's head bobbed. "That was her. I don't think she was sickly, though. I think it was more of her mother beating each page of her religion into a young Debbie. She married Phillip Brockman. He was a few years ahead of us."

"Okay. What does she have to do with shooting Stan?"

Thorny looked back with one eye closed. She saw the body of Danny, but the head had two large fuzzy ears. The last of a carrot and greens were disappearing. Thorny chuckled softly. "She doesn't, but her uncle is the sharpshooter. His name is Reggie Abbotsford. His sister was Debbie's mother."

Danny leaned in to look around Heather's head as he stuck another large carrot into her mouth. "I thought you said she was a Hudgins."

Thorny didn't move. She could see Danny working on the problem. His eyes opened. "Oh."

"Yes. The marriage thing. It changes some last names occasionally."

"Do we know where the uncle is now?"

"Great question. Stan's wife called to warn me he's headed this way. He can't get at Stan so we can assume I'm his next target."

Danny turned to look at the low-lying hills behind them. Well within the two-mile range. "So you just plan to sit out here in the open?"

Thorny's shoulders slumped as her head hung. "Were you always this quick, and I just didn't notice? He knew about the well in Buttermilk because he had been watching them drill, and he was there when they killed the crew. But unless there is some huge sign I haven't seen, pointing to this location and Heather, I seriously doubt his knowing about her or us coming here. Unless you let it slip out one night in a drunken rampage."

Danny hugged Heather's head and fed her the last carrot. "See Heather, I told you there was nothing to worry about."

Thorny closed her eyes as she reclined on the log. Danny wasn't sure if she had gone to sleep. The late summer sun felt good. Warm, but not hot.

THORNY SAT UP. "Frog? Did you forget to duck and hit your head on the bridge? I heard a large thump and some swearing about half an hour ago."

"Nope. A dumb rattler tried to kill my boot." The man walked around the large break of the brush. "I picked him up by the tail and sent him to his ancestors."

Thorny laughed. "Does the old crack the whip you used to do still work? I mean, you are getting old and slow now." The twenty-seven-year-old Paiute smiled.

Danny was still wondering how Thorny could have heard the man. Even close, the man was like smoke. Large smoke, but still silent smoke. "Crack the whip...?"

The Indian nodded. "Do it right, and the head pops right off."

"And if you do it wrong?"

Charlie drew his hand out of his pocket and held out a five-inch-long rattle. "Do it wrong, and the whole snake pops off leaving only the rattles."

Danny's eyes were large. "Large rattle. How big was the snake?"

The man held his arms stretched out. "But after I popped him a second time, he was about ten feet."

Danny felt the bullshit piling up and didn't want to touch it anymore.

Charlie put the rattle away and sat down on the grass looking north. "The front building is rigged. If he is stupid enough to nose around the mine, the first shaft looks like a garden path."

"Thanks, Charlie. I won't be going up without you until this is over."

"How soon?"

"Mr. Ferguson said the person who broke into my quarters in the barn was two nights ago. All the phony deeds and transfers were stolen. They left one of the laying hens on my bed. The head was torn off."

The man chuffed a growl. "Funny. I would have thought Reseda would have eaten the chicken and left the head. What do we do now?"

"We wait."

Danny threw the stick he had been toying with. "Why? We know who all the players are. We know what they have all done. Why not arrest them?"

Thorny looked out of the side of her glasses. "Do you have some special badge you're hiding in those fancy pants of yours?"

Danny looked over at Charlie.

Charlie coughed from stifling a laugh. "White man like his laws. White man like when red man knows his place and stay drunk on reservation." Thorny joined in the soft cynical laugh. "Besides, I'm only the chief of our reservation. We have never needed a police officer, so we have no sworn officers. And, even if we did, their jurisdiction ends at the fence line." He turned to Thorny. "He does have a point, though."

"How's so?"

"You know the crimes. You know who did them. They are provable..."

"And...?"

"Last time I checked, you're a sworn officer of the court. Your citizen arrest would carry almost as much weight as a sworn officer."

Danny fidgeted. "Enough weight to arrest Reseda?"

Charlie turned. "He's a wanted criminal under his real name. Now he has committed murder under his assumed name. I think a ten-year-old blind girl from Topeka, Kansas could make the citizen's arrest, and it would stick."

He looked at Thorny and thought a moment. Weighing his chances of survival, getting kicked in the crotch, or just slugged hard in the arm. The last did hurt, he had just learned not to show it. His stoic suffering was the only way he could get her back. "I'm actually surprised at you."

"Why?"

"For a white man, you don't think like a white man."

Thorny chuckled silently and pointed at her modest breasts. "Maybe because I'm a woman?"

"I didn't mean man as in male. But you aren't thinking much like a cowboy."

"Cowboy?"

"Yes, like John Wayne or Tumbleweed Baker."

"And how do they think?"

"When were they ever the sheriff?"

She never attended movies but thought about the movies she knew about. The lead role wasn't the sheriff. "Never."

"But they stopped the bad guys."

She and Danny both nodded in agreement. "Your point is?"

Charlie quirked his mouth and shrugged his one shoulder. "Go stop them and worry about the legality later."

Thorny liked the simple forward nature of the way Charlie saw life. If you're hungry—eat. Tired—sleep. Know about an evil bad man or men—go stop them. "How?"

Charlie laughed a short cough. "You never went to a movie, have you? You go stop them at the pass."

Danny frowned. "Sherwin pass?"

Charlie's face scowled at the man. "Why would he go there?"

Thorny jumped in—defending Danny. "Where then? Independence? He's already up here."

The big man's head rocked in agreement. "But where is he?"

"We don't know."

"Who does?"

"Reseda... but he wouldn't tell us. Besides, we need to stop him too."

Charlie rolled his head to one side and looked at Thorny. His mouth was a relaxed smile as he waited for her to figure out the next step.

"Debbie."

His finger pointed at her as his thumb dropped like the hammer of a revolver. "Bingo."

Thorny stood. Looking across the valley toward the ranches, she thought about what needed to happen. She turned back to Danny. "Where's Pete?"

"He took a prisoner down to Trona three days ago. He was going to come back up through Nevada. He mentioned Fish Lake Valley, but he also said there was something in Falon. I don't expect him back before tomorrow. Why?"

She bobbed her head but waved her hand as if shooing a fly. Her mind was working, as her eyes locked on a small chunk of wood floating in the river. Caught in an eddy, it kept going around and around. The tiny limb stuck up like a mast, with a single leaf sticking out horizontal to the water. In her mind, she saw it the way a child would draw a small boat with a triangle for a sail.

There was something there. Just outside the corral of her mind. She could feel it, just not see it.

She looked at Charlie. "You going back up to the mine?" He nodded. She knew he had more work to do.

She turned on Danny. "Can you drop me in town. I want to get the car in case I need to move fast."

38 HAMMER

Dinner with Monte and May on the back deck of the Bib had been an exercise of patience and distraction. Their patience with Thorny's distraction. The thought of a man using a small boat as his brand didn't make any sense.

She pushed the steering wheel and eased onto Highway six. Her eyes wandered over at the fueling station for trucks. There was a large gathering of trucks waiting to load up. At midnight, the new rations went into effect.

With the commercial loads, the stamps would be glued to a card and canceled with a date stamp. The time was written into space on the card, and the initials or marks were made by the driver and the station master. She had noticed a small green flag was flying over a tiny light. The flag meant there was fuel.

Thorny's car moved out on the dark highway. The hooded lights only gave off a modicum of light. She wasn't in a hurry. She glanced in the small rearview mirror. Only the small green flag fluttered in the night.

Thorny stomped on the brake pedal and pulled the car to the right side of the road. The Ford coughed and sputtered as it lurched to a dusty stop—the engine dead. The stirred dust hung in the air. She sat in the silence, looking at the small flag. The smell of the dust, the warmth of the night—the memory drifted toward her—full force.

HER FEET HUNG from the bench in the summer heat over the crack between the boards. The cool air pushed from the crawl space under the Indian church. Charlie sat across the table as they colored in the pictures. Thorny would use the blue Crayon, and then exchange pictures with Charlie who was using the red. Then they would close their eyes and pick new colors to use. Neither cared if the color they drew matched where it was supposed to be. Both agreed the sky was better yellow with a green sun. Any water was brown like the Owens River. People could be any color and usually were. They had once found a Crayon labeled *flesh*. They had put their arms together and laid the stick in the crack between them. It didn't match either skin, so they threw it out into the sagebrush.

One of the pictures depicted a few men in a small boat on a lake. There was a man with a beard, smaller than Ulysses's beard, standing on some rocks or something in the lake. Thorny asked the questions about the picture.

"Why is he standing on the rocks in the lake?"

The teacher was one of the churchwomen from in town. She was doing her 'God's work' with the heathen Paiute children and that yellar-haired girl. "He's not. That is Jesus, and he is walking on water."

"I walk on water when it rains."

The woman knew her lord was testing her. "But he is

walking on the deep water of the Sea of Galilee. He is calling to Peter."

Charlie put down his Crayon. "What does he call him?"

"He doesn't call him anything. He is calling *to* him to come walk with him."

Thorny snorted. "In the deep water of the sea of Golly...?"

"Galilee. The Sea of Galilee. You see, Peter is climbing out of the boat."

Charlie rolled his eyes. "I hope he knowed how to swim."

Thorny frowned as she looked at the printed drawing. "How do you know the water is deep—have you been there?"

"Nooo. No, I haven't. But the good book tells us it was deep."

"If it's deep, why is he out there standing on a rock, instead of being in the boat. I'd be in the boat."

The woman was coming to the end of her patience. "Because Jesus was a fisher of men. He gathered them in as he is doing with Peter. Do you understand now?"

Thorny looked at Charlie. Neither of them showed any response. "Yes, I think we do. Mrs. Pence, thank you for coming all the way out here for us lost souls."

"Well, you are very welcome..." She couldn't remember what the strange little girl's name was. The hand always gave her the heebie-jeebies. "You're very welcome, little girl." She turned to walk around the room before there were any more questions.

Charlie leaned over and whispered. "She's more chopie than a drunk three-eyed shaman."

Thorny snickered. "What kind of bait do you think he was fishing with?"

Thorny remembered the woman wore a green blouse. It was loose and hung where she should have had breasts. The green hung like the small flag hung over the light in the dead air of a late summer night.

In her mind, the small boat became the brand. The evangelist had been a fisher of men. The bait had been people's fears of pain, suffering, and death. The man had changed his skin, but not his spots.

SHE STARTED THE CAR. The lights only lit a few feet ahead, but she didn't need light to guide her. She knew every stride of the road, in sunlight or dark of night. The bright light of fresh snow or the rare drizzle of a rainy night. Thorny had walked the miles to town more than a few thousand times. She guessed she could close her eyes and drive true to where she needed to be.

She pulled to the side. The small light was on in the window. It moved as if drunk. Thorny knew it was a single candle. Too many homes had been lit the same way after the stock market had taken so much.

The door of the car squealed in protest as she stepped out. She was tempted to remove her boots. The silence of bare feet would be an advantage she wouldn't need. This was a frontal assault, not a sneak attack. She needed answers, and she wasn't going to ask like a neighbor asking about a missing cat.

She only knocked twice. Nice wasn't on her mind. The second knock she pounded the screen door with the side of her fist. She looked through the window. Debbie was at the table reading from a book. The two girls looked scared toward the door. The door wasn't going to open itself.

Nobody had locks on their doors. It wasn't the city—this was Bishop.

Debbie's head snapped up at the sound of Thorny's boot kicking the bottom of the door open. The girls jumped out of their chairs and ran behind their mother. Debbie half rose. Thorny could see the book she was closing. The black leatherette was common in all churches of all faiths.

"How dare you break into my—"

"Shut up." Thorny took five fast steps and was standing in front of the smaller woman. Debbie outweighed her, but Thorny was betting she had never raised a hand in anger. "Where is your uncle?"

"My uncle is dead." Thorny could tell she wasn't lying, just not talking about the right uncle.

"Wrong uncle, I mean your killer uncle—Reggie Abbotsford. Where is he? I know he is up here. Where is he staying?"

The woman flustered, and her face turned almost as red as the beet coloring of the stain. "I don't know. He never tells me anything."

Thorny grabbed the woman's arm with her claw. "Did he take his horse? The Palomino?"

She squirmed to get loose of Thorny's claw. Her eyes looked down like a sacred cow. Thorny realized she was afraid the claw would touch her skin. Touch her like the mark of the devil.

"Talk to me."

The woman's face flashed up with more fear. "No."

Thorny whipped around at the small tinkle of a belt buckle. The footsteps registered a moment later.

Reseda stood frozen in the doorway. He had been outside to the privy. His shirt was only half tucked in, his pants were closed at the button, and yet to be zipped. The belt hung in his two hands. His mouth was as round as a doughnut. His eyes were full of anger as well as fear.

"Who the hell let you in here?"

Thorny stepped over into his face. "Raymond Reseda, you are hereby arrested for three counts of murder in the first-degree. Give me your gun and surrender peacefully."

The man pushed her away. "The hell I will." He wrestled with the loose belt and holster.

Thorny rammed his chest with her shoulder and head. He stumbled backward onto the utility porch. Stopped by the screened wall, he drew his pistol and shot. The round went wide and high, but Thorny didn't want the next to be closer. She turned and pushed Debbie into the kitchen with the girls. She reached over and grabbed the heavy candlestick upside down. With the candle blown out, the room plunged into darkness as Thorny heard Reseda coming through the door. She swung backhanded.

The candlestick struck something soft. The wind exploded from his mouth a few inches above. She had been too low. She pulled back and swung again. This time she was too high, and the weight of the candlestick carried her around.

The next gunshot was near her ear. The flare of the muzzle lit the room in a wonky snapshot. Thorny could see Debbie huddled over her girls. They were safe, but she needed to take this fight outside. She felt for the bowl with a few late roses floating in the water. Grabbing the bowl, she threw it where Reseda's face might be.

The sputtering told her she had made a direct hit and where he was. She swung the candlestick. Hitting his upraised arm.

She ran.

A car's headlights crossed over the front of the house as she reached the door. The light half blinded her but created a silhouette for Reseda. The third shot didn't miss.

Thorny's left shoulder slammed into the doorjamb as her right smashed open the screen door and carried her out and around the jamb by an unfelt hand. She spun and stumbled down the three steps, hitting the ground. Her right foot curled under, and she fell to the ground.

Hearing the bellow of the fatted bull, Thorny rolled onto her back. The pistol in his hand misfired. He threw it at her, and she swatted it away into the dark.

Reseda bent and reached down to grab his nemesis. Thorny reflectively raised her feet and cocked her knees. As the weight shifted, she pushed out. The man stumbled back to the wall of the house.

The sweaty back of his shirt and the soft fat of his back folded over the twin wires running from porcelain knob to porcelain knob. The full effects of the 110-volts and raw amperage weren't sudden. His eyes flew as wide open as his mouth. His arms first threw out and then convulsed inward. The large body began to vibrate. The nearest circuit breaker on the raw electricity was somewhere on a pole down the street.

Just as the man seemed to light up, Thorny heard a pop and the dead mass tipped forward. The man was as dead as if Thorny had sent him up to the electric chair in San Quentin. The body flopped once and lay still. A light over the porch surged back on as the power resumed. Thorny watched the smoke from the twin burn lines until a motion caught her eye.

Turning, she saw a man who could pass for Errol Flynn. Tall and thin. Dressed perfectly, as if for a safari hunting big game. From the rifle, she guessed who the game was.

"I should have shot you the day you started drilling the damn well. I was on Chalk Bluff. To your car, it was only two miles. I could have made the shot. I've made longer ones."

Thorny rolled over and raised up on her left arm. The right wasn't working right, and she guessed the bullet had shattered her shoulder. "Is it because you're a coward? You only kill people from a distance? Is that what you did to Debbie's father —killed him from a distance?"

"Shut up. You don't know anything." He stepped forward under the porch light. "You're just a nosey little girl who thinks she can keep the land and water under it. Well, little missy, we are already reversing those deeds and transfers you made in Independence."

Thorny coughed wetly. "Sacramento."

"What about Sacramento?" His sneer was pure evil.

"They were filed in Sacramento the week before I county-conformed them here. I didn't have to file them here, it was merely a courtesy and formality. There is nothing you thugs can do about it now."

"Why you little shit. I ought to—"

"Poison me, like you did with your sister—Debbie's mother? Did you men think nobody would ever figure out how the woman suddenly became frail and seemed to go crazy? The water tested high in arsenic, but most around here does. But the nail in your coffin was putting the sulfate of mercury down the well. By now, all the wells on the lane have the poison in them."

Thorny could see the man was stunned. "They told me the mercury wouldn't leave the old bats well. They told me the well would naturally clear and by spring be back to clear water."

"Who told you, Holmes and Smith?" Thorny lied.

"No, Steve Spicer, the geologist at Water and Power. He swore only the old bat would be affected."

Thorny now had another name for her list.

The voice was small at the screen door. "Is it true? You killed my father and mother? You're my uncle, for God's sake."

Reggie's attention was split. He didn't know where trouble was coming from. He held up his left hand. "Debbie, it wasn't like that. There were circumstances. Just go back inside with your daughters. Let Uncle Reggie take care of this, just like he always has. Okay, sweetie. Go on."

He watched as the front door slowly closed behind the screen door.

Thorny could feel the grip in her hand but didn't know if she had the strength to pull the pistol from the holster. As she watched the man talk to his niece, the pistol slowly moved.

The man turned as his rifle raised. "As for you. It's time to take the trash out."

The .45 was braced on her hip. She didn't know if she could aim it, or even if it would stay in place once she pulled the trigger.

The man started to take a step. The screen door swung wide, and the barrel of a short shotgun stuck out. His eyes exploded at the sight as he started to raise his left arm.

Thorny rolled back and caught the lower part of the pistol grip and bottom of her right hand in her claw. She pulled it all toward her to aim at the man's chest.

The pistol jumped and settled back into place. His head snapped back as the hair on his head bulged up and back, and then came apart like an overripe fig. The shotgun's flame leaped out toward his guts. The man's rifle fell from his hand as his body was pushed sideways off the porch.

The body bounced and flopped twice on the lawn.

Debbie stepped out onto the porch into the circle of light. Her face was a mix of garish red stain and nauseous grayish white. The shotgun hung in her hands as she looked at what she had done.

Thorny transferred the pistol to her left claw and pulled herself to her knees. Taking a couple of breaths, she pulled her right foot around. A hand reached under her arm. She looked back at Pete.

"It looks like I was a little late. But the pie was good."

"How did you know I was here?"

"You parked your black car in the middle of the highway. I almost hit it."

Thorny looked at the twinkle in his eye. She laughed softly as he helped her up. She handed him the pistol and then held it to his stomach. He understood and stayed there.

Thorny stepped over Reseda and approached the porch. "Debbie?"

Her voice was that of a little girl. "He was my uncle."

Thorny eased up the steps. "Yes, but he was an evil man. He did evil things including killing your parents."

"But he was my uncle. He looked after me. He read to me. He bathed me and put me to bed."

Thorny froze at the revelation of an incestuous relationship. The shotgun took on a more menacing meaning. She glanced back at Pete. The deputy made no sign of having heard.

Thorny cautiously extended her claw. "Debbie, honey, give me the gun. It wasn't your fault, and he was dead before you pulled the trigger." She closed the last step. The woman looked up. All Thorny could see was an injured little girl. Thorny gently took the shotgun and heaved it out into the yard. It bounced once off the body and came to rest on the grass.

Pete moved to recover the rifle and shotgun. He watched as

the woman in the calico dress and white apron collapsed into Thorny and hung there.

They moved her into the living room and laid her on the couch. The two girls peeked from the kitchen. Thorny tried to wave them in, but her shoulder and arm were numb.

She turned to ask Pete to help.

As she turned, Pete barely caught her.

39 WHAT NOW

Thorny rolled her head and turned her body. There were sheets. Her one eye opened. The large brown face was soft and relaxed. The soft lips gently buzzed with each soft exhale.

Wherever they were, she knew she was safe. She moved her legs. There was no dog.

The rumble was almost a growl. "The dog is home. We have new kids. She's looking after them. Old Pokus will come over and feed them their milk. Stop wiggling, little lizard."

THORNY SAT in the lounge chair. Someone had found her some real pajamas. Her bare feet were pulled up into the large chair.

The knock on the door was soft.

Thorny looked up from the book to find two smiling faces. Stan laughed.

"I thought you were out of the sling?"

Ruth slapped him on the stomach as she rushed in. "Ignore him. He's just a man. How is the shoulder?"

Thorny moved to stand up, but the small hand pushed gently on her head. Without looking back, she smiled. "Stan is going to go find me a comfortable chair too."

From the door, the man rolled his eyes, and his body followed. "I'm just going down the hall to steal a chair for my loving wife."

The women laughed silently. "I have a great husband."

Thorny winked. "The fella you occasionally hang out with isn't so bad either. He's even cute—in a puppy dog way."

"I might even keep him."

Thorny feigned surprise. "Take him home even?"

"Only if he's house trained."

The asked-for chair slid up to her knees. Ruth sat. Stan sat on the bed. "So?"

Thorny pinched the bridge of her nose with her claw. "I don't know. Everything has an upside, but also, there are so many negatives."

Ruth rolled her index finger in the air. "Go ahead, dear. Just ignore the impatient one."

Thorny winced her mouth as she looked at the pain in the wounded husband's face. She also noticed the twinkle in his eyes. Being around his wife was doing him good.

"The mayor decamped the morning word got out. I'm guessing he was somehow tied to everything, but it would take too much useless work to figure it out. Anyway, the job, just like your boss implied, is also open. There are many women, who used to be Suffragettes, and now see getting a woman in as mayor as their new campaign. I'm not opposed to a woman in the office, but just not me. I'm not a speech maker, and unless the baby is a calf, colt, puppy or mule... I'm not kissing it."

Stan chuffed. "I hear Charlie got some new baby goats."

"They're called kids. I'll make an exception. His wife likes them."

Ruth screwed her head into a cocked position with a near frown. "Charlie? The giant of an Indian? He's married?"

Thorny flattened her lips into a smile. "Cutest husky this side of Alaska."

The woman hummed with one eye half closed. "You rural people have some funny ways." She turned and pointed at her husband. "Don't you get any funny ideas."

She turned back. "What were the other jobs besides police chief?"

"Teacher, sheriff deputy might be open soon, lawyer, judge, and there is a part-time position for county librarian. Which one will give you the flexibility and time to do your other job?" Stan sat back and smiled smugly.

Thorny thought about the question. "Is that your boss, my old boss, or Danny's father asking?"

"Take your pick."

"Did I just hear my name being taken in vain?"

Thorny smiled. "Mr. Rambino, how nice to see you. I think you know Stan, and maybe his lovely wife, Ruth?"

Ruth smiled. "Mr. Rambino and I go way back." She looked up. "How are you doing, Mike?"

"Well, it's done me good being up here these weeks. I've walked more each morning than I would in a week down in the city. My pants are almost falling off, and I think someone put some little springs in the soles of my shoes."

"Are you staying up here for the fall?"

"No, I'm heading back down. Danial and I thought we'd come in and say good-bye."

Ruth chuckled. "Give it up, Mike. We were just talking about the situation. She hasn't made up her mind."

The man held his hands over his heart as if in mortal pain. "Well, she's a water baroness now. She can afford to take her time thinking about how life should present itself." He pointed at Thorny. "Just don't take more time than some of us have left."

40 HAROLD

T he knock on the door was softened by the white gloves. The one pair was tatted lace. The younger out of calfskin. Thorny covered her surprise with a smile. "Bertha, Violet, please come in."

"We heard you were getting released today. We thought you might let us take you to the Bib for lunch."

Thorny peered out the window at the rain. "I don't think the back deck would be open today."

Bertha smiled. "It's Sunday."

"The Bib is closed."

Violet smiled. "Except for a private party."

THE FRONT DOOR INDEED OPENED. Monte turned with a few pieces of silverware in his hand. "Welcome to the Sunday Special Society."

Thorny's head turned slightly as her one eyebrow rose. The air smelled of freshly baked rolls mixed with bacon and…"

May walked out of the kitchen carrying a basket covered with a towel. The ubiquitous apron was removed. Thorny eyed the pleated slacks and bare feet. She noted out of the side of her eye that the foot attire matched the bottom of Monte's striped slacks.

She turned at the sound of shoes dropping on the hardwood floor behind her. Violet and Bertha smiled bashfully. Thorny turned on her uncle. "You have some explaining to do."

May harrumphed. "Not his to explain. He's coming late to the party also." She offered out her hand toward Violet and Bertha.

Bertha shied her head. "Can we at least start eating? I got up three hours ago, and I'm starved."

Violet snickered. "I told you that you should have taken the young man up on his eagerness."

Bertha frowned and buzzed her lips. "That young man is a boy. He is Tom Hollis's youngest, and I know for a fact he is only starting high school this year. I'm not training some kid like him for another two or three years… especially on a Sunday when he should be helping his father at the feed store."

The older woman fluffed her hands. "It's your business, but he looked like he could go at least ten minutes for the pair of sawbucks burning a hole in his pants."

Monte inspected the table one last time and looked up. "Ladies, no shoptalk or I'll start telling stories about bad haircuts. Come take a seat or go grab a dish."

Thorny turned toward the kitchen, but Monte stopped her. "Not you. You sit. You're the reason we are here today. Besides, you're wounded."

Thorny glared at him. She hated being babied and not pulling her fair share. "All healed. The doc even said so."

Monte pulled at the sling. "Haute couture scarf."

Thorny gripped the back of a chair to sit.

"Don't ever think you're too old or too big to be turned over someone's knee."

Monte leaned in and growled with a twinkle in his eyes. "Yes. It was true ten years ago when I told it to you, and it's true today. Now behave yourself and go sit at the head of the table where you belong."

May refilled the cups with a fresh pot of coffee. Thorny looked at Bertha with a slight frown. The young prostitute batted her eyes and smiled. "There are only a few businesses not regulated by ration cards. Mine is one of those. After you brought me over and introduced me to May, I have put on a couple of pounds eating better food. But in return, I found a new friend. A friend I would have never met, except for you."

Violet put her hand on her friend's arm. "Shortly after I finally met you, Birdy here brought me over. We had a wonderful lunch on the back porch. I had felt like I had been released from prison. Then May came out and joined us when she closed after the lunch. We talked about Bishop, and then it eventually got to Harry and the boys."

May sat and drew her napkin back over her lap. "That was when this all started to come together. This wasn't about the current and former town whore having lunch with the food server. This was about three women who knew the kind of Bishop the newspaper doesn't print. We not only know where the skeletons are buried, but we know what the skeletons look like."

Violet patted her lips. "And what they used to be like."

Bertha leaned in. "Honey, these two knew everything there was to know about the judge."

Monte grumped. "Meanwhile, I'm just chopped liver over here."

Violet's shoulders slumped. "Oh, poor little Eeyore, did Christopher and Pooh run off and leave you to rot at the base of a tree?"

Thorny laughed at the chiding. "Eeyore?"

Violet turned with a face of surprise and delight. "Haven't you read the book by Mr. Milne?"

She nodded as she pointed at Monte. "It is you."

"The four were ever so much some of the characters, I started calling them by them. Your grandfather was always about facts. He was Owl. Ulysses—"

Thorny squealed. "Oh my, he would have to have been Piglet. But what about the judge?"

Monte growled. "Nobody in the story was even close to Harry." The two older women nodded.

"So, back to why we're here. Or at least why I'm here?"

Violet put her two hands on her lap. "You, my dear, are why we are here. You were looking into why Harry hung himself. And make no bones about it. He did so by his own hand—there is no murder to detect here." Thorny looked to Monte who was sadly nodding agreement. "On the face, there was reason enough to doubt. But as we looked at the evidence, we are certain of our suppositions."

Thorny pointed around the table. "So you put your heads together and figured out why he would do such a thing? Why?"

"Because, we knew him—intimately. Well, maybe not intimately, but we knew enough of what the man was made of and the lengths he would go."

"No. Why would he kill himself? He had cleaned his house, done and put away his laundry, and stocked his pantry. Then he takes a bath, puts on his best suit and hangs himself? What man does such a thing?"

Monte sniffed. His voice was wet with emotion. "The kind of man who loves others so much, he was willing to lay down his life to protect them." He looked up. His eyes were wet. "Pardon my French, but those assholes in Los Angeles were going to expose him for the homosexual he was. It wouldn't take half a day in this town for people to make the connection to us other three. So he stopped it there. In his own house." His finger jammed into his other palm with each statement. "In his closet. On his own terms. It was no different than if he had jumped in front of a bullet in Cuba. I think for all and all, he turned out to be the strongest of us four."

Thorny slumped back with weight. Her shoulders slumped. She looked at Bertha.

The redhead shrugged her right shoulder and pointed at the other three. "I never knew the man. This case is all theirs."

"This case?"

May chuckled sadly. "Why, yes, dear. We're your Sunday lunch barefoot posse.

ACKNOWLEDGMENTS

There are times, research is spent digging in records, interviewing people, and compiling notes. This series is not one of those. Okay, the internet, Google, and Google Earth were used.

Some of the research for this mystery series stretches back to my childhood.

I'd like to thank two of my teachers who also shared their real passion of mule skinning with me. Bob Tanner, (seventh-grade PE teacher), for his stories of the Sierra Nevada Mountains and the part mule trains played in the building of trails and exploration. The other was more of a close friend than just one of my high school teachers. Jack Reeder taught me the power of sitting quietly in the desert, to let the noise level return to normal. His words still stop me today: "The person who talks about the silence of a desert never stopped long enough to hear the truth." I'd like to also thank him for introducing me to some of the older tribe members of the Paiute tribe. Even though we were sitting in the Indian Presbyterian Church, their beliefs ran into the undefinable and mystical.

Their stories of life are based on walking the same shores as I did and nothing to do with a place called See of Golly Lee.

In the nineteen-sixties, if you got gas in the middle of the night at the Chevron station, you probably had a bent old goat with a goatee. He moved like he was ninety and looked older. The man was Dick Swanson and was in his late fifties. After an accident that shattered his back, the most lifesaving treatment was from Dr. Bob Denton. Bob took Dick out into the desert and taught him how to hunt for arrowheads. Ten years later, Dick was still moving, had a collection the Smithsonian would drool over, but knew more about the ins and outs of the Owens Valley and its lore than any other walking soul.

Formally, I'd like to thank the person in Washington DC who understood the reservation might as well be where the Paiutes were already living. Growing up next door was like no other experience a person could have.

Finally, I'd like to thank another old desert rat, who, along with Dick Swanson, was my foundation for the character Ulysses. Elisha Cook Jr many would know from an enormous body of movies. But in Bishop, he was just Cookie. The day I told him that I couldn't wait to graduate from school and head to the big city, he rested his hand on my arm to slow me down. Taking a sip from his coffee, he turned on his counter stool with his wide eyes. "There are just as many stories in this valley as there are in Los Angeles. Only here, the bodies are buried deeper, or they are walking around in plain sight."

A special thank you goes to someone still very much alive. Joanne Lobeski became a Snyder. The ropey thin girl, who had the locker next to me in the basement of the high school, and used to shyly share her poems, slipped through the slots of my locker. She went on to be a teacher, and is the beta reader I needed. The earthier resonance of the valleys still hums in her, as well.

ALSO BY BAER CHARLTON

NOVELS

The Very Littlest Dragon: NEW 2019 Editions
(Newly edited editions available: an all-new full-color ebook, a paperback with coloring pages,
and a full-color Collector's Edition hardback)

Stoneheart
(Pulitzer Nominee 2015)

Angel Flights
What About Marsha?
Pirate's Patch
Dry Bridge of Vengeance

—

SOUTHSIDE HOOKER SERIES

Death on a Dime – Book One
Night Vision – Book Two
Unbidden Garden – Book Three
Boomtown – Book Four
One Day Under the Grass – Book Five

Southside Hooker Series: Books 1–5 Box Set
(Collector's Edition hardback & ebook available)

—

THORNY WALLACE SERIES

Death in the Valley – Book One
Light to Light – Book Two

BAER CHARLTON

ABOUT THE AUTHOR

Baer Charlton graduated from UC Irvine with a degree in Social Anthropology, monkeyed around for a while, and then proceeded onward with a life of global travel, multi-disciplinary adventure, and meeting the memorable array of characters he would come to describe in his writing. He has ridden things with gears, engines, and sails, and made things with wood, leather, and metal. He has been stitched back together more times than the average hockey team; his long-suffering wife and an assortment of cats and dogs have nursed him back to health after each surgery.

Baer knows a lot about many things in this world. History flows through his veins and pours out of him at the slightest provocation. Do not ask him what you may think is a simple question unless you have the time to hear a fascinating story.

You can find more about Baer at his website.
www.baercharlton.com

www.ingramcontent.com/pod-product-compliance
Lightning Source LLC
Chambersburg PA
CBHW031149120726
47905CB00006B/1878